BLOOD QUARRY

BLOOD QUARRY

C. J. Presson

Editor:
Nola G. Causey

Cover Design:
Katelyn Ketelsen

Blood Quarry
Copyright © 2019 Clennon James Presson

ISBN: 978-1-948440-02-8

Published by Black Shield Publications LLC
P.O. Box 20314 Roanoke, VA 24018

Dedicated to those who freely gave of their time
to encourage me in this endeavor and never
stopped supporting my goal. Thank you all.

Prologue

His light brown eyes squinted at the checklist on the clipboard in his hands. He scratched the bayonet scar beneath his eye; it always itched when he squinted, but the light was too sparse in the warehouse to help it. The scar ached a little as he scratched it, and he regretted, probably for the thousandth time, not pulling the trigger just a little bit faster. He remembered the searing pain he'd felt as the bayonet entered his cheek and the look of shock on the German's face a moment later, as the bullet struck true. He wiped the sweat from his brow as he shoved a shock of grey hair from his eyes and refocused on the task at hand, as new beads of sweat quickly began forming; despite the lack of light, the metal building intensified the already sweltering Virginia summer heat. It was only morning, and he didn't relish the oppressively humid hours to come.

"Careful with that!" He barked at a man wearing a green uniform that mirrored his own, but for the chevrons on his shoulder. The other soldier had only one, displaying his rank of private; the man with the scar had three. After all those years of service, he could hardly remember his time as a private. He checked his list once more between glances around the room to assess the progress of the soldiers in his command.

The warehouse was abuzz with men hefting crates, moving boxes, and coiling wires. The large room reminded him of how a bee hive must look on the inside when the keeper starts dousing it in smoke.

"Evans!" The sergeant snapped to attention. "Sergeant Evans, get them boys in the truck, and I mean now!" Major Henry Clinton's voice echoed off the walls. The major was an angry man at the best of times; shouting was his way, but this time, his tone was somehow different.

"We're packing up and locking the place down, now, sir." Evans responded in classic military style. He was obviously accustomed to the discipline of the battlefield.

"You got wax in your ears, Sergeant?! I said move out!" the grisly officer barked impatiently.

Evans was confused by the order. "How long do we have to close up shop, Major?" Evans was a good combat sergeant, but these peacetime military politics weren't his strong suit. In fact, he wasn't even certain whether he should return to his clipboard or stay at attention; he silently wished to be back in France or Africa rather than stuck on this detail. Major Clinton made Evans uneasy; he always had.

"The idea was that, if it weren't done yesterday, don't do it!" The Major spit the butt of a cheap cigar that he had been chewing right in Evans' face.

"Shouldn't we at least board the place up or something, Major?" Evans was obviously shocked that they would leave anything behind. "The lower levels are secure, but somebody could easily open them up, if they didn't know no better."

"I don't like repeatin' myself, Sergeant." The Major had lowered his voice to the point that Evans actually had to lean in to hear what Clinton was saying, but the quiet was no less threatening. In fact, being this close to his commanding officer made him very uneasy. "Now move your men out before I lodge my boot in your lazy hindparts." The major's face was beginning to turn purple in his frustration. Evans couldn't put his finger on it, but something about this didn't sit quite right with him.

A young corporal stepped out from a row of metal storage shelves with his arms full of boxes. "Major Clinton, there's some really dangerous stuff still boxed…" Clinton silenced the corporal's questioning tone with a backhand; the young soldier's jaw shattered with the force of Clinton's blow. And Clinton rounded on the sergeant.

"Evans!"

Evans' face was alive with fright as he snapped to attention. "Sir!"

"Scoop this pup up out of that puddle of blood and get your men out of here on the double!"

Evans jumped to work this time. He called a private over to help pick up the corporal and drag him outside; he didn't seem to be conscious, and Evans could hardly blame him. Evans had never seen anyone take a blow that brutal before. In fact, he had trouble believing just how brutal that blow really was; the corporal's face was little more than tatters of bloody flesh with crushed bones protruding from jagged holes. Whatever his misgivings, though, Evans wasn't about to risk the wrath of Major Hank Clinton, but he had a terrible dread in his stomach that leaving this base in tact was a big mistake.

It took only a few moments to get all of his men outside, and Evans was the last one out; he was in the habit of surveying a location last before moving out, as it helped prevent anyone from being left behind. At the door he couldn't help but steal one last glance at the pile of boxes the corporal had been holding. His stomach clenched into a knot, and it took every ounce of military discipline he had to restrain himself from countermanding Clinton's orders and closing up shop as they had planned. What he saw before turning away left him with the impression that it would haunt him for years to come; the boxes were splattered with blood from the corporal's broken jaw, but what really terrified the sergeant was the fact that one of them had broken open and was smoking.

CHAPTER I

Thomas Haynes hated working on his parents' farm. He hated plowing fields almost as much as he hated spreading manure, but what he hated most was the embarrassment of gathering eggs. Like most young men his age, doing yard chores didn't suit his idea of adventure, and being only 25 miles from the hustle and bustle in Richmond didn't help his flights of fancy. He had hoped to find a job in Williamsburg for the summer to help pay his tuition in the fall, but jobs were hard to find; there were too many soldiers back from France that hadn't returned to their own hometowns. He cringed at being too young to fight in the war himself. Tom would love nothing more than to run away and find himself in the midst of danger and intrigue rather than stay in Doughty and live out his life in the dull fashion he seemed doomed to endure. He frequently imagined himself like one of the heroes of the movies he'd seen, like *The Silent Man* or *The Secret Game;* that's probably why he tried to join the Army two years ago and head to Europe to fight *the Hun.* But passing for 18 was not the easy task he had thought; his biggest mistake was trying to grow a beard. He cringed again at the memory. The recruitment officer had barely glanced at him, but the doctor quickly spotted him as underage. The worst part wasn't the doctor telling him he was too young to join in front of all the other boys at the recruitment station, though; it was his parents' scorn and derision of his dream when the Doughboys delivered him back home. He still couldn't believe they'd throw around words like "suicide" and "felony" much less call him a bad example and influence right in front of his brothers and sisters; all he wanted was to get out of this backwoods, little town and see some action. His 18th birthday had come too late by almost two years.

Tom's anger got the better of him and the next egg he gathered was crushed before it made it to his basket. He shook off the broken yoke and growled under his breath, sounding more animal than human.

"This ain't even a man's chore." he grumbled. "If they're gonna make me waste my time around here, they could at least give me somethin' manly to do." He picked up another egg and slung it against the wall. He knew his father cut his pay for it, but he didn't care just then. Tom's moods were a bit like the Virginia weather; you could get almost anything, at almost any time, with little notice if you weren't very careful. Today the air was warm and the sun was bright. Were it not for Tom's foul mood, this would have been a gorgeous, summer, Friday morning.

"Tom!" his mother called from the back porch, but he was determined to ignore her. "Tom? You out there? I need them eggs!"

"For goodness sake." Tom said it as a sailor might say a swear. His parents had managed to instill a few virtues into him, not the least of which is that vanity and profanity are not the marks of a man, but there were times when he wished he'd never learned that lesson. "Here Ma!" He stepped to the window of the coop and waved.

"Mrs. Abernathy is comin' over later; I wanna give her some fresh eggs for the young'uns. How long you gonna take to gather them?"

Tom was suddenly very aware of his wages being cut for breaking eggs and was eager to keep his mother from crossing the yard and finding what he had done. "I'll be there in two shakes, Ma." Tom grabbed the eggs from the last few nests as quick as he could and started across the yard; his mother took a few steps to meet him, her long mane of red hair blowing in the breeze. Mollie MacClairn Haynes' parents had come to America only months before she was born, and her visage had more than a hint of the highlands about it. She wasn't a tall woman, but neither was she short. And she had a commanding Celtic presence that was hard to mistake.

"I'll take that basket, Tom. You'd best grab a little breakfast before starting on that fertilizer Gene dropped off yesterday." She smiled kindly at him and tussled his hair a bit. Tom hated when she did that. He knew she loved him like mad, but he wasn't a child anymore and didn't care for being treated like one.

"Ma, I asked you not to muss my hair." he would normally have been much more curt, but he didn't want to provoke his mother. His father was likely to take the cost of the eggs out of his wages, and he certainly didn't want to make it worse by getting into a row with his mother, especially on an empty stomach.

He tried to smooth his hair as he walked into the kitchen door of their old farmhouse. The house was almost 100 years old and had managed to survive the Civil War despite all of the fighting in the areas around and between Richmond and Petersburg. During the years before the war, this house had even been part of the Underground Railroad; in fact, it still had a hidden room in the basement where slaves had once been concealed on their way toward Canada and freedom. It had been nestled on a sprawling tobacco farm, but, with the economic aftermath of the war and the struggles of Reconstruction, the land had long since been parceled out and either sold back to the government at reduced rates or to carpet-baggers for matchstick houses that somehow all looked exactly the same to Tom. All that remained of the old farm now was the house and about ten acres that Tom's father had bought when he and his new bride moved out here from Norfolk 20 years earlier.

Tom loved this house, despite wanting with all his being to run away and leave it behind. He loved so many things about it that he would be hard pressed to list them all if his life depended on it. He loved the view of the fields and pond out his bedroom window; he loved the big fireplace in the den, and he loved the reading seat in the parlor's big bay window. But Tom could easily tell you what he loved best about that old house. Tom's favorite thing about living there had been the same for as long as he could remember; he loved that kitchen. The smell of the wood-burning stove, bacon, fried eggs, muffins, and fresh coffee lingered there for hours after the morning meal was finished and cleared away. The huge trestle table, which easily filled the entire middle of the spacious stone-floored room, was the only piece of furniture that was still in the house when his parents moved in, as it was entirely too big to get out any of the doors. It was a relic of a time past when a whole team of farm hands would gather every morning for breakfast and every night for dinner. This morning, though, it was only Tom sitting at the table, and that was exactly the way he liked it. Tom wasn't exactly what you might call a loner, but he did value his silence. He wolfed down his breakfast; ever impatient, he always needed to be going somewhere.

"Be outside Ma." Tom said as he made his way back out the door. He was intent on finishing his chores quickly and getting to town to see the fellas; one good thing about working for his parents was getting paid by the job rather than the hour. Usually, spreading a load of manure on the garden would've taken Tom the better part of the day, but that morning he was a man on a mission. The whole pile was depleted before eleven; he jumped into the pond on the far side of their property to cool off and get clean before heading to town. He sneaked back into the house using the kitchen door again, in order to avoid his younger siblings in the parlor where his mother was teaching his sister, Mary, to read and Kimberly was practicing her piano. He had no intention of spending today sitting at his father's writing desk and reading Dickens or Shakespeare; he had a goal today, and adventure was the only item on his agenda. He ascended the stairs to his room and dried himself before throwing on some clean clothes. He'd be soaked in sweat from the summer heat before he got to Garvin's Drug Store in Doughty proper, but it wouldn't do to start off with his shirt sticking to his back.

He retraced his steps to the kitchen as quiet as he could hoping to get on his way undetected. "Headed to town, Tom?" his mother asked before he was fully across the threshold; she must've been waiting for him.

"Yeah, Ma. I thought I'd go see the fellas now my chores is done." he wasn't sure what she wanted, but he was going to avoid it if he could.

"I cleaned up the egg, Tom." the words took a moment to register. How could she have found it without him seeing her go to the coop? He must have missed it when he was cleaning up in the pond. She looked disappointedly at him. That was nothing new for Tom, but it hurt just the same.

"Sorry, Ma." Tom felt sheepish. "I reckon you'll be cutting my wages, huh?"

"Not this time, Tom." Her face was impassive, but Tom was terrified. No garnishment? What could that mean? Was she serious or was this some new kind of punishment he didn't yet understand?

"What do you mean? I don't have to pay for the eggs?" Tom's voice came out a bit hoarse. His father was firm and bold and hard, but his mother was where the real fear lies. She was inventive and could make even his favorite activities miserable if she wanted. Tom tried not to show that he was worried, but that was a task much like hiding the scent of blood from a wolf.

"I know we've been tough on you, Tom. And I know that you don't like being stuck in this little town. I don't blame you for wanting to go out and find some adventure, and I don't blame you for being frustrated. You're man grown, and picking eggs and weeding gardens is hardly exciting at your age. So, this time and this time only, there's not gonna be any punishment." She paused for a minute collecting her thoughts. "I love you dearly, Thomas, but you can't carry on like this. You'll be on your own soon enough, but you can't do whatever you wish without consequence. Before you know it, you're going to be at university, then working a job and trying to support a family; losing your temper doesn't fit into that picture." Tom thought he saw tears in his mother's eyes, and that was one thing he could never stand.

"Sorry, Ma." he choked. "Won't happen again." He pushed back some tears of his own, as his mother stepped in and hugged him tightly. She wiped her eyes and patted down her apron trying to look nonchalant.

"Alright, son. Off to town with you." Tom began to duck out the door once more, eager to get away before she changed her mind about the punishment. "Tom wait!" It took all the gumption he could muster for Tom to turn back around and face his mother once more. "Could you take this to your father on the way to Garvin's." She handed him a lunchbox. "He forgot it again." She grinned, and Tom couldn't help but join her. Her smile was infectious, but in the back of his mind he had the sneaking suspicion that making him visit his father at work might be a punishment after all.

* * * * *

The walk to town was about three miles long but Tom liked the exercise, despite the heat and sore muscles he'd earned shoveling manure. He felt like something in particular was driving him today, but couldn't quite put his finger on what it was. Maybe it was the mounting boredom he'd been feeling for the last couple of weeks. Since graduation, he'd done almost nothing but work around the house, catch a movie here and there, and fight with his parents, his father in particular. Tom's craving for action was getting almost unbearable; summer break is supposed to be a time to get into and out of trouble and see what mischief you can work up, but Tom was stuck in a rut and desperately wanted out of it. His father's office was one block from the town square on Regency Street. Tom could never figure out what had attracted his old man to the law, but at least he made a healthy living at it, even in spite of giving his services away to some sob story indigent more often than not. Richard Haynes was the most respected attorney in town and was a friend to everyone he came across, but taking cases for free had never made sense to Tom.

The front door was made almost entirely of glass and had a huge brass doorknob. Tom entered and walked past Janey, his father's 70 year old secretary, another of Richard's charity cases.

"Pa." Tom didn't bother to knock before entering his father's office, though he might've had he known his old schoolmaster was inside.

"Tom, I'm in a meeting." his father didn't seem pleased by Tom's lack of courtesy, nor did Mr. Philps, and, for once, Tom felt the same way.

"Sorry, Paw. Ma wanted me to bring you your lunchbox." he held up the tin box as though his father needed to see it to understand the sentence.

"Alright, alright. Give it here and shut the door behind you." Tom complied quickly, exited his father's office, and pulled the door closed, but he didn't leave as his father and Mr. Philps had expected but listened at the keyhole, instead.

His father resumed the conversation, "Sorry for the interruption, Michael. Where were we?"

"The contract; the contract." Mr. Philps sounded incredibly agitated, and the idea of his father discussing a contract with the schoolmaster seemed very unusual to Tom.

"Ah yes. Well, let's have a look at it and see what they have proposed." Tom could hear the rustling of papers inside then several long moments of silence. "This cannot possibly be right." his father's tone had become somewhat strained.

"That's why I've come to you with it. I can't believe that they can get away with something like this." Mr. Philps' voice was beginning to sound a bit hysterical. "Can they really take my entire supply without so much as a dime of compensation and expect vague terms like 'later compensation' and 'patriotic duty' to cover my losses?!"

"Well, to be completely honest, I doubt we can successfully fight this conscription of supplies as long as the prohibitions against disloyalty in the Sedition Act are still in place." Tom had never heard his father sound so weary and irritated; he was usually a very fiery man who fought for his beliefs with a passion that frightened many of his contemporaries. "I hate to say it, but, as unjust and villainous as the terms in this contract are, the Army can do almost whatever they want these days."

"I can't bring myself to believe that our own government would take everything I own for some military project, especially now that the War is won." The Great War had raged in Europe for years, but the Treaty of Versailles had been signed by both sides almost a year earlier. "I mean what possible use could the Army have for ten cases of chemistry supplies?" Chemistry supplies?! Tom couldn't fathom a use for such items any more than Mr. Philps seemed to be able to do. His mind was racing and the voices on the other side of the doors began to go unnoticed while he pondered what could be behind this conscription.

Just then, Janey moved from her desk, and Tom had to abandon his listening post or risk getting caught, but he had certainly heard enough to get his mind to working.

Chapter 2

Tom's quick pace of an hour earlier was gone, as he strolled thoughtfully toward Garvin's Drug Store and the Soda Fountain. He'd heard enough through his father's door to know that something very odd was going on in Doughty, but Janey getting up from her desk cut short his eavesdropping before he got the full story. He knew one thing for certain; the Army had taken an active role in town, and he wanted to know why. He was downright baffled by the idea that the Army would conscript Mr. Philps' chemistry supplies, but, without knowing exactly what was in those cases, he didn't have nearly enough information to form any theories. Was there something special that they needed that they could only get from Mr. Philps? That seemed highly unlikely; Mr. Philps was just a small town schoolmaster, and Tom had trouble believing he possessed anything truly unique or hard to find. The next question that entered Tom's mind was whether they were conscripting supplies from other schoolmasters. With the War over, what could they possibly be doing that could require such a large amount of chemistry supplies? He had heard that, in the war, both sides had used gas and other chemical weapons, but he didn't fully understand how they had been made. Tom had more questions than he had answers, and his head was starting to spin; pondering this hard should be saved for university, and that was still two months away.

His thoughts distracted him to the point that he was almost past Garvin's store before he realized where he was. He pushed his father's conversation and the many questions it presented from his mind, turned around, and headed toward the panel glass double doors that fronted Garvin's Drug Store. The clock showed about five minutes after noon when the bell greeted Tom's entrance into his regular hangout.

Two voices greeted his arrival in unison. "Hey Tom!" James and Billy Wilson were identical twins; they looked so much alike that even Tom had trouble telling them apart sometimes, until they started talking. They were identical in looks right down to their identical blond haircuts, but they had nearly opposite personalities. They were Tom's age and graduated high school with him a few weeks earlier.

"Howdy fellas." Tom's voice sounded far away as he headed toward the counter. Mr. Philps' problem had affected him more than he was willing to admit. He cleared his throat and concentrated harder on the soda fountain and the possibility of an afternoon of adventure. He tried all the harder to push the chemistry supplies to the back of his mind where he could pick them up and mull them over more later.

"Tom." The young soda jerk nodded at him as he took a seat on the nearest stool next to James.

"Georgie." Tom nodded back. George Priestly was the only other boy in their graduating class and had been Tom's best friend since they were in diapers. Mr. Garvin, the proprietor of the drug store and soda fountain, was George's uncle, and Tom always had the feeling that the man didn't care much for him. The old pharmacist frequently voiced his opinon that people who aren't buying anything shouldn't be taking up space at the soda fountain.

"Uncle Garv is in the back, Tom." George eyed the back door warily between glances at Tom.

"Oh good grief." Tom's ability to make entirely innocent phrases sound like a string of venom when he was perturbed was uncanny. "If he's gonna be that way about it, just give me a malt, already." Tom's mood was beginning to fray again, and more reactionary narrow mindedness wasn't helping him keep it in check whatsoever.

"Well..." the voice was Billy's, and Tom knew that it was going to make a reasonable and well-formed response, and he wanted to knock Billy's teeth out for it. "...Mr. Garv is just trying to run a business. We can hardly blame him, if he doesn't want us blocking up the fountain without buying a dern thing, now can we?"

"Why do you always have to be such a goodie goodie, Bill?" Tom was taking his frustrations out on a good friend and he hated himself for it, but he didn't stop. "Garv is the richest man in town, and you know it. Why should he care if we sit here once in a while? There ain't nobody else in here anyhow, and there's stools a plenty."

"Okay fellas, there ain't no need in gettin' snippy with each other." When Billy was the group's self appointed conscience, which he seemed intent on being at just that moment, then James was usually the group's peacemaker.

"Fine fine. Just make me a malt and drop the whole business." George started making Tom's malt as the group searched for another conversation topic. In the absence of anything else to talk about, Tom's mind began to wander back to the hallway where he'd been hunkered listening at his father's keyhole. He absentmindedly picked up his malt when George sat it down and began slowly sipping on it. He was so engrossed, in fact, that he barely even heard a bell sound across the room.

"Well howdy fellas!"

Tom realized a second later than everyone else that the voice was addressing them and turned to see who had shouted the greeting. Walking toward them from the doorway was a tall red-haired young man with a thick ginger mustache. With his mind a jumbled mess of contracts and chemistry supplies it took him a brief moment to recognize Ralph Donnelson.

"Well, hey there college boy!" James had been good friends with Ralph before he went away to school, despite him being one year older. "When did you get back?"

"Been back for a whole week, but my pa has had me workin' my tail off repaintin' the barn since I got back." Ralph's ginger mustache twitched a little as he spoke. "We finished up the last coat yesterday, right before he and Ma headed off to Bristol to see my grandma; so, I been runnin' 'round catchin' up with folks all mornin'." Ralph had a broad easy smile and always managed to lighten the mood wherever he went; Tom genuinely liked him, and that was something that you couldn't say for just anyone. "How you boys been?"

"Pretty fair if you don't count being bored to death." George was smiling too, as Tom looked at him. Actually, all of them had goofy grins on their faces, Tom realized, even he was smiling. He chuckled under his breath and took another drink of his malt.

"Bored?" Ralph feigned shock at the very possibility of boredom. "In a town like THIS?! With sooo much to do?!" All the fellas laughed.

"So, what's Williamsburg like, Ralphie?" Tom wanted to hear of bustling and always having somewhere to go and something to do.

"Tell you the truth, it ain't much different than here, just a little bigger is all." Tom tried not to show his disappointment. "But enough 'bout Williamsburg; Doughty has plenty of trouble to get into, if you know where to look."

George obviously didn't believe there was anything resembling adventure in his hometown. "Finding adventure in Doughty would be like finding the Kaiser in your sock drawer. Pretty dern close to impossible."

"Oh? Then I reckon you might oughta look in your sock drawer." Ralph winked at George jokingly. "Don't reckon you fellas have been down to the quarry none lately, huh?" He grinned suspiciously.

Billy was aghast. "Of course we ain't." He had lowered his voice to a whisper in order to avoid being overheard but was no less emphatic than if he was screaming in Ralph's face. "Nobody but the workers are allowed in there. It's strictly off limits." The quarry had been in operation shipping iron and copper rich stone to Petersburg and Norfolk since the early days of the war.

"Yeah, well, that was before they pulled up stakes and headed out." This was news to Tom and the boys; they hadn't been to the quarry since they got caught trying to sneak over a fence a couple years back.

"Abandoned?" Tom questioned. "When did they pull out?"

"Looks like a few weeks at least. The place is a mess."

"We can't go down there though." Billy was adamant. "If we get caught, that foreman will have us arrested; he swore he would."

"Breathe now, Bill; just breathe. Tell me again. Who swore they'd have you arrested?" Ralphie was always good at convincing others to see things his way.

"I told you; it was the foreman. He's in charge over there!"

"Is he from Doughty?" Tom was beginning to see Ralph's angle; he took another sip of malt to hide his grin.

"No, he has a shack by the quarry." Billy hadn't caught on yet.

"So, he works for the stone company, does he?"

"Yeah, I reckon. Think I heard Grampa Jim say that they shipped him over to do the work."

"So, you figure he'd stick around if they stopped payin' him to work the quarry?" Ralph's smile was back and bigger than ever.

"You tellin' us that there ain't a soul down there?" James was excited; anyone who looked at him could tell he was about to burst at the seams.

"Not a soul. Place looks like a ghost town."

"You actually go inside and check the place out?" George was a bit more guarded than the rest of the fellas. He was cautious, but Tom could see that he was also intrigued by the possibility of an adventure right outside of town.

"Sure did! And you fellas won't believe what I saw down there." Ralph looked each of them dead in the face to make sure that they were hanging on his every word. "Let's put it this way. Do you know what a quarry looks like?" The boys all shook their heads a bit bewildered. "Well, they're takin' big chunks o' rock outa there, right?" Everyone nodded. "Well, they take it all from the same place too; it makes a big ole hole in the ground."

"What's so interesting about a hole in the ground?" Billy suddenly seemed to think that this might be a bunch of build up for nothing.

"Not just a hole, mind you, a BIG hole. I'm talking HUGE!" Ralphie's face was alive, even a bit wild. "And with a hole that big in a hill made of stone, y'all know what you get?" They didn't know, but he left it hanging there for a moment for the effect. Tom realized he was holding his breath, but he couldn't help himself. Finally, Ralph uttered a single word. "Cliffs." Billy gasped. George looked dumbfounded. And James grinned like a Cheshire cat. Tom wasn't entirely certain that he had heard Ralph right.

"Did you say...cliffs?"

"Yep. Honest to God. There's man-made cliffs down there." Ralphie's grin was so big that it defied belief.

"And when you say cliffs...do you mean like the falls? Over in Turner's creek?" George had somehow regained his powers of speech.

"Nope. I mean cliffs. Real ones, and big too."

"How big are we talkin'?" James could hardly contain his excitement. None of the boys had ever seen real cliffs. The closest thing around Doughty was the falls, but they couldn't be more than seven or eight feet high.

"In one spot, they're at least a hundred feet tall." Tom was surprised that Ralph could still speak with a grin that big.

"A hundred feet?!" Bill was as frightened as James was excited. Tom had to admit, he didn't blame him for being scared. George had accidentally knocked Billy out of Ralph's hayloft once and broke his arm, and that was only 20 feet; 100 feet could easily kill a man.

"Yep! But that's not all the way around. It looks like they just cut the side off of a hill then started diggin' down in the hole to get more rock out. And there's more!" He wasn't sure if Billy could handle much more good news, but Tom was more excited than he had been for a long while. "The hole is all full of water."

"Water? How'd it get full of water?" George was puzzling out the details still, but Tom could see the excitement growing in him too.

"Well, they redirected the creek after it leaves Miller's pond to fill the hole up. I could see fish swimmin' in there."

"We gotta check it out fellas." James was practically bouncing on his stool. He looked the way Tom felt. With an adventure this big so closeby, he couldn't imagine not going down there.

Tom suddenly had a thought. "Don't it seem weird to you fellas that the workers down there pulled up and shuffled off without us hearin' nothin' about it?"

"Well..." George was obviously trying to figure out an answer to that riddle. "...since we was banned, ain't none of us gone down there at all, right?" All of the boys nodded their heads thoughtfully. "And there weren't nobody from Doughty workin' there; they was all from outa town, right?" Tom was beginning to piece the puzzle together too. "It don't seem that far fetched that we didn't miss nobody from the quarry when we didn't know none of 'em anyhow, right?"

"Seems like good reasonin' to me." Ralph's ginger lip quivered with anticipation, as he obviously thought that all the boys would soon be hot on his heels headed to the quarry.

"But we're still banned! Even if there's nobody down there, we still can't go! It's against the law!" Billy obviously knew he was fighting a losing battle, but heights terrified him to no end.

"Give it a rest, Bill. You know we're goin'; can't pass up a chance like this." James, once again, settled the disagreement before it even got into full swing.

"You say there's fish in the water? Does that mean it's also safe to swim in?" George loved swimming. He often came over to swim in the pond with Tom and his brother and sisters.

"I'd guarantee it. In fact, there were some fellas down there this mornin' doing just that." His grin widened a bit more as Tom took another sip of his malt and listened intently. "In fact, they was jumpin' off the cliffs into the water at one spot."

"Who were these fellas?" Getting into trouble was the general idea, and Tom didn't mind company; still the wrong sort of people could ruin even the best adventure, and boys who would jump off a 100 foot cliff could very easily be the wrong sort. "What kind of fellas would jump off a hundred foot cliff?"

"Just some boys from down Petersburg way. They said they was gonna be there a few days sleeping in one of the empty buildings the quarry folks left. Sides, they wasn't jumpin' at the tallest spot. Where they was it's only twenty foot or so." Tom decided that a 20 foot drop wasn't so bad, and was about to say the same to the fellas when someone shouted.

"Buildings!" Tom turned to see an uncharacteristically enormous smile on George's face. The sight struck James as funny, who started laughing almost immediately.

"What about buildings?" Tom chuckled over the cackling that James seemed unable to control.

"Ralphie said buildings!" All the boys looked at George with mixed confusion and bemusement. "Oh, come on, fellas! What did we build down by the creek before the quarry people moved in?"

"Oh! The cabin!" Billy was suddenly just as excited as the rest of the boys. "We put so much work into that place. I hope they didn't tear it down."

"It's just south of the road, right?" Ralph hadn't helped them with the cabin, and the fences had been placed around the quarry before he'd become part of the group.

"Yeah, it's just before you get to the creek settled between two ole oak trees." Tom knew they'd told Ralph where it was before, but hearing how to get somewhere and going there yourself are two very different things.

"It's still there alright. Don't know what kinda shape it's in, but they didn't tear it down or nothin'. Saw it from a few yards off."

"I say we head down there right away and get the place set up to camp a couple days." James was brash, but Tom liked his take on this one; He nodded his agreement as he took another big swig of his malt.

George's smile faded a bit. "I can't go down there right now, boys. I gotta finish my shift here. Uncle Garv ain't gonna let me beg off early; you know how he is." George glanced back at the office door to see if his uncle might be listening; the coast was clear.

"No worries, Georgie." Tom was already formulating a plan. "The shop closes at five and it ain't dark 'til round nine." Tom had a good mind for solving problems when he actually cared to solve them. "Whatcha say we all meet by Miller's pond by the south end of the Petersburg road, headed out of town? I'll take some fresh eggs and tomatoes to you're ma and grab some clothes and gear from your room while I'm there." All the fellas seemed to be excited at the prospect of getting out of town, even if a plummet off of a cliff might await them the next morning. When you're 18 years old, what might come tomorrow always seems further away than it really is.

"How about me and James go on ahead and set up camp early so's we don't lose the light if somethin' holds you fellas up?" Billy was too cautious sometimes, but Tom thought he might be right about this.

"Might be a good idea, come to think of it."

"Hey! Think y'all can maybe get that good lantern from your paw?" Ralphie liked to read, they all knew, and the lantern would be helpful in more endeavors than just that one.

"Actually, he just bought a newer one from the General Store last week and gave us the old one." James said it as though he had talked his father into buying the new lantern, and, knowing James, he probably did.

"It's a plan then. I'll meet George at the pond round five-thirty and see you fellas at the cabin before seven." Tom downed the last of his malt, gave George a couple coins from his pocket to cover the drink, and headed out the door with Ralph and the twins, feeling energized. He was finally going to get the summer started; as adventures go, this one looked to be small, but Tom felt that it was a sign of big things to come. Little did he know just how right he was.

CHAPTER 3

Looking back at it as he sat by Miller's Pond, Tom chuckled at how differently his afternoon went than he expected. Sitting at the bar in Garv's shop earlier, he was certain that he'd have a time of convincing his mother to let him go camping with the fellas and miss a whole Saturday of work and was beyond certain that George's mother would be even more skeptical. He had never been more mistaken.

When he had arrived home, it had been about 1:30, and Tom had kicked around in the barn for a good fifteen minutes practicing what he would say to his mother before he braved the kitchen door. As the screen creaked open, he was talking before he was fully across the threshold.

"Ma, I know I was wrong this mornin' and all, but Ralphie just got back from University and me and the fellas were thinkin' that we'd take him campin' as a welcome home thing. I'm way ahead on my chores, and I'll work double hard on Monday." He'd said it all in one breath and commenced, almost at once, to panting heavily.

"That sounds fine, Tom. You all have a good time."

"It's just one day!" He exclaimed without realizing what she had said. "We're just gonna be campin' and maybe fishin' some!"

His mother turned to look at him and chuckled. "I already said yes, son."

"Oh, yeah. Okay thanks Ma!" He stumbled over the words as well as his feet as he headed toward the hallway door and raced upstairs before she could change her mind. It wasn't often that he had a day off work entirely, aside from Sundays.

Once in his room, he began throwing odds and ends in an old haversack that had belonged to his grandfather Haynes when he marched with Lee, Jackson, and Longstreet. He grabbed clothes, a pocket knife, a hunting knife, and a sleeping roll before tearing his way back out of his room, down the stairs, and into his father's study to retrieve his Winchester pump .22 rifle; he thought he might shoot some rabbits or squirrels for dinner. He plunged out the front door and strolled around the side of the house to the root cellar where he stowed jars of potatoes and beans in his haversack before grabbing eggs and tomatoes for George's mother.

George's family and Tom's had always been close, and the friendship only intensified when George's dad was killed in the war. Tom's parents had taken it on themselves to help out the Priestlys as much as possible; that's how Tom started delivering eggs and vegetables about twice a week to the house up the street.

"Well Tom!" Agnes Priestly exclaimed as he trotted up the walkway toward the front porch. "We didn't expect you to be bringin' no more vittles for a couple days."

"Well, Mrs. Priestly, I was comin' by anyway; so, I thought I'd bring you some fresh stuff while I was at it." Tom gave her his most ingratiating grin.

"Well, that's mighty thoughtful of you, Tom." She took the basket and seemed, for the first time, to take note of his pack and rifle. "Where's a young man like you headin' with a gun and haversack on a day like today? You ain't figurin' on signin' up again are ya?" She gave Tom a teasing grin.

"No ma'am. Me and the Wilson boys are takin' Ralphie Donnelson campin' as a welcome home kinda thing." He knowingly looked at his shoes for a brief second before kicking at the dirt between the pavers on which he stood. "It's a real shame that Georgie has to be workin' today and can't go too. He'll be awful bummed out to miss a good campin' trip." He looked back up at George's mother who seemed to take his meaning.

"And just why can't George go along?" she asked a little more hastily than she had intended.

"Well, ma'am, he's stuck workin' the soda fountain 'til five and won't have time to get his stuff packed and meet us afore we need to be headin' into the woods. Can't rightly set up camp after dark, you know." Tom gave her an innocent look, and she took it hook, line, and sinker.

"Now Tom, I'd have thought you were a mite smarter than that. You're here already; you can just grab George's things for him and meet him when he gets off work. That should still give you boys plenty of time to get into the woods and set up before dark, unless you're thinkin' of marchin' on Richmond." She chuckled lightly at her own joke, and Tom joined her.

"No ma'am, we're headed south to stop Sherman in Georgia."

And that was that. Tom grabbed George's things quick as a whip and stowed them in a shoulder duffel that George's father had carried when he went off to France. It had been returned to the family by a chaplain and a courier. Tom then passed back by his own house on his way south toward Miller's Pond. It took him well over an hour to walk the distance. He marched past Doughty proper and a whole slew of fields and houses before he caught up with the trickle of water known as Doughty Creek. The creek fed into Miller's Pond then flowed past the small dam toward the quarry. Tom stayed on the road until he hit the pond. Then laid down his double burden and flopped onto his back in the soft grass by the pool.

He'd been there on his back for quite a while watching the clouds and whistling to himself when George's familiar hum accompanied the sound of shuffling feet on the road.

"Took ya long enough, Georgie." Tom didn't bother to sit up before speaking. "Thought I'd be layin' here 'til doomsday." Tom chided his friend.

"Give a fella a break, will ya?" George shot back. "Besides, I'm early. It ain't a minute past five-fifteen."

Tom checked his wristwatch and realized it was earlier than he'd thought. That was good; the pair would have another hour at least to hike before getting to the cabin. Tom tossed George's duffel to him and they set off at a brisk pace.

* * * * *

The cabin was, in Tom's humble opinion, a work of art. They had stumbled on the perfect spot one day while hunting and knew immediately that it would never realize its true potential until they had built the cabin to end all cabins beneath the canopy of the twin oaks. It took them the better part of a whole summer to down, skin, and age the logs and gather the bits of lumber and nails that they needed to build their masterpiece, and they had done an impressive job. The cabin stood stately before them as Tom and George approached; it was even bigger than they remembered. George had frequently expressed his disbelief that they had managed to build such a huge structure without at least one of them falling to his death from atop the rough shingled roof.

"Ho-Ho!" Ralphie was hanging out of one of the windows, Ginger mustache twitching with excitement. "Words don't do this place justice fellas! I mean, it's big from the outside, but it's ENORMOUS once you get in here!"

"Told ya so!" George threw back. "Hard to believe that us four knuckleheads managed somethin' like that, huh?"

"You said it. We could house half the town in here, if we needed." Ralphie's near constant smile was mixed with a little disbelief and just a dash of bemusement.

"Well now! There you fellas are." James had stepped out onto the porch and was leaning against the rail. Tom remembered how hard it had been to come by the sturdy upright posts they needed to frame that railing.

"How's the place look, Jimmy?" Tom was cautiously optimistic that they would have minimal work to put into the place.

"Looks almost just like we left it." James grinned down at them. "There was a few spiders and a couple birds to run off, but the webs and nests were all we had to clean up."

"Ain't no damage to the flooring or roof at all?" George's voice cracked slightly betraying his excitement at finding the cabin so in tact.

"Not a thing wrong with it." Billy's voice preceded him out the door. "Even I wouldn't be scared up on the roof here as long as I stayed away from the edges."

That was good enough for Tom. "Well, then let's get our stuff stashed inside and have a look at the quarry."

The other fellas had chosen their rough bunks and laid out bedrolls already. Tom slung his haversack on one bunk, and George tossed his duffel up onto another before heading back out into the forest and heading off a little further south to see the scene of what they would recall as the biggest trouble of their lives. None of them was truly prepared for their first glimpse of the quarry proper. Even Ralph took a deep breath when he saw it again. The hillside had, indeed, been totally removed to its peak, and the cliffs that were left behind were every bit of 100 feet high. If the cliffs were the only thing that awaited them, the boys may have been able to keep their composure, as they had been warned by Ralphie of what they were to see, but the lake was totally unexpected. Ralph had said that there was water, but he had failed completely to explain just how much water to expect. The lake covered a full five acres in the middle of the forest and was bordered by a few ramshackle shacks and one warehouse with a road running off to the northeast.

"Ralphie you genius!" James was beside himself. He had excitement bubbling out of every pore as he jovially punched Ralph in the shoulder. "This place is spectacular!" He hooted and hollered continuing to assault his friend's left shoulder.

"I didn't know. I mean, I didn't expect." Billy was at a loss for words, and that said volumes.

"Tommy boy, are you seeing what I'm seeing?" George obviously didn't believe his eyes.

"I think I am, but I don't believe it." Tom thought he'd stumbled across an adventurer's heaven practically in his own back yard. He'd soon learn to tell heaven from hell.

Suddenly, someone started shouting at the boys. They all scoured the edge of the lake and cliffs trying to locate the owner of the voice as it was joined by several others. The task of spotting the criers was made more difficult by the echoes caused by lake and cliffs. Ralph located them first.

"Hey hey! There they are fellas; there they are!" He was pointing to a portion of cliff with a large stone outcropping that hung out over the water. Standing atop it was a group of young men who looked to be two or three years older than Tom and his cadre. "Come on fellas! Let's see what they've got to say for themselves!" Ralph started strolling toward the water's edge but didn't seem to be interested in climbing the hillside to where the others were standing. A moment later, the rest of the group realized why, when the men atop the cliff began jumping into the water below. Tom noticed that Billy had become as white as a sheet and stayed that way until the jumpers began to surface and swim toward shore.

"Thought we might find you boys down here!" Ralphie hailed as he helped the first of them up out of the water and slapped him on the back. That was when Tom and the others first realized that this lake was unlike any other they had ever seen. There was no gradual entrance into this water hole, because the edges that were immersed in water were just as sheer as the cliffs that loomed above them.

"Howdy fellas!" A very tall man with a thick lowland accent and arms twice as thick greeted them as Ralph helped him from the water. "Name's William Sweet. Friends call me Wil. And who're you lot?"

Ralph did the introductions and Tom tried his best to keep Wil straight from Mike, Harry, and Hosea. "So, how long y'all fellas stickin' around for?" Ralph asked Wil after pointing out Tom, George, James, and Billy.

"Long as we don't have nothin' better to do, I reckon." Wil chuckled.

"Yup, or 'til we run outa food. Whichever comes first." Tom already couldn't remember if that boy was Mike or Hosea.

"What about you all?" Tom was pretty sure that the fella asking this question was Harry.

"Well, we just got here; so, I reckon the sky's the limit." James was right at home with these older men Tom had to admit that they reeked of confidence, and he hoped that some of it would rub off on him before he headed off to university.

"That's the spirit!" Wil seemed to be taking a liking to the group.

"I don't see a camp, nowhere. Where you fellas sleepin'?" Tom forced himself to sound older than he felt.

"See that warehouse over there?" Wil pointed. And, was it Hosea that pointed with him? Tom was really bad with names. "We've got our stuff stowed in there, bedrolls and all."

"How'd you get in there? I would figure that the stone company would've locked it up tight when they left." Billy suddenly seemed twice his age. Tom never realized how mature being a constant worry and nag sounded until right now, and, for perhaps the first time, he envied Billy Wilson.

"I figured the same, but the place weren't locked up or nothin'." Wil had snagged a shirt from a pile on the ground and was stepping into his boots. "Actually, it looks like they left in a real hurry, to tell ya the truth."

"What would they have to hurry about? It ain't like nobody was chasin' 'em away." James wore his puzzlement plainly on his face, and Tom wished he'd stop looking quite so young.

"Dunno, don't care to be honest." gabbled Mike, or was it Harry? Tom desperately needed to get better at committing names to memory.

"What if something did run them off though?" Billy's tone reminded Tom of his father. When did his friend become such an old man?

Ralphie was the first to answer. "We chatted about that last time I was down here. We don't see no evidence of a fight or anything that might could hurt a man."

"Sides from a stray big cat or two, that is, and if those are around, then the best place to be at night is inside somewhere secure." One of the older fellas, Harry or Mike Tom figured, threw out the statement as if they all knew about the cats, but Tom and the others knew that there hadn't been a mountain lion seen around there in years. If there was one about, it was news to them.

"Where'd you see cat tracks at?" Ralph was too curious to let it pass.

"Didn't see no tracks; we saw ourselves a cougar on the far side of the lake this mornin'." Tom had all but given up telling the others apart by names; so, he started calling them by their attributes in his head. This was the stocky one. Thick arms and thick chest; Tom wasn't sure about the look in his eyes.

"Saw one? It didn't come after y'all?" George's Uncle Garv had been mauled by a cat when he was younger and had scars down his leg to prove it, but he survived, which was more than could be said for the cat that had become his bedroom rug. Cats were notoriously aggressive, but Garv was moreso.

"Nah. Well, it might woulda, but Wil here shot off a round from his pistol and it took off." Said the one with the dark hair. Dark was the wrong word, Tom thought; his hair is more like the black of raven's wings.

"Well, a cat would be a problem, but it ain't likely to scare off any miners." Ralph brought it back around to the point, but Tom heard something in his voice that said he wasn't fully sure that he believed the boys.

"Right, and we done been here three days." Wil's confidence would've easily put Tom's misgivings to rest, but for the rising suspicion he had that something about their story didn't quite add up. "Don't y'all reckon that we'd have done seen anything dangerous by now? I mean a big cat ain't good, but, with all us together, it ain't gonna hurt nobody."

"He's got a point. I don't see any signs of nothing except for a few miners done pulled up stakes. Ain't no reason to fear a place where ain't nothin' gone wrong." James was not about to give up on this place, but even he seemed to have pulled on a cloak of caution. Had the older fellas known him, Tom was certain that they would have been just as unsettled by James' adoption of anything other than a recklessly cavalier attitude.

"I reckon y'all are both right." Wil seemed to have formulated a new take on the situation. "Way I see it, there ain't no sense in gettin' run off by something we ain't even met yet, but it might also be a good idea if we all made room to sleep in the same place." George gave Tom a knowing look to which Tom replied with an ever so slight head shake.

"Well where y'all stayin'?" Tom was fairly sure it was Hosea who'd asked the question; at least he kinda looked like a Hosea to Tom.

"We're campin'!" Ralphie was many things, but foolish wasn't one of them. Nobody had bothered discussing with him the fact that the cabin was a well-guarded secret amongst the group, but Ralph had good instincts about such things.

"Well, that don't exactly sound like the safest idea with cats about." Tom was pretty sure, now, that Hosea was the one with the thick shock of black hair.

"Whatdya suppose?" Tom looked to Ralph.

"Well, I ain't keen on leaving the campsite; it's the best one around, and I also ain't keen on sleeping in an abandoned warehouse." Ralphie's smile stayed put, but Tom noticed an ever so slight cautious glint in his eye and twitch of his mustache. That was enough for Tom to make up his mind. He liked these fellas, but he didn't really know them and was not about to sleep in close quarters with a group of boys that could easily be up to no good. And with the uncertainty in their story, he was as sure as ever that these fellas should stay somewhere other than the cabin and that the cabin was exactly where he and the group should stay.

"We didn't bring tents or nothin'; so, campin' is out of the question for us." Wil obviously hadn't caught the silent conversation that had just passed between Tom and Ralph. "But, heck fellas, there's plenty 'o room in our warehouse. And it ain't as uncomfortable as you might reckon. At least come and have a look see at it." With that Wil and his cadre set out at a stroll toward the building. Tom and the boys exchanged quick glances at each other and fell into their wake. Tom was suddenly aware of and thankful for his rifle. It was a small caliber better suited for shooting squirrels than men, but it was something. He didn't actually expect a conflict, but something had certainly set his mind on edge.

The warehouse seemed innocuous enough on the outside, but Tom felt chills go down his spine when he approached the door. It took more effort than it should've for him to step across the threshold into the building. What he saw was not what he had expected. He thought the building would have been completely empty; he was never more wrong. It looked like the mining company had left everything behind when they pulled up stakes and left. There were metal shelves that stretched from wall to wall standing about 30 feet in front of him with a ten foot alleyway running down the middle of the room. There were boxes and packing crates strewn about, most of them intact and sealed or padlocked shut. He noticed a pile of boxes broken up and tossed aside in the middle of the aisle between the shelves, but didn't quite know what to make of it. The older boys had turned right and headed toward the front corner of the building when they entered; so, Tom followed. When they got to the corner, they closed in around a cluster of bedrolls, Tom had a sudden realization; these fellas had been in the war. They all had tattered duffels, much like George's, and they all had mismatched pieces of uniform laid on their beds.

"You fellas doughboys?" Tom asked.

Wil chuckled. "Nah, but we was a while back. We got discharged when the war was over, but we ain't found no decent work since."

"Yep, we been wanderin' 'round lookin' for work ever since." Tom was now certain that Wil's second mouthpiece, the black-haired one, was Hosea. He picked up a field shirt from his bed and put it on; he had been a sergeant.

"How did y'all end up here?" James liked soldiers; he always had, and this new realization seemed to have softened some of his misgivings about the men.

"Walkin' down the road from Petersburg one day a few weeks back, we saw a bunch of trucks come pullin' out of the gate up the way." Tom still couldn't tell Mike from Harry.

"Right, and they all said 'Rock Quarry' on the sides." Whichever was which; they'd both pitched in now.

"Yep, and the Lieutenant here and myself got to talkin' and decided that we could move stone as well as anybody else and came lookin' for a job." Tom's realization that Wil was an officer was a shock, but he kept it off his face as best he could. "Course, when we got here, the place was deserted. But we found some food in one of the shacks and figured we'd rest a while and regroup 'til we run out of food, then move on."

"So, that's our story. Now, it's gettin' late; so, y'all better either go grab your gear and bunk here or you better get back to your camp while you can still find it." Tom thought himself a fool for not noticing before how Wil was used to being in command.

"We thank y'all for the invite, but we really were excited to have ourselves a camping trip. Don't y'all worry though; we're safe from animals where we're at." Ralph had eased up too, but he and Tom were of the same mind. The cabin was where they oughta be, and these fellas seemed intent on staying here, anyway. Tom figured he'd try to talk them into sleeping in the cabin the next night; he might even invite them to church Sunday.

As they stepped back out the door, it occurred to Tom that it was worth checking out the cougar sighting. "Hey Harry!" Tom called back inside, and the stocky one came strolling up; at least he now knew which was which. "You saw that cat right?"

"Yeah, saw him by the shore right over there." Harry pointed to the opposite shore, about 300 yards away.

"You said it was this mornin' right?"

"Yeah, bout half past five, I reckon. Dawn was just about to break."

"So, the light weren't that great?" George now knew where Tom was headed and pitched in a helping hand.

"Nah, well, I could SEE, but the details was a bit fuzzy."

"How'd you know it was a cat?" Billy was keen on the investigation now.

"Well, it was about the size of a man, and looked to be a kinda yellow color. And it was crawlin' kinda funny; you know, like stalkin' somethin'." Harry looked off into space trying to remember some details. "Ya know, I don't think it realized I could see it. It was movin' real slowlike."

"When Wil fired off the shot, how did it react?" Billy was better at asking the right questions than the rest of the fellas.

"Well, it took a start at first. You know, it kinda jumped a little like it was shocked."

"Then what? Did it take off quick into the woods?" Tom remembered seeing cougars when he was younger; whenever someone took a shot at them, they ran like the wind.

"Nah, I figured it would, but it just kinda glared at us, then turned and crawled off like it was disappointed or somethin'."

"Hmmm, that's curious for a cat. I reckon we might wanna take a look over there on the way to camp." Tom set off at a quick gait and waved back at Harry. Harry returned the wave and stepped back inside. The more Tom thought about it, the more he felt he might've been a little too mistrustful of those fellas and would try to make it up to them the next day. He began to almost regret not inviting them to the cabin that night, but he was sure they would've declined anyway.

It took a few short minutes to cover the distance to the section of shoreline where Harry had seen the stalker that morning. The sun had begun to drop, but there was still plenty of light to see the muddy ground, and, as Tom had suspected from the start, there were no cat prints.

"Hey Tom." Ralph waved him over a few feet away. "You're the best tracker, whatdya make of these?" He pointed to a set of boot tracks and what looked to be giant raccoon impressions.

"Dunno, never seen anything like it before in my life." Tom scratched his head. "You figure the boot prints might be one of the doughboys'?"

"Could be." George was looking down over Tom's shoulder now, and James and Billy were walking over to see what the fuss was about. "They look about the right size, and are definitely made by some sort of boots."

"Could be army boots, huh?" James seemed to be thinking the same as the others.

"I'd say one of them probably came over for a look." Billy pitched in.

"Could be. We can ask 'em tomorrow if needs be." Tom looked to the other tracks. "But what I'm really puzzlin' over are these other tracks."

"Oh man. I didn't even see those at first." James had a cryptic and twisted look on his face. He was obviously thinking very hard about their little mystery.

"Looks like raccoon, don't it?" George took the words right out of Tom's mouth.

"That'd be one tolerable, big raccoon." Ralph looked astounded at the mere possibility as he scratched his flaming red hair.

"Well, it's gettin' too dark to find out tonight." Tom stood and stretched his back a little. "We can find out more in the mornin'. For now we at least know there ain't no cougar around. Let's get to the cabin afore dark."

As it was, the young men had taken almost too much time getting back. The sun was almost gone when they shuffled back into the cabin, and James had just enough light to get the lantern burning brightly before night had fallen in earnest. The fellas made a small meal of bread that Billy and James had pilfered from their mother's pantry and some canned sardines that Ralph had bought at the General Store. When they turned in, they all drifted off within moments. The first day of their adventure had been an interesting one, and the next would hold even more, Tom was sure of it. In hindsight, he would think that a wiser man would've wished for less excitement.

Chapter 4

Tom awoke around dawn as the early light fell across his eyes. He was thoroughly tangled in his blanket and reeked of nightsweat. He had some half remembered dream of screams in the night lingering in the back of his mind as he rose from his bed and disentangled himself. The others were still asleep when he slung his rifle around his back and emerged from the cabin. He thought that a hunt would do him some good and a little fresh rabbit and potatoes would make a good breakfast. It didn't take him long to find his quarry. A thicket near their tree proved an ample source. Tom was strolling back with four conies slung over his shoulder within minutes and was skinning them on the porch when George exited the cabin. Tom could tell it was George by his gait.

"Mornin' sunshine!" Tom chuckled at his friend.

"Dunno what's good about it. I hate mornings." George's speech was slurred to the point of being almost garbled.

"Ain't much of a mornin' person myself." Tom commiserated. "But I always figured that, once you're up, there ain't no use in doin' nothin' aside from stayin' up. And, if I have to be up anyway, I might as well get somethin' done."

George chuckled a little to himself, still a bit groggy. Tom turned from his skinned rabbits to look at his friend. George looked to have had a terrible night.

"You not sleep well, Georgie?" Tom asked with more than a twinge of concern in his voice.

"Tell you the truth, I don't recall ever having slept worse." George yawned out the last couple words.

"I didn't sleep so hot neither." Tom stood and clapped George on the back. "C'mon, let's get breakfast started."

George followed Tom into the treehouse to find the other three men in similar disarray. Billy had bags under his eyes. James had somehow managed to tear his shirt in the night. And, most disturbing of all, Ralph wasn't even cracking a smile.

"Well, we're a sorry lookin' lot." Tom chided. "I reckon that next time we oughta bring a couple nice feather beds with us; so's we get a little better sleep."

"My bedroll was just fine." Billy shot back. "What kept me tossing all night were those awful nightmares."

Tom and George stopped in their tracks as they were heading to the pot-bellied stove in the middle of the room. "You had a nightmare too?" George seemed almost unhinged.

"I had one myself." Ralph croaked out, ginger mustache bristling slightly.

"Me too, I had one too, fellas." James' face was hard to read. He looked half excited and half terrified.

"What happened in your dream, Billy?" Tom was not yet ready to concede that the nightmares were anything other than a coincidence, but he had to admit that there was something fishy about it.

"It's kinda hard to remember any details. All I really recall is lots of screaming." Billy shuddered slightly. "Yeah, just screams in the dark."

Ralph turned to look at Billy with eyes that looked as though he'd seen a ghost. "That was MY dream." he whispered.

"Mine too." said James in little more than a squeak.

Tom looked to George who seemed to have lost all capacity for speech. George slowly turned his head to look at Tom and gave the slightest of nods. The other fellas seemed to stop breathing when they saw George confirm his dream.

"I had the same dream, fellas." Tom heard Billy gasp. "I don't know what's going on here, but something isn't right."

"I say we skip breakfast and go see if them army boys had any dreams last night." James never did anything halfheartedly, and, right now, he was in a wholehearted panic.

"Calm down now fellas." Tom didn't want to look a fool by barging in on the doughboys in a panic crying about bad dreams. He was sure something was up, but he didn't want to look like a ninny in front of his new friends. "We'll go down there, sure enough, but we've got to pull ourselves together. How about we just calm our nerves a little with some breakfast?"

"Hang the breakfast!" Billy was almost unhinged. "Something is invading our dreams! Who can eat at a time like this?!"

Ralph punched Billy in the shoulder; it seemed to do him some good. "Get a hold on yourself, man." Ralph was older, and Tom was thankful for it; maybe his age would translate to authority. "Tom is right. We're awake now, and I don't hear no screamin'. Do you?" He looked to James who shook his head. "No matter what went on while we was sleepin' we need to eat something before heading out. And I, for one, ain't goin' runnin' in on a bunch of doughboys fresh off the front with tears in my eyes about a little nightmare."

"I'm with Tom and Ralph." George was still visibly shaken, but his resolve was starting to kick in. "A few minutes to eat ain't gonna make a hill 'o beans difference, anyhow."

James nodded, and Tom and George got to work on the fire while Ralph chatted with Billy, trying to calm him down a little more. Tom elected to set the rabbits on an old cast iron griddle and shove them right into the fire. They would be slightly charred this way, but the sooner they could eat and go check with the other fellas the better. Breakfast was fast and quiet as the boys all shoveled their rabbit and raw canned potatoes into their mouths, all except Billy, that is. Billy took a few bites, true enough, but he was far from enthusiastic. Once they had eaten their fill, the group headed toward the quarry as fast as they could go without breaking into a run. Tom felt like a foolish child, rushing like this. He hoped that he and the others wouldn't make idiots of themselves, barging in with tales of shared dreams, but he knew that the others were too frightened by the experience to listen to his take on things. He'd just have to suffer through and hope to find some answers.

The group made an enormous racket as they stomped through the woods to the quarry. Normally, the fellas would have been quite good at not announcing their presence as they traveled through a forest, but the morning's events had them all shaken and distracted, even Tom. As they exited through the treeline into the clearing that surrounded the quarry, Tom fully expected to see the doughboys milling about, cooking breakfast, fishing, or even jumping from the ledge as they had the day before, but there was no one in sight. The clearing was eerily still and quiet, Tom thought, but the others seemed not to notice as they headed toward the warehouse. Tom caught Ralph by the arm and spoke just loudly enough to get the attention of the others. "Don't it seem awful quiet around here, boys?" His gaze quickly darted between shacks and cliffs while pausing briefly to make contact with the eyes of each of his companions. George cocked his head to the side a little and listened. "You're right, Tommy. I don't hear nothin' at all."

"Right. Don't y'all figure them fellas would be somewhere out and about by now?" Tom looked to Billy to intimate his meaning.

"Not just that Tom." George interrupted the moment before Tom could tell what Billy was thinking. "I don't hear nothin' at all."

"Yeah, that's what I just said, Georgie. How's that different?" Tom hadn't quite followed George's meaning yet. "No, I mean anything at all. No birds chirpin' or nothin'." George slowly looked around them in a circle just above the heads of his compatriots. "The whole forest done gone quiet."

Billy's eyes got wider as he took it all in. "Normally only a big predator can make birds stop their chirpin' like that." He began scouring the treeline with his gaze. "You don't suppose that the doughboys really did see a cat and we just missed its tracks do you?"

That was a thought that none of them relished. Ralph still hadn't cracked a smile since they had dragged themselves out of bed. "If there is a cat around, that might explain why them fellas ain't outside yet."

James looked as though a hurricane of doubt and fear was swirling behind his eyes. "You don't figure it's stalkin' us do you?" His eyes were as wide as saucers.

Tom motioned for them all to gather close and take a knee. He began to whisper. "Look, we're here now, and we'd be safer if we can get under cover and quick. I say we move real quiet like over to the warehouse and get in there with them doughboys." He looked from man to man gauging their agreement. "I mean; if we can get ourselves in there, we'll be safe and we can find out about what's going on around here from them boys." The fellas all looked back at him with a mixture of agreement and fear plastered on their pallid faces.

Tom slowly stood to his feet and took in the landscape. He motioned for Billy and Ralph to follow a few feet behind him and for George and James to take up the rear. He unslung his rifle from his shoulder and checked that it was ready to fire; it would be tough to kill a big cat with a .22 caliber, but something was better than nothing. He started off slowly toward the edge of the lake; it would be much more difficult for a predator to ambush them with one side guarded by water. The boys fell in behind Tom silently, all of them alert. The tension in the air was palpable. Tom took his steps slowly and carefully. He moved so quietly that a nervous looking squirrel didn't notice his approach until the boys were mere feet from him. When they reached the shoreline, Tom began to breathe just a little bit easier. He didn't know for sure if the rumor was true, but he'd heard that mountain cats hated getting wet almost as much as house cats; he hoped with all his fervor that it was true and that the presence of the water would deter anything from attacking.

He was just a few yards away from the warehouse when he first noticed the door. It was closed, as he had expected, but it also had deep gouges and monstrous dents in the metal. Something had definitely gone very wrong here. Tom stopped and stooped low taking in his surroundings; the others followed his example. After a few moments of scanning the area, he turned slowly to look at the other fellas. Ralph seemed steeled by the concrete evidence that something was legitimately wrong. Billy was as white as a ghost, but he had his jaw tightened enough to crack a tooth; he was afraid, no doubt about that, but he was also determined. James looked to be a bit less terrified than his mirror image, but he was certainly less excited than he could usually be found when in the middle of an adventure. George was a rock; the walk seemed to have taken all of his fear and turned it into a suit of armor through which even Tom couldn't read his emotions.

Tom's voice was barely audible as he whispered. "We need to get inside there." The boys all nodded their agreement. "Alright. Georgie, you and Ralph take the lead to the door. Billy and James follow. I'll take the rear and watch for danger until we get behind that door." The boys nodded again, and George slowly stood and began silently walking toward the door; the others fell into their positions. Tom lagged behind to have more view of their surroundings without obstructing it with the warehouse. George and Ralph had reached the door and were knocking on it, quietly at first and slowly getting louder. After a few attempts, when there was no answer, James hauled off and slammed his fist against the door. It opened a crack. It wasn't locked! It was obvious from the way it had lurched open that small distance that no one had pulled it inward. Tom felt as though a lead weight had just dropped into his stomach, as George looked back at him with hollow eyes; the plain fear he'd worn earlier had returned. Tom got to his feet and walked to the door with his rifle leading the way. He and Ralph pushed it harder and the door swung the rest of the way open. What the group saw beyond the threshold would haunt their dreams for years to come. To say the place looked like a war zone is an understatement. The room was filled with more blood than any of them had ever seen; the sticky smell of iron was so thick that Tom could literally taste it. There was dark scarlet sprayed all over every surface they could see; the blood had been there for several hours, but there was no sign of the doughboys. Tom carefully tip-toed through the bloody carnage until something caught his eye; Wil's revolver was laying amidst the bloody mess on the floor, the only distinguishable relic of its owner. Tom stooped and picked it up, wiped off the bulk of the blood on his pants, checked that it was fully loaded, and handed it to George who immediately understood. They weren't staying; this place was no safer than the outdoors, and they had to get back to town as soon as possible. Tom turned to leave without going another step toward the bowels of what was now little more than a cavernous slaughterhouse. He heard retching just outside the door; apparently Billy couldn't handle the sight of so much blood, and Tom could hardly blame him. As he approached the door Ralph grabbed his arm.

"The screams, Tommy boy." His eyes locked on Tom's then gazed around the room.

Tom nodded his agreement. "Yeah, I think you're right. We didn't dream them at all; we all HEARD these poor fellas in our sleep."

Ralph was never one for sentiment or pointless posturing, but, as he turned away, Tom was certain that he saw tears in Ralphie's eyes. He knew that his tears would come too, for these boys he'd barely known, but, just then, he had more pressing concerns; whatever got the best of four trained soldiers was out there, and Tom was not about to stay here and wait for it to come back for seconds.

In retrospect, Tom would always remember the journey back to the cabin then to the Sheriff's office in shades of grey. He would come to believe that, after the vividness of the deep red horror he had so recently witnessed, no color in the world even permeated his fogged mind. In reality, the silent walk back to the cabin was fraught with frayed nerves and darting glances as the boys trained their gazes on every fluttering leaf or dark shadow they encountered sure that, at any moment, they would come face to face with what Tom imagined must be the Devil himself, in all of his demonic terror and hate; he could not fathom that anything less could have reduced even one man to such complete annihilation, much less four.

When they had arrived at the cabin, the frightened departure of just an hour past seemed almost like a jolly memory compared to what they now felt. George had taken the pistol inside first and made certain that it was safe before Billy, James, and Ralph helped collect all of their things. Tom stayed crouched at the base of one of the twin oak trees with his eyes peeled and ears perked until they had all safely rejoined him. He handed his rifle to James for the few seconds it took to sling his haversack over his shoulders.

The rest of the trek through the forest was a blur of anxiety and fear until they arrived back at Miller's Pond and simultaneously broke into a run that didn't relent until they had arrived back in Doughty. As they came up to the door inscribed *John Thompson Sheriff Doughty Virginia* in three lines across the glass, not one of the boys had a breath left in their screaming oxygen deprived lungs. Tom had a side stitch so severe that he thought he had broken a rib, but he didn't hesitate for even a second before ripping the door open and barging into Sheriff Thompson's office. John Thompson was about 40 and rarely had anything to do in the sleepy town that was Doughty; so, when four men came charging at his desk out of breath, soaked in sweat, carrying guns, and looking as though they'd just seen the Kaiser marching half of Germany down the street, he was understandably taken aback.

"Whoa boys! What's all this about?" He looked from face to terrified face inquisitively.

Tom tried to answer more than once through his wheezing and coughing and gasping for breath, but his lungs wouldn't cooperate. James was the best runner and was the first to choke out a response. "They're dead." The two words came out through gasped breaths, but it spoke volumes.

The middle aged lawman looked as though someone had hit him broad-faced with a two-by-four. "Dead?" His visage darkened as the comprehension began to wash over him that something untoward had happened. He glanced at each of their faces once more. "Who's dead?" he said to no one in particular.

Tom was finally beginning to feel the spasming contents of his chest begin to slow as his lungs took deeper and deeper draughts of air. "The others. The others are dead." He couldn't manage any more than that just yet.

"Doughboys . . . *gasp* . . . by the quarry . . . *gasp*" George sounded like Tom felt, scared and on the brink of collapsing a lung.

"What doughboys? I haven't heard anything about no doughboys in town." The sheriff was beginning to recover from his initial shock and ask the pointed questions he needed in order to get to the bottom of the matter.

"They was from Petersburg." Ralph choked on his words; he was still overcome by emotion as much as he was by the lack of oxygen.

Billy nodded vigorously sucked in a deep gasp of air and blurted out what he could. "They were veterans of the War." That little exertion pushed him into a coughing fit, but James seemed to have almost recovered his composure, at least physically.

"They were looking for work and had bunked in an old warehouse." He took a couple deep steadying breaths before continuing. "Something killed 'em." More deep breaths braced him. "Something big...and vicious. Maybe a wild cat." He choked a little and took more breaths.

Tom picked up where he left off. "Maybe a big cat, sure, but..." He coughed a little and gasped again. "...but I never seen anything like that in my life."

"Like what, Tom?" The sheriff's question was still all business, but the concern on his face softened his tone considerably.

"Blood, sir. So much blood." Tom shuddered; he felt the emotions rising again but refused to let them sweep him up just yet. "There's nothin' left of them boys. I mean nothin'." He shook his head violently a couple times to clear his eyes and senses. "The whole place is covered in their blood, though. They're dead, sure enough. It looked like someone got a mind to paint the place red and figured blood would do the job."

The sheriff was plainly beginning to get the picture. "At the quarry you say?" His mind was clearly trying to work out the details. "What were you fellas doing down there?"

"We was campin'." George answered first, but all of them had opened their mouths and nodded agreement without the slightest hesitation.

Georgie's answer seemed to be satisfactory for Sheriff Thompson. He stood from his seat behind the desk and went to the gun rack on the wall. He slung a revolver around his thick waist and chose a pump shotgun which he quickly loaded with buckshot. "Come ahead fellas. We'll run you home. I need some more armed men with me if this is a wild cat, anyway."

He grabbed a couple more shotguns and handed them to Ralph and James along with a field bag full of buckshot and headed out the back door past the holding cells which were, as usual, empty. Tom took up the rear feeling that he had enough leading today to last him a lifetime. As they filed out the heavy steel door, Tom realized that the sheriff had them loading into the back of a big truck. He waved Tom to the cab and motioned toward the passenger seat before climbing in himself and cranking up the behemoth.

"How bad was it Tom?" He said earnestly as they pulled out of the parking lot behind the office fighting with the tempermental clutch and gear shift.

"Bad sheriff. Very very bad." Tom's eyes began again to well up with tears. *"No!"* his mind screamed at him. *"Not yet. The time will come but NOT YET!"* Once again he choked down his tears and made his face as much like stone as he knew how.

"How many of them doughboys were there?" Tom had the impression that the sheriff was trying to keep his mind on the particulars and facts in order to delay his own realization of the tragedy that had occurred.

"There was four of 'em, Sheriff." Tom thought again about the men he'd met...was it just yesterday? It felt so long ago. He remembered Wil's jovial face and the way he led the others. He remembered Hosea's thick curly black hair and Harry's thick features. He recalled Mike last of all; he'd barely said ten words to the doughboy, but Tom felt his loss all the same.

"You ever seen a wild cat attack before?" The sheriff seemed to be puzzling something out in his mind.

"No sir, not in person. I've heard tell of 'em and have seen a bobcat den a time or two." Tom thought he knew where this was headed. He took a second and looked out the windshield as the town fell back around them as they headed north toward George's house and his own.

"Did it look like the bobcat dens at all? Maybe just a bigger version?" The sheriff seemed to be holding his breath waiting for Tom's response.

"No, it surely didn't, Sheriff." Tom sighed deeply. "It didn't look like anything I'd ever seen before, to be honest. It was the most gruesome thing I ever saw, and I work with my paw when it's time to slaughter the hogs in the Spring." He shuddered a bit; it felt like a cold chill had run down his spine.

The sheriff nodded slightly and commenced chewing his bottom lip as if afraid he'd say something he shouldn't. They continued in silence for a couple more minutes before arriving at Tom's house. His father was just pulling a horse-plow out of the barn as they pulled up. Sheriff Thompson left the engine running and opened his door. Richard Haynes' face showed an uncharacteristic bewilderment as the young men and Sheriff Thompson poured out of the truck toting their guns and looking about warily.

"Sheriff." Tom's father nodded. "Something amiss?"

"Mr. Rick, I'm afraid there's been an incident this mornin'." Sheriff Thompson cleared his throat and glanced at the fellas before continuing. "The boys here found what looks to be a killin' while they was campin'."

"A killin'?!" Tom spun on the spot to see his mother looking more shocked than he'd ever seen her before. She was usually so steady; he'd come to think of her as his rock amidst the storm, but this was a very different woman standing before him. "What kinda killin', John?"

"Everything's gonna be alright now, Mollie." Tom's father was crossing the yard to his mother. "The boys are safe now. Don't get your nerves unsettled."

Mollie Haynes calmed herself a little and took two deep breaths. "Sorry, Sheriff. You was sayin' somethin' about a killin'."

"Yes ma'am. Four outa town fellas seem to have been killed by somethin' down by the quarry." Tom cringed waiting for his mother's wrath; all of the fellas knew their parents would normally warn them away from going to the quarry after they'd been run off by the foreman, but Tom's mother didn't bat an eye at the word; she struck Tom as far from impassive, though. There was something deep behind her eyes that Tom had never seen before. Was it fear? Worry? He didn't know, but it scared him.

"How'd they die?" Tom's father sounded all business, but Tom thought he saw fear behind his steely grey eyes as well.

"That's what I mean to find out, Rick." John Thompson grunted a little and adjusted his gun belt before continuing. "The fellas say it mighta been a big cat, but they ain't rightly certain." The Sheriff motioned to the still rumbling behemoth. "I'm lookin' to bring a truck-full of men and guns down there and see what we can see. You mind joinin' me? It'd be awful nice to have a lawyer with me on this one. Never know what we might find, and I'd appreciate your take on things."

"Sure, whatever you need, John." Tom's mother stiffened almost imperceptibly, but Tom knew she didn't want his father anywhere near that place. "It's alright Mollie. There will be several of us. We'll be fine." He brushed a lock of hair behind her ear and looked her in the eyes for a moment before starting up the steps into the kitchen and calling over his shoulder. "Tom, you better bring that pea-shooter inside and grab something that can actually do a little damage."

~50~

CHAPTER 5

The rest of the morning was spent gathering up men and guns and dropping George, James, and Billy off at their houses. It seemed that everyone was on a party line sharing the gossip; by the time they were headed southward out of town, there wasn't a soul on the street, and every shutter in the county looked to be closed up and latched tight. Tom's heart seemed to have taken up permanent residence in his throat, and it beat so hard that he could hear it ringing in his ears. He glanced left and right at Sheriff Thompson and his father as he sat in the middle of the cab's bench seat. Over his right shoulder he knew he'd see Ralphie with his jaw set like stone. The discovery of the Petersburg boys had taken a toll on his joyful spirit, and the absence of his ever-present chuckle and smile made Tom feel as though he'd lost five friends rather than four. Tom adjusted his M1895 lever-action .30-06 rifle as it leaned against his knee. The rifle was usually reserved for deer hunting, but, as his father had said, he needed a gun with a little power, if this was actually a big cat attack. A big cat's power was only matched by its speed; Tom certainly didn't want to need a second shot if he was being charged by a fully grown mountain cat, but, in the back of his head, he had a thought brewing that what he was soon to face would be much, much worse.

It was almost noon when the truck lumbered around the left-hand turn where the Petersburg road passed Miller's Pond. Tom could almost taste the tension and fear exuding from his father and the Sheriff. The two men had taken a few minutes alone and away from the others before leaving Tom's house that morning to discuss what the fellas had told the Sheriff. Ostensibly, the private conversation was to spare Tom's mother and younger siblings the gruesome details of that morning's discovery, but Tom had a sneaking suspicion that there was much more going on here than they claimed. Each of the group was called over in turn to answer a few short questions for the two older men.

"Did you see any prints, Tom?" His father had asked when his turn came.

"No sir, not one. Well, not this morning anyway, but I was not about to go poking deeper into that warehouse with nothing more than my .22." Tom sniffed hard and wiped his nose trying to hide the fact that he was, once again, on the verge of tears.

His father cupped him bracingly on the shoulder. "So, there was blood everywhere but no prints in it near the door?"

"No, not one."

"And no sign of the fellas that had been sleeping there?" The Sheriff had more than a twinge of concern in his voice.

"Not nothing except some shredded bedrolls and that pistol that Georgie has."

"Okay, thank you, son." Tom recalled his father's face. There were more lines in his furrowed brow than in the fields they had freshly plowed. Tom couldn't recollect ever seeing his father more worried.

Tom's musing about his recollections of the morning's events was interrupted as the truck took the hard right turn onto the rough and muddy quarry road. The tires settled into the ruts in the dirt causeway with a thump, and the sheriff pulled to a slow stop as they pulled up in front of a pair of metal gates set into high wire fences that stretched off to Tom's left and right.

"Hey Garv!" Sheriff Thompson called out his open window. "Mind grabbing the gate for us?"

"Don't mind if I do, so long as these fellas keep their eyes peeled and guns ready. I been grabbed by a cat once afore, and I don't relish killin' another one with just my field knife." Garv was a brusk man, but, in the field, there was no one that Tom respected more, not even his father, who had fought with Roosevelt in Cuba.

Garv hopped down from the truck bench. He always moved a bit gingerly. He had been barely older than Tom when he had been attacked by the last big cat he had killed; that had been 30 years earlier, but the damage caused had left him permanently injured. Tom suddenly had a pang of guilt for thinking badly of George's uncle the day before. Billy had been right; there was no reason to blame a man for trying to run a business, and Tom could easily afford a soda or malt whenever he had a mind to loiter at the fountain.

"They ain't even latched, John!" Garv hollered back from near the gates as he cautiously approached them. He stepped up and swung them both wide open with almost no effort. "They weren't even pushed all the way to, fellas!"

Tom's father and the Sheriff exchanged knowing glances. "Seem odd to you, Rick?"

"Odd's the word for it, I'd say." Richard Haynes looked out his side window and seemed to be scanning the treeline beyond the fence. "I don't like it, John. I don't like it one bit."

"Let's get a move on Garv!" The sheriff called out the window brusquely. "I don't want anyone in harms way for longer than they have to be."

Mr. Garvin climbed back into the giant green monster and took his seat on the bench, and Sheriff Thompson violently shoved the truck into gear and started rumbling down the path once more. It took only a few minutes before Tom caught a glimpse of the sun flickering on the surface of the quarry lake. He could hardly believe that he had thought this place so beautiful just yesterday. The view as those cliffs came back into view now filled him with nothing but dread, where there once had been excitement at the coming adventure.

"Where we head from here, Tom?" The sheriff's voice had startled Tom, but he managed to pass it off as just an adjustment in his seat.

"Just over there, sir." Tom pointed to the group of ramshackle shacks. "The warehouse is behind that cluster of buildings."

The sheriff pointed the truck in that direction. He had slowed up considerably, and he called back to the bed of the truck. "Hey y'all fellas! This is it, now! Keep them eyes peeled as taters, and give a loud shout if you see anything at all!"

As he approached the buildings, Sheriff Thompson swung a little wide and hugged the shoreline, as Tom had done that morning. He was moving at barely more than a crawl now. Tom figured that he could easily walk faster than the pace at which they were currently moving. He was unsure if he'd rather hurry up and get it over with or take as long as possible before he had to re-enter what was now little more than a slaughterhouse where his new friends had been so brutally killed. Tom could now see the warehouse clearly and the shapes of the windows and that nearly destroyed door were beginning to become more distinct.

"We oughta stop here, sheriff." Tom didn't want to approach on foot, but he knew that it would be best if they took their time and scoured the ground leading to the warehouse for prints, as he and the fellas had not taken the time to do so that morning.

"Ain't we still a little far from the place, Tom? That's it there, right?" The sheriff had slowed to a near stop as he pointed at the warehouse.

"Yessir, that's it alright, but I figure that we oughta check for tracks. Me and the fellas were more concerned with gettin' outa here alive this mornin' than we was about findin' out what happened." Tom felt ashamed of having left in such a hurry, but he knew that he had made the right decision. He knew he couldn't help the doughboys, and he knew that getting himself killed too would do no one any good whatsoever. But deep down the shame of having left without trying to save them, dead or not, had a hold on his guts, and he wasn't sure he'd ever be able to shake it.

The sheriff swung wide right and turned the behemoth around before finally pulling to a stop and hopping out his door. Tom turned toward his father in anticipation of exiting too and getting the search under way. His father held up his hand and motioned for Tom to wait. "Tom, I know you feel guilty about what happened to those boys; I felt that when we lost friends in battle. But you can't let it cloud your judgment. You've got to keep a clear head. You hear me, son?"

Tom nodded. "I hear you, Paw." Tom tried to look as impassive as he could. His father patted his knee and opened the truck door.

As Tom climbed out and held his rifle at the ready, he felt exposed. He startled a bit when Ralph came up from behind and patted his shoulder. "Sorry, Tommy boy. I didn't mean to scare ya." Ralph said, sounding more than half dead.

"You okay there, Ralphie?" Tom could barely recognize his friend's face without its characteristic grin.

"Fine, Tommy, just fine. I just want to get whatever tore into them fellas and make it pay." There was certainly sadness and grief deep in Ralph's eyes. Tom had seen that look before, but there was something else bubbling there too. Tom had never seen anything quite like that look, but he supposed it must be hate. He wanted to say something to help his friend, but he couldn't quite find words that sounded anything less than absurd in his head. Just as Tom finally started to open his mouth, Ralph shouldered his shotgun and began to slowly walk toward the skirmish line the sheriff was organizing.

"Bill! Sam! You two fellas stay with the truck and keep an eye out." Sheriff Thompson hollered to the only men still near the truck. "We don't wanna get cut off from our escape if we gotta leave in a hurry." The sheriff turned on his heel and resumed organizing the skirmish line. "Not quite shoulder to shoulder, now, men." John Thompson was lining the men up a few feet between them. Tom stepped into place on the right end of the line and began, once again, his wary scouring of anything and everything he could see. He glanced in a wide circle spinning slowly on the spot. He saw the warehouse, the shacks, the treeline, the lake, the truck with Mr. Garvin and Mr. Abernathy standing guard high up in the bed, the skirmish line, and, finally, the warehouse once again.

"Okay now, fellas, we're gonna take it real slow and deliberate like. Every second man, look to your feet, but keep your ears open and never stop stealing glances around yourselves. The rest of you keep them eyes running circles. Don't want nothing taking us by surprise." He glanced up and down the line slowly checking for questioning looks and giving bracing nods where needed. "Okay, now, real slowlike. A few feet at a time, no faster than a crawl. Move out." The sheriff turned on his heel and waited for the line to catch him up before moving forward with it.

Tom inched forward looking here and there and trying to scour the ground for prints. He felt as though his head was quite literally on a swivel. He neared the corner of the warehouse and glanced down between it and the nearest shack toward the treeline to the west. Nothing moving. He snapped his view back to the ground just in time to see it. A footprint!

"Sheriff! Sheriff stop the line!" Tom had thought earlier that his heart would never beat faster than it did as he stood gasping for breath in the sheriff's office, but he had been wrong. His heart felt, quite literally, as though it would pound out of his throat, as it had not yet resumed its residence in his chest.

"What is it Tom?" Tom's father was just two places down from him and had stopped on a dime. The men at the other end of the line had gradually come to a stop and all eyes were looking at him.

"Prints!" Tom's voice was a hoarse whisper, but his tone was more intense than if he'd shrieked the word.

The sheriff cautiously walked toward where Tom stood as many of the other men scanned their surroundings. He stopped abruptly right in front of Tom's father and studiously took in every inch of the ground separating him from where Tom just realized that he was pointing. He and Mr. Haynes then began very slowly to step forward until they saw what Tom had seen. A bootprint.

"Boots." Sheriff Thompson stated flatly.

"Yessir. Same as we saw yesterday when we was looking for cat tracks. One of the doughboys thought he saw a big cat yesterday mornin'. That's why we figured that a cat mighta done the killin' inside. But we didn't see no cat tracks at all. Alls we found was some boot tracks and what looked like giant raccoon tracks over by the lake."

Tom's father and the sheriff looked again to the ground, as did Tom himself. "Stay where you are men." Tom's father called out. "We've found something curious. Don't move; we don't want to damage any tracks."

The three began moving in unison splitting wide around the boot print. Then, Tom spotted it. There, plain as day, were the same queer tracks he'd seen the day before. There were two of them side by side right in line with the boot track. "There we are!" Tom pointed to the raccoon-like tracks. "That's what we saw yesterday too!"

The sheriff and Mr. Haynes stooped down to get a better look. Sheriff Thompson stared at it intently, but Tom's father began looking ahead and behind for the next prints. Tom followed his father's example. They both spotted their quarry at almost the same instant. About six feet along there were two more boot prints spaced about a yard apart.

"There we are, John. More boots." Tom's father pointed at the prints.

The sheriff looked back behind him. The last boot print was six full feet behind them. "Who's got a stride twelve feet long?" the sheriff said not even attempting to conceal his disbelief. "Is it even possible?!" His voice had begun to sound a bit strained.

"I've never seen a man that can move like that." Tom's father was quick on the uptake, but Tom himself was intent on the raccoon tracks at his feet. He couldn't make heads nor tails of them, and it worried him to no end.

"You figure that these boot prints could've been made by them doughboys?"

"I wouldn't think so, John." Tom's father spoke up before Tom could formulate an answer. "These tracks aren't very old; they were probably made late last night."

"Well, we know whatever done the damage probably made these queer tracks, and it looks to me like there was someone with it who was wearin' army boots." Tom suddenly realized that the answers they wanted would be inside not in this line of tracks. He stood and began slowly following the line of the wall toward the door. Sheriff Thompson and Tom's father followed.

"Okay, men. Keep the pace. I want two of you with us inside when we get to the door. The others of you stay outside and keep a lookout." The sheriff was worried, and Tom didn't blame him in the least; after all, he felt like he'd been trying to swallow his heart since early that morning, and was having no more success than if he'd been trying to swallow the Moon.

They walked forward at a steady pace until they got to the door. Tom's father stood by the right-hand doorjam and looked Tom in the eyes. Tom nodded and took his spot on the other side of the door, shouldering his rifle, aiming it at the ground, and waiting for the time when that door would be shoved open once more. In retrospect, Tom would wonder why he didn't realize that he and the others hadn't pulled the door shut when they left earlier, but here it sat closed tighter than when they had first arrived that morning. Ralph and Mr. Philps left the others standing in a circle, backs to one another and moved toward Tom, Mr. Haynes, and Sheriff Thompson. Tom's father held up his left hand when they were a few feet away from the door, where the sheriff was kneeling and looking intently at the near shredded door. Ralph and Mr. Philps knelt on the sheriff's right and left.

Tom took a deep breath, held it, closed his eyes for a moment, then exhaled slowly. When he turned his head, Tom locked eyes with his father who nodded; Tom returned the nod and turned very slightly toward the door.

The next few seconds were a flash of fear and determination. It seemed that all at once his father kicked the door open, entered, and turned to the right, Tom followed him inside and turned left, and in their wake, the three behind them came charging through the gaping doorway. Tom looked deep into the shadows in front of him scanning for any signs of movement and listening for breathing, while his trigger finger twitched, but he heard nothing but his companions, and saw even less. The only one of his senses that seemed to deliver any response whatsoever was his sense of smell; he smelled blood, stale blood, and lots of it. The room had been awash with sticky redness a few hours earlier, but what he saw now had begun to turn a sickening shade of brown. Tom turned slightly to be able to see his companions and a little more of the warehouse itself. He noticed the sheriff and Mr. Philps choking a little on the smell, but his father was steeled as ever as he peered into the carnage around them.

"I never seen this much blood in all my life." Sheriff Thompson broke the silence. "If there was only four of them boys, then they's all dead, for a certainty."

"I agree." Mr. Philps seemed to have recovered a bit; that was good. Tom had thought that the poor man might be sick a moment before. "Most people don't have but a few quarts of blood in their whole bodies. There's enough here to bleed six men to death. I'd wager that they each sustained massive wounds."

"True enough, but we've got bigger worries at the moment." Tom's father's tone was all business. "Where are the bodies for one. And just where did the attacker or attackers disappear to?" Mr. Haynes had stooped slightly and was looking across the floor. "There are no return prints in the blood; so, they're either still here or went out another door or maybe a window."

Mr. Philps stiffened visibly. Tom could tell that the prospect of being in the room with a killer animal had him scared to the bone. If he was being honest with himself, Tom would have to admit that he was equally afraid at such a possibility. He followed his father's example and stooped as low as he could without touching his knees to the bloody aftermath in which he stood. He crouched as low as his legs would let him, staying on the balls of his feet; he wanted a better view of the floors, but he wasn't about to sacrifice his mobility to get it. Looking across the shiny floor he saw nothing at first. All he saw for a few moments was sticky, half-dried blood covering the floors and walls and spattered across the ceiling. He extended his gaze toward the shelves and noticed that they too were covered with blood, though only about halfway up. All of the aisles were clean though, except the widest one that went down the center of the room.

"Paw?" Tom was only half aware that he had spoken as he turned his head ever so slightly to his right and glanced at his father. Their eyes locked. Mr. Haynes' face had adopted the expression it wore whenever they went hunting; he had a searching squint in his eyes and a jaw set like steel, though Tom knew his teeth were not quite clenched. "That middle aisle's the only one with blood, Paw."

The others all looked down the aisle together and wordlessly began creeping forward through the bloody mess that had once been four doughboys. Tom hated the sound of it; everything was so quiet except the squish and squeak of their boots against the floor. He felt like a fiend with every step. Under his feet were good men; they had been genuine and gracious to Tom and the fellas, and he wanted nothing more than to wipe the blood from his soles and never set foot in this building again. But he kept willing his feet forward; he kept peering into the shadows around him. He looked left, then scanned forward, then scanned upward, then scanned left again, and kept that pattern as he stepped ever closer to the shelves. Every single step was a battle, but he refused to stop.

Suddenly, "My supplies!" Mr. Philps exclaimed so loudly that Tom thought his heart might stop dead in his throat. "My chemistry supplies!" Philps began to move forward more quickly when Mr. Haynes grabbed his arm and stopped him.

"What are you talking about, Michael?" Tom's father seemed not to be following the schoolmaster, but Tom immediately recalled the conversation upon which he'd eavesdropped the day before.

"My supplies! The one's the army seized! They're right there!" Mr. Philps was pointing to a broken wooden box a few yards away. Its contents were strewn about and mostly shattered against the floor. There were a few other crates and boxes nearby that appeared to have some very old blood splattered on them.

Tom looked down the aisle intently. The doughboys' blood seemed undisturbed as it stretched out in front of him. It covered the metal flooring quite evenly, stretching about ten feet from where he stood; then it suddenly stopped. There was a square on the floor that had no blood spatter at all but was ringed in blood for another foot or so. About ten feet beyond that was Mr. Philps' box and the other boxes. Tom was sure that the blood on those boxes was from some other event.

"Paw?" Tom spoke amidst the chatter that he had tuned out between the two men as he investigated the floor in front of him. Mr. Philps was almost beside himself, and didn't stop when Tom spoke. "Paw!" Tom's raised voice stopped the conversation.

"What is it Tom?" His father seemed almost upset at having been interrupted.

"Look at the blood, Paw." Tom pointed to the peculiar shape ahead of them, and Mr. Philps gasped. Ralph and the sheriff seemed nonplussed, but his father became quite silent for a few moments.

"John." Mr. Haynes finally ventured.

"Yeah Rick."

"I think the killer is still here." His father's voice was barely more than a whisper, but the impact of his words hit Tom so hard he thought he might be sick.

"Still here?!" The sheriff was obviously shaken by the thought. "Where at? Did ya see somethin'?"

"Only the same thing that Tom just pointed out." Richard Haynes had a cool tone in his voice, but Tom thought there might be a twinge of fear there too. "See that odd shape in the blood?" The two older men nodded and seemed to begin to realize what it was that laid before them.

Ralph tucked his chin a little; Tom had never seen him this determined before in their lives. "There's a cellar, ain't there, Mr. Haynes?" Ralph reminded Tom of what a volcano must look like right before it explodes, and that thought scared Tom more than even a mountain cat.

"There surely is. Looks like it's supposed to be a secret. If it weren't for the blood there, we might never've spotted it." Tom's father was still nodding when the two of them took their renewed steps toward the trap door.

Almost immediately the metallic smell of blood was joined by another more acrid smell that Tom couldn't quite place. "You smell that, Paw? That queer smell?"

"I do." The voice behind him Tom recognized as Mr. Philps. "That's the smell of sulfuric acid. I had a big bottle in that box when the Army took it from my office." Mr. Philps inched past Tom; the thought of the killer still being closeby seemed to have restored the caution he had momentarily lost. "Look just there!" Mr. Philps was pointing to a spot near the broken box where there was some shattered glass and the floor was discolored. But Tom noticed something more.

"There's a crack in the floor!" He felt like this was a puzzle, and he was unsure if he really wanted to complete it.

The sheriff was then moving past Tom and the schoolmaster with a large section of a metal pole. Ralph was right behind him carrying another of the same. "We can figure this mess out once we catch or kill whatever's down there, y'all." Sheriff Thompson was right, by Tom's reckoning. If there was something dangerous down there, then they should be shooting it rather than talking about it.

Tom moved to help the sheriff, while Mr. Haynes stepped up beside Ralph and put his shoulder into the metal rod. The floor-plates creaked loudly and began to give way. They swung the metal slabs upward. Tom found the weight of the doors to be almost unmanageable. Each of them must have weighed every ounce of 200 pounds or more. Tom was very intent on staying as far to his left as possible, as Mr. Philps was behind him pointing his Springfield rifle at the ever widening gap between the doors. Finally, when Tom thought his arms were about to fail him, the doors reached their apex and fell to the sides against the metal shelves.

Tom stepped back, unslung his Winchester, and aimed it intently into the cellar that had opened before him. The chasm was lit from below; it looked to be electric lights from where Tom stood. But what really caught his eye was the thick layer of blood caked on the stairs, the bodies at their base, and the same queer footprints leading down the staircase.

"That ain't no wild cat." The sheriff finally said what Tom had seen brewing behind his eyes while they drove to meet Tom's parents that morning.

"It surely ain't." Tom had suspected something else was going on almost from the start, but the idea that a cougar could have been the culprit had been, somehow, comforting. Tom felt as though the floor had fallen out from under him, but the worst was yet to come.

"I don't care what it is. I'mma kill it dead." Ralph's words rasped out tinted with hate and garbled with tears. "Dead!" He shouted, full of rage.

Tom looked at his friend to find his eyes locked, full of tears at the base of the stairs. To this point, Tom had managed to not look directly at the bodies, but he could no longer will his eyes away from the terror that awaited him there. Tom felt his gaze traveling toward the brokenness that had been new friends only a day earlier; he hoped against all he knew and everything he'd ever known that what he would find there would be something else, but his hope was futile. He locked eyes with Mike's hollow gaze. When Old Lady Givens had died the summer before, Tom had attended the viewing. She was a kindly old lady who always brought hard candies to Sunday meeting for the kids who all fought for the chance to sit by her during the sermon, and, as she lay there peaceful in her casket with her eyes closed, Tom felt that she could almost sit up and hand him a candy. This was different. The boys were in the most chaotic pile Tom had ever seen. Arms were here, legs there, often not attached to anything at all, and there was so much blood. It looked almost as though they were swimming in a sea of red. But Tom couldn't tear his gaze from their eyes. Wil, Harry, and Hosea each held the same hollow terrible gaze as Mike. There was no mistaking that gaze for sleep. The boys were dead, and Tom felt his stomach lurch, flip, and tie into a knot all at once. The man wearing those boots and whatever pet he had with him would pay for this. These boys survived fighting the Hun for freedom over there just to be torn limb from limb where they should have been safe for the rest of their days. Tom became aware of the fact that Mr. Philps had just become sick behind him. Tom didn't blame him, but he knew he'd never been further from losing his stomach. This new emotion had steadied him. Was it hate? A thirst for vengeance? Or was is something else? Tom didn't know what to call it, but he knew it was deep and powerful and was keeping him on his feet. If it *was* hate, then it surprised Tom. He'd always thought he hated doing tedious chores around the farm, but what he felt right now filled him with strength and action where hate had always filled him with angst and sloth. No, this was not hate. This was something much more basic.

"Paw?"

"Yeah, Tom." His father sounded old, all of a sudden. Tom looked to him. His eyes had softened some. He looked sad...and sorry.

"We gotta get them outta there Paw." Tom was resolute. He had never felt more driven in all of his 18 years. He suddenly felt more like a man than ever before, and it somehow frightened him.

"It don't look to be a very big room, Rick." The sheriff's words rang true. The room was very small, and Tom saw nothing there but the mangled bodies of his friends. "Might be the killer tossed 'em there and went out another way, like ya said."

"Could be." Mr. Philps was still obviously queasy, but he seemed to be putting his mind to task in order to settle his stomach. "Could be there's another secret door somewhere."

"First things come first." Mr. Haynes had resumed his staunch and iron-like demeanor, but Tom still saw hurt behind his eyes. "Those boys don't deserve to be trussed up like animals. We get them out of there; then we search that room for more clues." He looked up and took note of each of the men before him. His eyes lingered briefly on Ralph and Mr. Philps. "Michael, take Ralph outside for some air and send in Dr. Wilson and Doug Samson."

It took Mr. Philps some time to pull Ralphie away from the cellar doors, but, in the end, Tom's horror-struck friend consented to go help stand watch outside. Tom resumed his scanning of the room, but he somehow knew that the killer was not coming to attack them. He had a feeling somewhere he couldn't even identify that the killer wanted them to find this massacre; he felt like the killer was toying with him. No, he *knew* the killer was toying with him, him personally.

"Paw. There ain't nothing gonna attack us today." Tom's shoulders slumped a bit as he turned to face his father. The sheriff seemed not to notice their conversation as he peered into the shadows around them.

"Tom, are you okay?" His father's eyes were searching his own more deeply than he'd ever done before.

"I'm fine, Paw. I just want to get them out of there and find what did this." He was surprised to find that he was almost telling the truth when he said he was okay. In the moment, nothing seemed to matter but the task at hand. He knew he'd be a wreck later, but, for right now, he was all business.

"Good man." His father had let his gun hang in his right hand and clapped Tom on the shoulder with his left. "If you need to go outside at any point, just go. There's no shame in it, Tom. You kne these boys, and nobody'll think you less a man for stepping out."

"Honest Paw, I want to help them. I know I can't save them now, but they deserve better than...well...than that." Tom waved his hand at the hole and choked for a minute. "*NO!*" His mind screamed at him. "*It's not the time! Those boys are counting on you, Thomas Richard Haynes! You pull yourself together and be a man for them. You owe them that much.*" Tom took a deep steadying breath and straightened himself up. As his eyes met his father's again, what he saw there surprised him more than anything else he'd seen in this bizarre day. Deep in his father's strong grey eyes Tom saw something he hadn't seen in an age, *pride.* His father's jaw was tight and brow was furrowed, but his pride in his son was practically beaming. That sight steadied Tom even more, and made him feel as though his chest was swelling too large for his shirt.

"Rick?" Dr. Wilson called to Tom's father and the moment was broken. "Philps said that it was pretty bad in here."

"Yeah, Jack, bad barely scratches the surface." Mr. Haynes began describing what he thought would be the best approach for disentangling the boys and getting them back to town, but Tom's mind wasn't in the conversation. He was vaguely aware of the blood on his hands and the bizarre feeling of carry an arm or leg to the thick bags the doctor had brought with him, but his mind was somewhere else. His mind was focused on that look in his father's eyes. He somehow knew that he would never forget that look, and he determined that he would always strive to make his father feel that same sense of pride in him.

~67~

Chapter 6

After searching the cellar walls thoroughly and the ground around the building for no less than hour and finding no sign of the attacker, Mr. Haynes and Sheriff Thompson agreed that, for safety's sake, they had best return to town. Tom had spent the entire search inside the warehouse. He knew somehow that there was more to be found in that cursed building, but he couldn't, for the life of him, find what he was seeking. He went over the walls of the cellar a dozen times, searching them inch by inch, aided by the electric lights that were suspended from the ceiling in metal grates. He studied them so intently that one pass was surely enough to be sure that they were solid, but Tom would not relent. He even stooped down and felt along the floor wrist deep in blood, but, if there was anything to be found there, he couldn't feel it. The futility of the search irked him, and his temper was almost raw, but, unlike most days, the anger he felt deep down made him, somehow, more effective, rather than less.

When his father had called to him from the door that it was time to call it a day and return to town, Tom begrudgingly emerged from the hole where he had spent the afternoon slogging through the butchery. He shook the blood from his hands and wiped them on a shop towel that was hung haphazardly over one of the shelves before hefting his rifle once more. He had left it on a shelf to keep it clear of the blood; though he was sure that it was simply psychological, Tom couldn't bear the thought of it being tainted with the blood of his friends. He shuffled wearily toward the ravaged metal door. The sunlight still shone in slanting through the windows and doorway, but he could tell that dusk would be upon them in barely more than an hour. He didn't want to stop the search, but the wisdom of getting to shelter was undeniable.

As he emerged from the carnage, he realized that he had become so accustomed to the smell of death that he'd almost forgotten how good it felt to breath fresh air. He flared his nostrils and took a deep labored breath. It was then that he noticed that his heart had sunk back to where it belonged; he had no idea when his pulse had slowed and his fears had abated, but he felt human again and was thankful for it. He looked to his feet and realized that his boots were a near ruin of sticky red and brown. He started toward the edge of the lake to rinse them, and a few of the others followed suit. He dipped his feet one at a time up to the knee and let the now old blood slough off. The cool water soothed his aching feet and helped remind him that there were still good things in life, but, though some other time he might have lingered here for hours, he cut his relief short and strolled back toward the truck. For the first time since Mr. Philps pulled him out the door to get Dr. Wilson and Mr. Samson, Tom caught a glimpse of Ralph Donnelson. He looked dejected, angry, and confused all at once.

"Ralphie?" Tom called as he approached the tailgate. "You alright, buddy?"

Ralph looked up slowly. His eyes were somewhat sunken and tired, but, deep within, Tom could still see the fire he'd seen earlier, before they had kicked in the door for the second time. "Oh. Hey Tommy." Ralph's voice was hoarse; he sounded half dead.

Tom reached for his canteen. "Have a drink Ralphie; you sound a bit rough."

Ralph accepted the canteen and took a long draw off of it. "Thanks Tommy, I needed that. Reckon I forgot about drinking." He wiped his mouth with his sleeve and slowly handed the canteen back to Tom.

"Mind if I sit back here with you, Ralph? I could sure use some fresh air." Tom patted him on the knee, and Ralph scooted in along the bench that ran along the right side of the truck bed.

As Tom climbed up, he noticed the ache in his legs once more; between the tense state he'd been in since discovering the massacre, the run that morning, and the hours spent stooped low scouring the cellar for signs of a hidden room his legs were nearing their failing point. Even if the sun wasn't beginning its downward trek toward the horizon, his fatigue alone would be reason enough to call off the search until the next morning. The next morning? As he slumped onto the bench next to his friend Tom suddenly remembered that the next day was Sunday. Would they be attending meeting with all the other families? Was it safe to gather like that? The strangeness of this new experience impressed itself upon Tom, once more. He'd need to remember to speak with his father about it when they arrived home.

"Tom." Speaking of his father, Tom turned to see that Mr. Haynes was approaching with the Sheriff; everyone else was already aboard the truck.

"Yeah Paw?"

"You alright?" Tom's father had a tired look in his eyes, but a shadow of his earlier pride still lingered in the corners.

"Alright Paw. You?" Tom patted his father's shoulder as he came up to the tailgate.

"Alright. Just tired." Richard Haynes wiped his brow on his sleeve. "You riding back here?"

"Yeah, thought I'd get some fresh air. Been inside that building too long." Tom spoke the words as though that was all there was to it, but his father read in Tom's gaze that he wanted to be close to Ralph on the drive. His friend was obviously taking the days events very hard.

"Okay son." His father nodded knowingly and closed the tailgate. "You keep a weather eye out, now, and your gun at the ready. There's no tellin' where that monster might be." His father's tone was awash with concern, sorrow, fear, and anger.

"Will do, Paw. Will do." Tom had kept his trigger hand on his rifle without pause since he gathered it inside the warehouse, but he now shouldered it once more as though he'd see his quarry at any second.

"Good man." His father said clear as day before lumbering to the cab, climbing inside with Sheriff Thompson, and slamming his door. Tom saw pride in his father's eyes once again. He knew his father loved him, but those were a different kind of words. Those words meant respect, and Tom valued them more than he could possibly express. The day had already been a roller coaster ride, full of twists and turns, ups and downs, but Tom knew that two things he would not soon forget came today, not from the beast, whatever it was, but from his own father.

Tom realized that he had kept his gaze searching the entire time he'd been musing about his father's new-found perspective of him. He consciously stole a glance at Ralph between his furtive attempts to see movement in the trees or between the buildings. The usually jovial young man sitting beside him was somewhat slumped in his seat, but Tom thought he saw his spirits buoyed slightly by his friend's closeness. *That, at least, seems to be something.* Tom thought to himself, as the Sheriff once again cranked up the monster, roughly slammed it into gear and started off toward Doughty, worried mothers, wives, siblings, and a hundred frighted families.

It seemed only moments before they were once again driving through the metal gates William Garvin had opened hours earlier. Tom eased his searching gaze for a few moments to let his eyes linger on the gates as they drove through them.

"Oughtn't we to close the gates and keep folks from going in there?" Tom called out to no one in particular.

Garv was the first to answer. "Did closed gates keep you boys out?"

The answer was obvious, but Tom felt obliged to answer it just the same. "No, sir. They sure didn't."

"As I see it, Tom, the only folks likely to be headed to the quarry through the gates are the quarry workers, and them bein' left open like that is apt to warn 'em that somethin' is up." Garv scratched his nose, and Tom mused that the only time that Mr. Garvin looked like a pharmacist was when he was behind the counter wearing his white coat. Right now the grizzled man looked more like a character out of some dime novel Western.

"I reckon that makes pretty good sense." Samuel Abernathy interjected. Mr. Abernathy, Mr. Garvin, and George Priestly Sr., Georgie's father, had been the best of friends from the time that they were all boys. Abernathy and Garv were several years George's senior, but they had all been intent on adventure, much like Tom and the fellas, even after Mr. Garvin's unfortunate run-in with the mountain lion.

"Still." Garv continued. "I reckon we oughta bring some signs back down here next time to keep folks out." Tom reasoned that would be the best course of action, as they left the rutted dirt road and made their hard left turn back toward town.

The rest of the drive was made in silence as the men all kept their eyes on the ever darkening woods. Every few minutes one of the men would startle slightly at something, likely imagined, moving in the forest, but nothing came charging at the truck. If he was honest with himself, Tom would have to admit that he more than half hoped that the culprit would do exactly that, and sooner rather than later. With this many men and guns close at hand, even a bull elephant would be hard-pressed to do any damage before being dealt a fatal blow, but that would be too much to ask of a hardened killer, such as this.

There were lights burning behind shuttered windows as the behemoth lumbered back toward Doughty proper. Tom looked in the bed just behind the cab where the four body bags lay. He knew that Dr. Wilson would be up late into the night trying to determine exactly what happened to the doughboys, and Tom did not remotely envy him his job. No, Tom felt very keenly that he had done his duty to the boys in getting them out of that den, but he didn't think he could stomach spending any more time among the dead just now.

The truck came to a rolling stop in front of the Williams boarding house; Janey, Rick Haynes' septuagenarian secretary, and her two grandnephews, now well into their 50's, ran the old house. Five families had taken up residence there this morning as the men prepared to seek out the killer. Mr. Samson, the butcher, jumped down from the truck to greet his wife who was on the verge of tears, while Mr. Abernathy joined him on the ground and strolled toward the entrance where his family waited, a bit more stoically. Mr. Philps joined them in the street.

"Oh, Doug!" Mrs. Samson exclaimed. Tom had never seen her look so distraught; in fact, Tom had barely ever seen the woman when she wasn't laughing. At the butcher's shop, she and her husband were practically a comedy troupe.

"It's okay, Maggie. It's okay." Mr. Samson ran his hand over his wife's hair as he tried to comfort her. "We all made it back safe and sound, darlin'. We didn't see hide ner hair of the beast."

"Doug, I was so WORRIED. Y'all been gone for HOURS!" Margaret Samson's fear and worry was quickly turning into anger. Mr. Philps, Mrs. Samson's brother, stepped forward to lend his brother-in-law his support.

"Now Maggie, that's not fair, and you know it good and well." His tone was softer than his words, but there was no mistaking the reprimand for anything else. "Your husband has been doin' what any good man should do. If you wanted a man who'd always be home safe and sound, then you shoulda married a coward."

Mrs. Samson blushed a bit at the rebuke, but it was clear that her brother had cowed her unfair indignation, at least for the moment. "I reckon you're right, Michael." She conceded as her eyes swelled once again with tears. Tom couldn't quite tell if they were tears of fear, shame, or pride, but her face quickly began leaking anew. "I was just so worried is all." She bawled and buried her face into her husband's shoulder.

Mr. Philps stepped forward and patted his sister gently on the back. "Everything's fine now, Mags. Everything is alright." Tom heard a sound unlike anything he'd ever heard before exuding, ever so quietly, from beside him. He turned to see Ralph's face alight, once more, with rage. The sound was that of Ralph's teeth grinding as he clenched his jaw so tight that Tom feared he'd do himself some sort of damage.

"You alright Ralphie?" Tom was almost afraid to approach his friend, but he knew that he had to do something before Ralph exploded.

Ralph turned his face to Tom. The fire in his eyes frightened Tom to no end, but Tom held his gaze, nonetheless. "Do I look alright to you?" Ralph growled his response then swore under his breath. "Nothing is *alright*!" Ralph's volume was still inaudible to the rest of the townsfolk, but his tone was unmistakeable. Ralph's new-found vehemence was now targeting the Samsons and Mr. Philps.

"Look, Ralphie, I know what you're feeling; I really really do, but it ain't their fault, pal." Tom was not about to let go his grip on his rifle, though he couldn't quite say why, but he gently prodded his friend with his elbow as a gesture of friendship. "I knew them boys too, and what happened to them was a crime. But these folks're just scared. They don't mean nothin' by it."

Ralph's jaw eased up a bit as he glanced from Tom to the small huddle and back. "Yeah, I know you're right, Tommy boy, but they ain't got no idea what they're talkin' about." He punched his thigh so hard that Tom was sure it would leave a deep bruise.

"I know. I know, buddy. But you can't let it get to ya. We've gotta keep our heads clear, pal. If we don't, alls we're gonna do is wind up gettin' ourselves killed as well. Ya hear me?" Tom was worried about his friend, but Ralph's face seemed to register some impact from Tom's pleading.

"Yeah, you're right, Tom. You're right." Ralph's eyes sank from rage back to sorrow in little more than an instant. "I'm a wreck buddy. I dunno what's wrong with me."

"I do. You'd made friends out there, Ralphie, and now they're gone. That ain't easy. We all deal with that sorta stuff our own way, but ya gotta keep your head straight. These folks ain't the enemy, pal. The enemy is out there somewhere." Tom gestured to the pastureland behind them and suddenly realized that it was dusk. The sun would be gone in less than 30 minutes.

"Tommy, we need to get a move on." Ralph's voice was almost shaking, and Tom saw terror in his eyes.

"When you're right, you're right." Tom looked left and found his father standing by waiting for the people nearby to get to their respective locations. "Paw!"

Mr. Haynes turned his head suddenly to look Tom in the eye. "What is it son?" His face was impassive, but his tone betrayed the uncertainty he felt.

"The sun's settin', Paw. We gotta get a move on." Tom pointed toward the treeline where the sun was setting.

Without hesitation Mr. Haynes hollered loudly enough to silence everyone mid-sentence. "HEY NOW!" All eyes jerked to Richard Haynes, and many hands jerked to their weapons. "This reunion stuff is all well and good, but it's better done indoors. Don't anybody set foot outside a door before morning, and, until we get this thing, don't nobody go anywhere alone nor without a gun."

"Rick's right folks. Everyone inside and locked tight 'til mornin'." Sheriff Thompson seemed to have woken from a slumber. Tom knew that it was simply a feeling of relief at being home, but that relief was premature.

Those who were staying the night at the boarding house tucked themselves inside and locked the doors tight; the rest of the men closed the tailgate, loaded into the cab, revved up the engine, and headed toward the last two stops. The last stop would be Billy and James' house, where Dr. Wilson kept his office and examining room; with his family out of town, Ralph would be bunking with them, and Sheriff Thompson would stay the night there and assist the doctor in determining just what happened to the doughboys. But first the truck stopped at the Haynes farm where Tom, Mr. Haynes, and Mr. Garvin were greeted at the door by Tom's mother, Mrs. Priestly, and George. Garv ushered everyone inside as fast as they would move, and Tom was glad; the sun had fully set, and the only light to be seen was from the truck's headlights and the gas lamp by the front walk.

Almost as soon as he was inside with the door shut behind him, Tom's mother pulled him and his father into the tightest hug he thought he had ever experienced. For a moment he thought she meant to smother him, but, just as soon as her arms had tightened, they became limp and he felt her sobbing against his shoulder and his father's. Just then, Mark, Abigail, Kimberly, Ruth, Mary, and little Hannah Haynes all poured down the stairs in their night shirts followed closely by Paul and Grace Priestly. Amidst shrieks of "Poppa!", "Uncle Garv!", and "Tommy!" the whole foyer devolved into a mess of tearful reunions and embracing family members. For a few furtive moments Tom found himself in the middle of a tangled web of little arms pulling at him and little voices asking what happened. Thomas feared that some of the smallest children might be hurt in all the hubbub and snatched up his youngest sister and hugged her tightly. Mark was the second oldest Haynes child, at 14, but Hannah was only three years old.

"Alright now! That'll be quite enough shouting!" Tom's mother tearfully silenced the noise. Tom had always wondered why, when the noise stops, the action always slows along with it. Everyone straightened up, and little Hannah buried her tiny pink face against Tom's neck. "Okay, now. Haynes children, all back in bed, right this instant. It's after nine o'clock, and every one o' y'all has chores to do in the mornin'." There was some grumbling, especially from the older children, but they all obeyed. Tom began to follow them upstairs as well, "Tom. Not you son. You should get cleaned up and have some dinner first."

Tom remembered food, just that instant. The days events had driven food from his mind, but at the word "dinner" his desperately empty stomach began to growl loudly. He descended back into the foyer where George clapped him on the shoulder as Mrs. Priestly ushered her two youngest back upstairs. Once they were far enough away to be out of earshot George whispered, "Besides that, we got some talkin' to do, as well, Tommy boy." George's wan smile was far from bracing and betrayed the fear and grief that lurked behind George's eyes which were scanning the dried blood stains all over Tom's clothes, but Tom was grateful for the gesture. He had seen too few smiles that day, and, he suddenly realized, anything felt better than enduring Ralph's sullen rage.

Tom followed his mother into the kitchen where she busied herself at the stove, warming three plates of food for the men who she shooed toward the basement where they found clean clothes, a big brass tub full of hot water, and three wash basins. Tom's mother was nothing if not thorough. The men washed and changed in silence. It felt almost unreal to be clean again. Tom had only gotten blood on his hands and feet, but he washed himself so vigorously that even his skivvies were too wet to go unchanged; the older two men were not as thorough, though they had spent much less time in the blood today than Tom had. Before heading upstairs, Tom and Mr. Haynes left their blood-stained boots to soak in the tub with a tin-cap of lye.

The kitchen table was set for them when they reemerged, and Mrs. Haynes, George, and Mrs. Priestly all sat awaiting them, Mrs. Priestly at the end nearest the back door, George opposite his mother, and Tom's mother at the opposite end of the bench nearest the basement door. Tom took a seat between George and his mother, while his father sat at the head of the table next to Mollie Haynes' end of the bench and Garv sat next to his younger sister. For a few minutes the only sound was that of forks and knives. When the men had finished eating, Mrs. Priestly rose, kissed George on the cheek, squeezed her brother's shoulders and headed to the front staircase.

"Agnes doesn't want to hear about them boys." Mollie Haynes. said in a matter-of-fact tone. "To tell you the truth, I don't much wanna hear about it neither, but I'll stay for the time being."

"Reckon there ain't no more sense in puttin' it off is there?" Bill Garvin sighed deeply and vigorously rubbed his face with his hands for a few moments. "Well, I say we get to the rat killin', before we think about it too much."

"I agree, Bill." Tom's father pushed his plate to the side and placed his linen napkin in a pile atop the small remnants of his supper. "Mollie, you should know from the outset that what we have to talk over is gruesome at points."

Tom's mother swallowed hard and nodded her head slowly. "I understand, Rick. Say what needs to be said." His mother's voice was choked with emotion, but she held back her tears.

"Tom, I think it would be best if you told George the basics before we get into the discussion in earnest." Richard Haynes' eyes pierced Tom to the core, but the thought they betrayed was one of apology.

Tom straightened himself up and cleared his throat. "Ahem! Ummm, well, I reckon the best place to start is to just say it outright. We found 'em, Georgie; we found the doughboys." Tom was starting to get choked up, but he cleared his throat again.

"I reckon since you didn't come in whoopin' and hollerin' that we was right about 'em. They're dead, ain't they?" George had done his best to put on a face of stone, but there was a well of tears in the corner of one eye that he surreptitiously wiped away, hoping no one would notice.

Tom pretended not to see his friends tears while choking back tears of his own. He nodded through a quivering jaw and steeled himself for what must've been the thousandth time that day. "They're dead." He heard the words more than he said them. They rang in his ears and shattered the near silence of the night. The words felt wrong in his mouth. They felt evil and wretched and foul to the greatest extent he could imagine. He coughed a bit and wiped his nose before gathering himself once more. Looking back to his father to indicate that his portion was done, he saw it again, pride. This time he saw it, not only in his father's eyes, but in the eyes of his mother too, as tears streamed down her face. How had he missed that look all of these years?

"Thank you Tom. I know how hard those words are to say, but I knew you'd want them to come from you." Tom nodded to his father, and Mr. Haynes nodded in return. "Alright. So here's the real business. Those boys were killed very viciously. I've seen a lot of things in my life, but, short of a man being hit full in the face by cannon fire, I've never seen anything that disturbing." Tom's father coughed a little and took a sip of water from the glass sitting next to his plate.

"True enough, Ricky. True enough." Garv broke the silence with his brusk voice. "I've seen many a troubling sight myself, but what I hear 'bout the state of them fellas is the likes of which I ain't never heard before." Even harsh, grumbling Mr. Garvin seemed to have some emotion in his voice as he said those words.

"I ain't seen much myself, before today, but that was a horror I ain't like to forget anytime soon." Tom didn't know what made him say it, but he knew he felt better once it was out. His mother reached down the table and patted his hand. He appreciated the touch, but it made it harder to keep in his tears.

"Garv, you're the best hunter I know. What do you think could do that to a man?" Tom's father was looking directly at Mr. Garvin who returned his gaze.

"Only thing I ever heard of could have a den like that is one of them big African lions, Rick. Y'all know, like them big man-eaters they done shot that eat them hundred rail workers some years back."

"I read about them, but how could something like that get to Doughty without anybody noticing?" Tom's father had a puzzled look on his face. He usually wore that expression when playing chess with Mr. Philps after meeting on Sunday evenings.

"I dunno, Ricky. I just don't know." Garv scratched his nose.

"How bad could they have been?" George asked incredulously. Tom could tell that the thoughts swimming in his head were still those that Tom had been expecting when he thought a big cat was responsible. "Georgie." Tom cleared his throat again. "Georgie, they was in pieces. Something tore them to pieces." Tom grunted hard to keep the tears at bay. Try as he might, he couldn't stop them all, as one solitary tear trickled down his right cheek for everyone to see. Tom lost his patience with himself and slammed his fist down on the table. The pain helped, somehow, to keep his tears where he wanted them.

"Pieces?" His mother's voice was strained. "What does he mean 'pieces', Richard?"

"He means what he said, Mollie. Something pulled them apart, limb from limb." Mr. Haynes took his wife's hand and squeezed it slightly as she gasped, but Tom's gaze was still on George. George's face was frozen in the most horrible expression that Tom had ever seen. The only word that came to mind to describe that visage was aghast, but even that fell short.

"There's more though, ain't there, Tom?" Garv wanted this conversation over, and Tom tended to agree with him.

"There's more. We saw them same footprints as yesterday, Georgie."

"The weird coon tracks?" George seemed to recover a bit with the renewed discussion.

"Yeah, them and the boots. Them boots didn't belong to the doughboys." Tom gave George a knowing look whose eyes widened. George snapped his gaze to his uncle, who nodded, then to Tom's father, who nodded as well.

"I'm confused, honey. What does that mean?" Mollie was speaking to Tom, but it was Mr. Haynes who answered the question.

"It means, my dear, that our doughboys were murdered." To Tom's knowledge, it was the first time the words had been spoken aloud, but he'd known that truth since fist they opened the butcher's cellar that afternoon. Murder had come to Doughty, and the killer was still on the loose.

Chapter 7

The conversation had lasted another hour, but the rest had been little more than precautions for securing the house and plans for the next morning. Mr. Garvin and Tom's father would take turns through the night sitting up to listen for any signs of danger. It was quickly agreed that it was important for them to all be in attendance at Sunday meeting in the morning as the topic of the attack and what it would mean for the community was likely to be of primary discussion; Pastor Burton would almost certainly have Sheriff Thompson give some instructions on how to behave until the beast was captured or killed. It was also decided, almost without discussion, that all the men should carry their guns to meeting with them; anything that could so brutally murder four soldiers would not hesitate to tear its way through a church full of unarmed people. Once those issues were settled, Mr. Garvin signaled the end of the discussion by standing, stretching, and reaching for his shotgun. George was the first one to head toward the staircase, as Tom wrapped his mother in one more bracing hug. As he left the kitchen, she and his father were clearing away the few dishes left on the table and Garv was unloading and reloading his shotgun, making certain that he was ready should any unwanted visitors come calling.

As Tom staggered into his room, it finally struck him just how exhausted he really was. George was stretching out his bedroll on the floor between Tom's bed and that of his brother, Mark. Tom knew that the other children would all be in either the nursery or the guestroom with Mrs. Priestly. But Mark had chosen to huddle in his own bed.

"Tommy?" a quiet voice came from beneath the pile of sheets and quilts that was the younger boy.

"You oughta be asleep Marky Larky." Tom chided gently, sitting on the edge of his brother's bed.

"Was them boys really tore apart like you said?" his tone betrayed the tears and fears the sheets were hiding, and Tom felt his heart fall into his stomach. Tom slowly pulled the bedclothes away to see the tear-streaked cheeks of his little brother.

"You shoulda been in bed, not sittin' on the stairs listenin' in on that, little brother." Tom wiped his brother's cheeks gently with his soft linen sheets.

"I know it. Now I wish I had been, but I's curious." Mark looked as though he might tear up again at any moment, and the sight of it began to cause tears to well in Tom's eyes once again.

"Now you listen to me, Mark Haynes. There ain't nothin' gonna hurt you. You hear me?" Tom's words were solid, but his tone was softer than lamb's wool as he cajoled the frightened boy.

Mark nodded slightly. "I hear you, but that thing's still out there somewhere ain't it?"

"Something got them fellas, sure enough, Marky, but it ain't gettin' you nor me nor anybody else in this house long as I got anything to say 'bout it. Understood?" Mark nodded once again. "Alright now, you dry them eyes and get yourself some sleep. We gotta be at the church early in the mornin' for meeting. We can't be missing our Jesus time cause we stayed up all night scarin' ourselves silly, now can we?"

"Okay, Tommy. I'll sleep; I promise." Mark sniffled slightly, but he was putting on a brave face; Tom knew he'd be alright. Tom patted his brother on the shoulder and rose wearily from the bedside.

George was already tucked into his bedroll and sounded to be snoring lightly as Tom flipped off the lights and crawled into his own feather bed. Finally, at the end of what Tom would always remember as the day that manhood was thrust upon him in a grisly crimson haze of death, he began allowing himself to feel once again. He felt all the things he'd been fighting through the whole day. He felt it all, as if for the first time, and he covered his head with his pillow and began to weep. He wept tears of fear and anger and loss and sorrow. He wept the silent tears of a man. A man's tears do not come easy in the face of hardship and danger, and Tom finally began to remember what it meant to feel. All the emotions and hurts he'd buried inside leaked from his eyes and puddled silently on his linen sheets as he laid there alone in his anguish feeling spasms of grief wracking their way through his stomach. Several times he felt that he might wretch from the pain of the sorrow he felt, but, in the end, the exertion of the day overcame him in a fitful and nightmare filled slumber of heartache and misery.

* * * * *

As the light assaulted his eyelids, Tom knew it must be morning; the loud crowing of the roosters confirmed it. He couldn't say how long he'd been awake, asleep, or even if he'd slept at all; in fact, at that moment, he could not quiet tell how much of what he remembered was real and how much of it he had dreamed. What he did know is that he felt ill-equipped to face another day. The scraping sounds from outside his door told him that someone was up and about in the hallway, and the smells of bacon, eggs, coffee, and biscuits told him that his mother, and probably Mrs. Priestly for that matter, had been up preparing breakfast for some time. Tom rolled onto his right side, away from the bright window, and covered his face with his arm.

"Tom?" George broke the spell of the morning and Tom begrudgingly opened his weary sleep-laden eyes.

"Yeah, Georgie?" his throat was dry and his voice was hoarse. It was only then that he realized how drenched his bedsheets were; he must have cried himself to the point of dehydration before finally surrendering to that near restless night of sleep.

"You probably better get up, buddy. We gotta leave for meeting in 'bout an hour." George's words sounded pretty dry as well.

Tom began to wonder if his friend had been faking his snores the night before. Had George cried himself to sleep as well? Tom would never ask the question outright, but he thought he knew the answer. George was a strong fella and brave, but he felt things deeply, Tom knew. Grunting as he put forth the first real effort of the day, Tom pushed against his bed as he sat upward haggardly and began rubbing his sore eyes.

"I think we're the last ones up, Tommy boy." George was stowing his bedroll in the corner as Tom swung his legs over the side of his soft feather bed and stretched his aching feet toward the smooth floorboards.

"Mark already downstairs?" Tom was trying desperately to sound as though today was business as usual, but he felt as though his ordeal the day before had cut him off at the knees.

"Yeah, I woke up when he headed downstairs, 'bout an hour ago to help keep watch and help hitch up some wagons to take us to meeting. Your Pa came and got him up." Tom slipped into his Sunday best and was beginning to feel a little more awake, despite the subtle melancholy that had taken residence in his chest.

"Well, let's grab some breakfast and get the day started." Tom attempted a wan grin at his friend.

"A fella once told me that once you're up, there ain't no use in doin' nothin' else other than stayin' up. Ain't that right, Tom?" George's reminder of his own words bolstered Tom a little, and the two of them chuckled weakly as they started down the stairs.

Tom hadn't seen the kitchen this full since Christmas. He had a sudden realization that, when his home was a real farm, it probably looked much like this every morning; he could imagine the farm hands getting ready for a long day in the fields as he watched the children bustle about and tussle with one another here and there around the table in their eagerness to get the day started. The thought of simple farm life gave Tom an uncharacteristic longing for a quiet day of chores and the sun on his face; he felt older than he had over his breakfast of rabbits and potatoes only one day earlier and ever so much older than the last time he'd taken breakfast in that kitchen, his favorite place in the world.

"You fellas best get some food before these others eat everything." Agnes Priestly shouted toward the young men as they stood in the doorway.

Tom and George squeezed their way onto one of the long benches and began filling their plates. Tom nodded with a weak grin across the table to his brother who responded with an appreciative grin and nod of his own; at least Mark seemed to have had a decent night's sleep. The food looked even more delicious than it smelled, and Tom's stomach felt, once again, as empty as if he'd never eaten in his 18 years of life, much less the night before. He shoveled a monstrous portion of cheese laden scrambled eggs onto his plate beside several slices of bacon and two biscuits that he practically drowned in chipped beef gravy. The room was chaotic with children eating, running around, and vying for second servings of whatever remained on the table while the youngest ones kept running up to one mother or the other asking for help combing hair, tying ribbons, or finding shoes. Tom and George devoured their breakfasts in silence, placed their messy plates in the wash basin, and headed to Mr. Haynes' study where they were certain they'd find the older men.

"Come on in boys." Richard Haynes called quietly as they approached the door. He sat behind his wide cherry desk in his black Sunday suit. Garv sat opposite him in a leather winged-back chair dressed in an ill-fitting pair of slacks and a threadbare tweed jacket; he had apparently not thought to bring meeting clothes with him the day before, but some of Mr. Haynes' older clothes fit modestly well and would certainly get him through the day.

"I reckon you fellas best get ready for the day too." Garv laid his shotgun across his lap, waved them into the room, and motioned to the edge of the desk where there laid two holstered revolvers. Tom then noticed the holsters strapped around his father and Garv's waists.

"Pistols?" Tom asked a little puzzled, looking to his father.

"Just a precaution, Tom. We'll be carrying our rifles, but, with the bootprints we saw, William and I think it best to carry pistols too." Tom's father rose and handed each of the fellas one of the revolvers. Tom had shot them with his father at cans on the back fence many times before, but he'd never carried one, until that day.

"Where's the one that belonged to Wil Sweet?" Tom looked to George first then to the older men.

"I locked it in the cabinet for now." Tom's father stated gently. "I thought it best to keep it safe, in case we find his family or someone who might like to have his things." Tom nodded his approval, as did George.

The two boys selected long guns as well. Tom grabbed his M1895, once again, loaded it, and stuffed his pockets full of extra shells. George chose, instead, a Browning Automatic-5 12 gauge shotgun, but he followed Tom's example when it came to extra ammunition.

"Paul and Mark will be driving the wagons this morning." Garv stated matter-of-factly. "They's old enough to handle a team, and we want you lot helpin' watch for anything that ought not be lurkin' about."

"You boys will ride one in each wagon." Mr. Haynes sounded all business. "George, you're with me; Tom, you're with Mr. Garvin. That way we'll have a shotgun and rifle in each wagon as well as the four revolvers." Tom's father paused for a moment to be sure that everyone was understanding his instructions. "We'll be keeping our guns at the ready and eyes peeled. I don't expect to be attacked in broad daylight this far from the quarry, but we're better safe than sorry."

"What do we do once we're at the church?" George sounded nervous.

"We keep a weather eye open until everyone is inside and stay alert during meeting." Garv made it sound like a Sunday stroll, but Tom's palms were already starting to sweat slightly. Protecting two wagons full of women and small children was a far cry from being in a fast moving truck filled with armed men. He had thought the day before was a test of his mettle, but he found himself thinking that watching his own back was a cake walk compared to protecting his mother and siblings. He wiped one hand on his pants then the other, swapping his rifle to each in turn.

"Well, it's about that time." Garv rose and hobbled into the hallway and back toward the kitchen. Tom's father filed out right behind him, while Tom and George followed in their wake.

"Mollie." Richard Haynes caught his wife's attention at the kitchen door. "Are y'all ready to go? Everyone dressed and know where they're sittin'?"

"Yes, Rick, we're as ready as we're gonna be." Tom's mother looked a bit uncertain, but she began herding the children toward the door, nonetheless. She picked up little Hannah just before she got to where Tom was standing. "You do as your father tells you, now, Tom." She kissed him on the cheek and joined the queue at the front door.

Mr. Haynes and Garv had led the way down the hall and were the first to step onto the front porch. Tom and George shouldered their way through their siblings and followed the two older men out the door. They took a brief look around for anything out of the usual before climbing into the wagons and motioning for the rest of their families to join them. The youngest children seemed to have slept off all the fear of the night before, but the older ones still had a look of fear behind their eyes as they stepped into the sunlight and glanced in every direction for some hidden terror. Tom, George, and the older men kept an eye out as the mothers, Paul, and Mark helped the rest of the children into their respective spots in the wagons. The two young drivers hopped into their seats and urged the wagons into a slow meandering pace toward the church, three miles away.

CHAPTER 8

Tom was not really sure what he had expected Sunday meeting to be like that day, as he looked back on it, but he certainly expected things to be much less normal than they felt as he entered the small sanctuary that Sunday morning. He had always loved the stained glass windows and the rich colors they cast around the room as the morning light shone through them. He couldn't be sure, but he mused that the splashes of green and red and blue might have taken the edge off the fact that all the men had carried their guns into church this morning. Tom nodded his greetings to James and Billy as they walked over to their usual spot with their parents, each shouldering guns of their own, and he clapped Ralphie on the shoulder as they walked past his normal spot at the end of his family's pew. His drooping ginger mustache and hollow eyes told Tom that his mood had not improved much since the night before; Tom said a silent prayer for him as he found his way to the second pew and took a seat between his mother and Georgie. The children went downstairs with the Abernathys and Sheriff Thompson just before Janey began playing hymns on the pipe organ to start the service. Certainly, the presence of so many guns in the room was a reminder of the danger that lurked somewhere outside, but it didn't hold up the service in the least. The whole town had turned up, as usual, and they sang the hymns as though nothing unusual had ever happened in Doughty. Pastor Oscar Burton preached a powerful message about God's love and grace, and everyone said their amens and hallelujahs where it was appropriate. Tom felt almost as though he had left the horror of the butcher's cellar behind him for good as he sat their soaking up the message, but he knew that it was only a temporary fix, until they found the killer. His stomach tightened slightly as he thought about the killer.

"No!" he thought, *"No good can come on dwelling on revenge."* He blinked his eyes hard to force the thoughts from his mind and returned to the service. The pastor's message was powerful, and Tom didn't want to miss even a single word of it.

At the very end of his sermon the pastor brought the reality of what had happened only a day earlier back home to the congregation. Tom had known this portion of the service was bound to come sooner or later, but he found himself wishing that it could have been later rather than sooner. The kindly clergyman became very silent for a few moments before saying something that touched Tom in a very real way and threatened to force his heart back into his throat once more.

"Yesterday some of our own young men stumbled on some of the hardness and evil that lives in this world." Pastor Burton pulled out his handkerchief and wiped his forehead. "Our young men had befriended four veterans of The Great War, and yesterday morning they found the scene of a brutal attack against those brave boys fresh back from France." The pastor halted for a moment collecting his thoughts. "I would like to encourage you all to say a prayer for our young men; they are all with us right now. Pray for them to feel God's love and mercy despite the pain and anger they must be feeling right now." he appeared to Tom to be very close to tears. "And I want us all to pray for one another. Pray for safety from whatever has committed this horrible crime. Pray that our young ones might be spared the horror of seeing the kinds of things that our young men were forced to see yesterday. And pray that God will visit His swift justice on the evil that has come to Doughty."

The pastor was taking another moment to compose himself when the doors to the church were flung open with such great force that every man in the room trained their guns on the portal. Standing where Tom was certain the Devil himself would be at that very moment was, instead, an Army officer accompanied by several soldiers, including a grizzled old sergeant.

"Ladies and gentlemen!" the officer began. "I am Major Henry Clinton, United States Infantry." He began walking toward the pulpit, chewing a stubby cigar, and trailing the other soldiers in his wake. "I am here looking for information about the goings on at the Doughty Rock Quarry."

"Major, I appreciate you being here, but we are in the middle of a service." Pastor Burton's rebuke was kind but firm.

"I understand that, sir, but we have more pressing matters to attend to here." the Major's dismissive tone, however, was not kind. He stepped up onto the platform and leaned on the side of the pulpit.

The pastor was not having any of the major's insolence. "Sir, I don't know who think you are or why you're here, and I don't care." His tone was steady, but the authority it carried was unmistakeable. "This is the house of God, and we are in the middle of a service. There are NO more pressing matters than God's work. If you want to wait until after we are finished, you are welcome to pray with us, but you will not be interrupting my service any further."

Perhaps it was his unmoving resolve, the heavily armed townsfolks whose expressions affirmed their support for the elderly clergyman, or perhaps Clinton was just taken aback by the rebuke he'd just taken from a man 20 years his senior, but the Army officer complied and stepped down from the platform and took a seat on the front pew. Tom could hear the other soldiers closing the church doors and taking up posts on either side of the doorway. The sergeant seemed to be directing them to keep an eye out for trouble.

When everything was quiet once more the pastor continued. "Everyone, I ask you now to pray that God will save Doughty from the scourges we find ourselves amidst." Tom thought he saw the pastor throw a glance in the direction of the major. "Pray for the families of those who lost their lives. And pray that God's gracious will be done." He then knelt beside the pulpit and bowed his head. All around the room the congregation bowed their heads and closed their eyes. "Our Father in Heaven" the pastor began, "I pray that Thou would visit with us this day. I pray that Thou would comfort those who are weary or frightened or touched in some other way by the tragedy that we are facing." The pastor's voice quivered, and Tom was certain that the old gentleman was crying. "Our Father, I pray Thee give us strength to face the coming days, and I pray Thou will give us the wisdom we need to faithfully trust in Thee in this time of strife. In the name of our gracious Savior and Lord, Jesus Christ, we pray all these things. Amen."

Tom raised his eyes to see the major sitting stonefaced and unmoved on the front pew. He may not have continued his open defiance of the pastor, but it was apparent that he was far from being cowed. "Can I now have a word, father?" Clinton's tone dripped with rage.

"I'm a pastor, Major, not a priest." Pastor Burton's patience seemed to be fraying, but he was still keeping his composure. Tom doubted that he would have been able to keep from screaming at the belligerent officer if he had been the pastor. "Now, I would like to invite all of you ladies and young folks to join together downstairs for coffee and cakes while we men discuss how best to approach our current situation." The pastor's tone was shepherdly as he addressed the congregation, but it became more strained when he turned back to Clinton. "Major, you are welcome to join with us and address the men with whatever concerns you might have."

Most of the ladies and many of the younger teenagers filed downstairs noisily, leaving the armed men from Doughty and the soldiers alone with the pastor. After a few moments, the major made a dramatic show of returning to the pulpit, which he, once again, leaned against irreverently.

"I just came from the warehouse at the quarry, folks." he began flippantly. "Do any of you hayseeds know what I found there?"

"The scene of a murder, I'd imagine." Sheriff Thompson's voice preceded him up the back stairs. He stepped past the soldiers in the entryway and began slowly walking down the aisle to the front of the church.

"Well, I don't know about any murder, but I sure did find a mess the likes of which I ain't seen this side of the Kaiser's Hell trenches." the Major was hard and sharp, and Tom did not think he was ever apt to take a liking to the officer.

"Well, you can take my word for it, mister; there's four boys on a table down at the doc's office that says there's been somethin' murderin' folks." Sheriff Thompson had a no nonsense tone to him that Tom was unaccustomed to hearing; it made him think that the sheriff was as unsure about this Army officer as Tom was.

"That's right Major." Dr. Wilson had risen to his feet. "There are four bodies in my office that tell a mighty grisly story."

"Bodies?" the Major seemed taken aback, but Tom was almost certain that he saw a tiny smile crease his lips for the briefest of moments before returning to his customary stone visage. "You tellin' me that somebody killed four boys in my warehouse?" Tom was unsure that he'd heard the major correctly; how could it be the major's warehouse when it had been built by the stone company?

"The warehouse was placed by the Petersburg Stone Company on land owned by the Town of Doughty. How, exactly, does that make the warehouse yours?" Tom's father seemed to be thinking the same thoughts as Tom himself. Rick Haynes had also risen to his feet and, hands pressed on the back of the pew in front of him, was leaning menacingly toward where the major stood.

"Petersburg Stone is under the direct supervision of the United States Army. Their lease of that property was on the behalf of my unit, and the same goes for my warehouse." Major Clinton flung the answer out there as if it should cure any doubt immediately; perhaps it did in some, perhaps even in Rick Haynes, but Tom was not convinced. "Be that as it is, if somebody's gettin' murdered out there, it don't matter who owns the place. It looks to me like I need to know what all you folks know about things, and you need me and my soldiers to help find a culprit." Tom couldn't deny that the idea of having a few armed soldiers helping locate the murderers sounded appealing, but he was very uncertain about this cigar chewing brute of a major.

"You offering to help me in my investigations?" the sheriff sounded skeptical, but Tom could tell that the idea had peaked his interest.

"That's exactly what I'm proposing, officer ... what's your name?" Clinton's tone was condescending and flippant, but John Thompson seemed not to notice.

"Sheriff John Thompson." the sheriff tossed his name out there the way a sworn enemy might throw out an olive branch. It meant peace between the two men, but Tom could already tell that it was an uneasy one; he wondered how long it was likely to last.

"Fine, *Sheriff*." The Major drew out the title with a leer and a few of his soldiers hooted in laughter from the back of the church. "I propose that you make use of the training and expertise I and my men have to offer, and I say we start by you telling me everything you know."

"That sounds reasonable, *Major*." The Sheriff had followed suit with his tone as he emphasized Clinton's rank, and Tom heard Jimmy mimic the hooting laughs of the soldiers. "But now ain't the time for that. Right now we best be gettin' on with tellin' these men how best to protect their families."

Clinton scoffed but motioned to the platform as though inviting Sheriff Thompson to join him there. The sheriff, however, was much more reverent than the abrasive major; he stepped up in front of the pulpit but remained firmly planted on the floor. "Men, by now y'all know the goings on of yesterday." John Thompson cleared his throat. "Four doughboys got killed out at the quarry, yesterday."

"Doughboys?!" Major Clinton seethed. "You telling me that you expect to keep jurisdiction over my warehouse when the boys killed out there were Army?!" His voice echoed off the walls of the church so loudly that Tom was sure that even the women and children downstairs must have heard the racket. "I should have known better than to trust a bunch of bumpkins to handle anything like they had a lick of sense between them!" The officer's face had turned a deep shade of red, and Tom was afraid he was about to throttle the sheriff. "You stay away from that quarry. You hear me?!" Clinton shook his finger at Sheriff Thompson as though he was brandishing a sword. "Sergeant!" Clinton slammed his fist down on the pulpit as he shouted the word; the force of the blow cracked the old wood deeply, and Tom heard the pastor gasp. "Load them useless boys up, NOW!" With that, Clinton marched resolutely back out the doors of the church, which slammed shut behind him and left an echoing silence behind in their wake.

After a few moments, the sheriff regained his composure and began anew. "As I said, four boys was killed out there at the quarry. We don't know what did it just yet, but we're pretty sure that it ain't human, but it's probably got a man with it." He paused a moment, cleared his throat, and continued. "Best to stay indoors until we catch or kill whatever's responsible for them killin's, and keep y'all's guns at the handy too. We got food set up downstairs for everybody. If you can, plan to stay together with friends and neighbors for the time bein'." The sheriff looked around the room impressively. "Strength in numbers, right?" He paused again letting the idea sink in. "Alright now, let's get some of them vittles before them young'uns eat everythin'."

* * * * *

"Tommy!" James hollered from across the room as he and Billy edged their way through the crowd to where Tom stood with George.

"What do you make of that major?" Billy asked Tom and George with a sidelong glance at the people standing nearby.

"Don't like 'im. Don't like 'im one bit." George mumbled through a mouthful of fried chicken.

"I'm with Georgie." Tom said. "Don't like him, and don't trust him."

"Don't trust him?" Billy asked, meaningfully.

"Nope. Something ain't right about him. He reminds me of a wolf." Tom paused a moment looking for the right words. "You ever seen a wolf in a field near a chicken coop?" Billy nodded, and George and James followed suit. "Ever notice how a rogue wolf will run off foxes and weasels in a field?" They all nodded again. "Yeah, he'll run off all those other critters, but it ain't because he's feelin' generous. He runs 'em off so's he can have all the chickens to himself." Billy's eyes grew wide; Tom guessed that he hadn't looked at their situation quite that way before.

"You don't reckon he could be worse than whatever killed them fellas do ya?" James was incredulous.

Tom shook his head slightly, "I dunno, Jimmy, but he makes me nervy." Tom noticed a fiery red head of hair sitting at a table in the corner. "Has any of you fellas talked to Ralph today?" Even James looked sheepish in response to Tom's question, and he knew the answer without them ever opening their mouths. "He's not hisself, boys." Tom shook his head.

"We figured that out, Tommy." Billy's tone was as matter-of-fact as ever, but Tom sensed a little fear behind his eyes. "He hasn't cracked a smile all day."

"Yeah, Tommy boy, he didn't even look at me when we was eating breakfast this mornin'." James was noticeably concerned for his friend. "Wonder what's botherin' him so much." Jimmy looked at Tom with a pondering look.

"Well, you saw that place." George seemed to realize that Tom wasn't up for discussing the butcher's cellar again quite yet. Tom was grateful for him redirecting the conversation from him. "It was a right war zone in there, and Ralphie knew them doughboys better than us. He's bound to have a hard time." George briefly locked eyes with Tom and they exchanged the slightest of nods.

"Welp, I reckon I'd better go talk to him." Tom handed Billy his plate and crossed the room, praying all the way. Ralph didn't even look up when Tom stopped across the table from him. "Anybody sittin' here Ralphie?" Ralph shook his head such a small amount that Tom thought he might have imagined it, but, real or not, Tom took the seat anyway. "Don't look like you slept any better than me last night." Tom chided amiably.

Ralph shook his head again and cleared his throat wearily before speaking, "Didn't sleep none at all, Tommy." Ralph unconsciously began to tug on his mustache with his right thumb and forefinger. "You still see 'em when you close your eyes?"

Ralphie sounded on the verge of tears, and Tom knew that he wouldn't be able to hold back his own if Ralph started crying in earnest. "I try not to think about 'em in that state, Ralphie." Tom choked a little. "They wouldn't want us rememberin' them like that, buddy. Let's just remember 'em the way they was before, you know happy and friendly and ... alive." Tom cleared his throat and willed back his tears once more.

"We gotta find whoever killed 'em, Tom." Ralph choked the words out trying to hide his tears; he was having more trouble than Tom, as a few strays dripped into his thick ginger mustache.

"You're right there, Ralphie. We sure do gotta find whoever done it and make sure they don't ever hurt another person again." The knot of sadness that had been growing in Tom's stomach suddenly changed. He began to feel an insatiable desire for justice taking its place. He clenched his hand into a fist under the table.

"I've been thinkin', Tommy." Ralph's tone had changed too; he sounded more resolute, more determined, more...present.

"What you been thinkin' about, Ralphie?" Tom didn't have the slightest idea where this conversation was going, but he liked hearing Ralph's voice have a little strength behind it.

"Been thinkin' about them soldiers and that big major." Ralph looked Tom in the eye for the first time. "What do you make of 'em?"

Tom didn't hesitate in the least. "Don't like 'im. Don't trust 'im."

"The major?" Ralph asked earnestly.

"Yep. I don't trust 'im anymore than I'd trust a wolf in the chicken coop." Tom liked talking over a familiar subject with Ralphie. He hoped this would help Ralph get back to feeling like himself a little bit.

"Did you pay any attention to the other soldiers?" Ralph asked with a very sober tone in his voice that took Tom off guard.

"The ones by the doors?" Ralph nodded in response to Tom's question. "I didn't pay them no mind at all. I was too worried about that troll of a major. Why do you ask about them?"

"There was this sergeant." Ralph left it out there as though Tom needed to come up with the rest on his own.

"Sergeant?" Tom wondered aloud searching his brain. "Was he the older fella? The kinda rusty lookin' one with that scar?" Ralph nodded his response again. "What about 'im? He didn't do much of nothin' did he?"

"Not much." Ralph agreed. "But he didn't seem pleased with the major interruptin' the pastor."

Tom gawped at his friend for a moment trying to figure out where he was headed with this discussion of the old sergeant. Suddenly, it dawned on Tom. He turned around in his chair and saw the other three boys milling about where he'd left them trying to look as though they weren't watching Tom and Ralph. He waved to them to come over to where he sat with Ralphie.

"If you're right, Ralphie, there might be somethin' bad wrong goin' on in Doughty." Tom tried to keep his voice down, but he felt the adrenaline beginning to surge through his veins.

He felt a hand on his shoulder. "How we doin', Ralphie?" James asked a little too gently. Tom cringed.

"He's upset, and he oughta be. But he's also a genius." Tom tried even harder to keep his voice low as he turned to face the fellas. "Ralphie here just gave me an idea, but it probably ain't the sanest thing I ever came up with."

~102~

Chapter 9

Tom spent the rest of the afternoon trying not to look suspicious or call attention to himself. He was constantly aware of his parents, Mr. Garvin, and Mrs. Priestly. He was paranoid about not looking paranoid, and he felt like that was a losing battle. He tried to distract himself with one activity or another, but he mostly failed in those attempts. The idea he'd shared with the fellas weighed heavily on his mind. He could feel his parents' eyes on him from time to time, even without actually seeing their gaze. He felt a twinge of guilt at keeping this secret from them, but he was sure he would never get away with what he had planned if they caught even a whisper of it.

"Am I insane?!" he thought silently while absent-mindedly losing a game of dominoes to Mark. "Do I really think I can get away with this?" He threw a covert glance at his father reading in his chair by the window with his rifle leaned against the sill. "Maybe the real question is whether I think I can manage not to get us all killed with this cockamamie idea." Tom played a tile that he had meant to save and locked eyes with George on the other side of the parlor. George seemed to be doing a better job of working a jigsaw puzzle with his mother and siblings than Tom was with his dominoes. "Of course, he's not the one who came up with the plan that's likely to get all of his friends killed and torn limb from limb." Tom mentally kicked himself as he tried to return his attention to the game. Mark only had two tiles left; Tom, however, had eight. Tom redoubled his effort to focus on the game.

He finally played a tile that made sense and resisted the urge to glance at his father again.

"Tommy?" Mark half-whispered.

Tom looked his brother in the eyes and noticed more than a little worry hiding behind them. "Yeah, Marky?" Tom had a sinking feeling in his stomach and felt that the jig was up.

"I been thinkin' 'bout what you said last night." Mark still seemed serious, but Tom was beginning to think that this was about something other than his plan. "And I been thinkin' 'bout them soldiers." Tom nodded along, encouraging his brother to continue. "Well, I don't think I like that major too much."

"Cause he interrupted Pastor Burton?" Tom asked the question only to feel like he was part of the conversation, because he was certain he knew the answer.

"Yeah, that, but also cause he argued with Sheriff John and Paw."

Tom was flabbergasted. He lowered his voice even more, "Mark Haynes, were you listenin' on the stairs again?" His brother lowered his eyes and nodded his answer. "I'll be! If that don't beat all. The Army oughta recruit you as a spy, boy. You're better at hearin' conversations you ain't 'sposed to than anybody I ever knew." Tom tried to sound as though he wasn't impressed, but a small grin wrinkled his lips nonetheless, and his younger brother returned it.

"So, I was wonderin', do you figure that major ain't all he seems to be?" Mark had flabbergasted him a second time in as many minutes.

"Marky, are you sure you're only thirteen years old? Cause you been thinkin' like a man twice your age." Tom ruffled his brother's hair proudly, and Mark beamed in appreciation. "Me and the fellas were thinkin' the very same thing, as matter of fact."

"You think he might be trouble?" Mark's concern was evident on his young face.

"I think he might be. I figure the best way to tell is by talkin' to some o' those doughboys and seein' what they got to say about things." Tom blurted it out with barely a thought. He wished he could stuff the words back down his throat, but it was too late now. He held his breath and waited.

"Is that what you and the fellas is plannin' on doin'?" Mark stated it so matter-of-factly that someone listening in might not even realize the idea was crazy.

"Well, yeah, actually. That's what we figure we oughta do. We figure we owe it to them boys, since they died when it could just as easily been us." Tom didn't know where this conversation was going to end up, but the worry that his brother was going to tell their parents about the plan was slowly dissolving.

"You sneakin' out tonight; so Ma and Paw don't try to talk you out of it?" Mark said bluntly.

Tom was, once again, flabbergasted. When did his baby brother get so smart? "To be honest with ya, Marky, that's exactly what I was plannin'." He held his breath, once again.

"How ya gonna do it? Somebody's gotta be standin' watch all night, ya know?" Mark's tone didn't sound much like he planned to tattle.

"That's the only part I ain't quite got worked out yet, brother." Tom's brain began churning again, and had the beginnings of an idea on that front. "I don't reckon you'd be willin' to help me with that, would ya?" Tom gulped hard; Mark echoed him.

"What you want me to do, Tommy?" For the first time, Mark's face revealed a little worry. Suddenly, Tom realized that they had stopped playing dominoes. He glanced around quickly to see if they'd been detected. Only George seemed to be aware of him and Mark. He returned to the game before answering the question. He placed another tile.

"Your turn, Marky." He looked back to his brother who nervously placed a tile. "Do you think you could stand watch a few minutes tonight while we slip off?"

Mark gulped even harder this time, set his jaw, and nodded. "I could do that, if you give me a rifle." They locked eyes again. Tom wasn't sure about leaving his brother alone with a rifle, but it would only have to be a few minutes, ten at the most. And, with himself and George out walking around in the night, Tom was sure that they would make a more inviting target than the well-secured house anyway.

"Okay, Marky Larky, you can carry one of mine while me and Georgie head out." Mark nodded and Tom locked eyes with George once again. They both gulped hard, and Tom realized that George must know what had just transpired in his conversation with his younger brother, because he nodded once more. Tom looked back to his tiles and said a quick prayer for safety. He hated leaving Mark on his own, but he couldn't think of another way to get out of the house without getting caught.

* * * * *

Tom, George, and Mark had all gone to bed earlier than normal, but their parents and Mr. Garvin seemed to accept their excuse of a rough previous night's sleep and the need to be up in a few hours to stand a watch. They had agreed that Garv and Mr. Haynes would stand three watches and the boys would stand two. Each watch would last an hour and a half. The fellas' second watch would end at 5:00 am, and they'd head out just before they were set to wake Tom's father and George's uncle. Mark would stand the last ten minutes of the watch and wake the older men once the boys had a slight head start.

Tom's palms began to sweat halfway through their second watch, and, no matter how many times he wiped them on his canvas britches, he couldn't get them to stay dry. As soon as he heard his father and Garv close their bedroom doors, Tom had sat down at Mr. Haynes' desk and written a letter explaining that he and George and the fellas were going to investigate some things and would do their best to stay safe. He intentionally left out the part of the plan that included the soldiers in hopes that the older men wouldn't set out to find them. He also instructed Mark not to tell them what he knew; he was just to wake them in time for the next watch, give them the letter, and tell them that Tom and George had convinced him that they needed to do something to keep them all safe. Once the letter was done, he retrieved his .30-06 Springfield bolt-action for Mark. It wasn't as fast on the second shot as his Winchester, but it was a solid rifle and would deal a lot of damage. Tom knew that Mark was a good shot and had a steady hand; he'd killed two wolves that summer already. He also knew he could trust his brother to watch the house for ten minutes, but that didn't stop him from worrying.

Tom paced the floor as he listened to the clock ticking away the seconds. He had a sense of dread rising up in his chest that he could only describe as second thoughts. He knew the plan was sound, but he was afraid. He was so very afraid, but he also knew he needed to look resolute and confident to keep Mark's courage up. He set his jaw and kept his vigil; it wouldn't do to get caught off guard. He tried to focus on the watch rather than the clock, but he kept glancing at that ticking menace as it wiled away the minutes. It read 4:30. He paced some more; wiped his sweaty hands, one at a time, on his britches; glanced again, 4:38. He looked out the window into the darkness; paced again; wiped his hands; glanced back, 4:49. "Already?!" He thought.

"It's time, Georgie." Tom half-croaked the words. He cleared his throat quietly, and looked to Mark. "You ready, little brother?"

Mark nodded, wiped his hands on his britches, and hefted the Springfield. "You can count on me, Tom."

Tom beamed at his brother. "I know I can, Marky. You'll do fine. Just don't tell anybody where we went before lunch. Okay?"

"Okay, Tommy." Mark set his jaw in determination, and Tom clapped him solidly on the shoulder.

George had stepped up to the front door and was looking out the window. "Don't see nothin' Tommy." He looked left and looked right. "Now's as good a time as any."

Tom nodded, and George swung the door open as silently as he could manage. The creaking was barely audible, but it seemed to Tom to be akin to a scream in the silence. He cringed and hoped that no one had heard it. He wiped his hands once more and stepped over the threshold. For the rest of his life, Tom would try to capture with words what he felt that moment as he stepped from the safety of his home to the unknown outside his front door. The closest he could ever come was to say that he felt invigorated. His senses, that had been dulled by the hours of waiting, were suddenly more alive than he had ever felt them before. He was intimately aware of every sound, every hint of movement, and every smell. The tiny hairs on his arms and the back of his neck tingled ever so slightly. He was aware of the friction between the soles of his boots and the boards of the porch decking. He was aware, all at once, of something moving to his left. He startled and swung his gun to his shoulder. Just before taking aim, Tom realized that it was his father sitting in his rocking chair with his rifle laid across his lap.

"Morning Tom." Mr. Haynes said nonchalantly.

"Paw?!" Tom's heart had taken to beating about twice as fast as normal.

"Not to worry, Tom. I know what's going on. You and Mark were not as quiet this afternoon as you thought." He smiled at Tom gently.

"Sorry, Paw. We just figured..." Tom hung his head.

"I know full well what you figured, and I figured the very same thing. Bill and I talked it over and figure that you've got the right idea. Your mother and George's aren't too happy with the plan, but we figure that you five'll be safe enough this far from the quarry. Find out what you can about Major Clinton, but don't cross him. Be careful, and be back by dinner."

Tom couldn't believe his ears. "You mean you want us to go?"

"Want? No, I don't *want* you to go, but it's a good idea. We need to learn more about what's going on here, and it'd be a mistake to trust that oaf of a major to be up to anything but trouble." Tom's father stood smirking and stepped up in front of his son. "Tom, you're a grown man, and you've more than proved yourself these last few days. I have faith in you. Be safe. Look out for one another. And, by all means, be back here by dinner, or your mother will roast me alive." He grinned and clapped Tom on the shoulder. And there it was again, that look in his eyes; Tom saw pride in his father's eyes once more. "Mark, I think it's high time we get you a good rifle of your own." With that Richard Haynes stepped inside, closed the door behind him, and left Tom and George dumbfounded on the front porch.

"Do you believe that?" George was practically beside himself. "Our *moms* agreed to this." His face was a comical mixture of bemusement, fear, and sheer confusion.

"Well, I reckon we'd better head out before one of them changes their mind then, hadn't we?" Tom punched George in the shoulder and started down the porch steps. He set off at a pace as brisk as the night air that surrounded him. He felt alive. He felt clear. He felt...calm. Suddenly he realized something; his palms were dry. They had stopped sweating. He hefted his Winchester more confidently and quickened his pace with George hard on his heels touting his shotgun.

Billy and James were waiting near the empty Abernathy house as the boys strolled up through the night. "Mornin' glory!" Jimmy chided in a hoarse whisper. "Lose your way in the dark? You're five minutes late."

"My Paw stopped us at the door. He knew all along. He told us that he figures this is a good idea and sent us on our way." Tom still couldn't believe what had transpired. The looks on the twins' faces told him they were having just as much trouble with the concept.

"He let you go?" Billy asked in sheer disbelief.

"He *told* us to go." George interjected before Tom could answer. "He told us that we'd probably be plenty safe and sent us on our merry little way."

"Well don't that beat all." James seemed to have been energized by that news. Tom wondered whether he'd sported that same look of excitement himself as he stepped off the porch a few minutes earlier.

"Alright now, let's get a move on." Tom commanded calmly. "We can't be standin' here all mornin'. Ralphie's waitin' for us near town, and I don't like 'im bein' there by his lonesome."

And just like that, the four set off into the darkness hefting rifles and shotguns, wearing pistols around their middles, and scanning their surroundings warily.

Chapter 10

Ralph was leaning against the back wall of the schoolhouse in the misty morning gloom, as Tom and the others approached. He had needed to go by his own house to grab his gear after leaving the Wilsons'. From a distance, Ralphie's stance looked almost casual, but the closer they got the more Tom could see the hard set of Ralph's jaw and tension furrowed deep in his brow and between his eyes. Where the morning before Tom had seen despondency and heavy grief, a new sense of purpose seemed once more to have given teeth to the anger and bubbling hate that seemed to have taken up residence deep in his friend's heart. There was a fire burning in his eyes that threatened to fly into a flull blown rage at any moment.

"Okay there, Ralphie?" George called in a hoarse whisper as they padded closer.

"Where y'all been, fellas?" Ralph's tone was more irritation than fear, but Tom could tell the waiting had worn his nerves a little bit ragged. "Been standing here for a good half hour." Tom could hear a slight quiver in Ralph's voice and realized how unnerving it must be to be outside alone with a killer on the loose.

"Sorry, Ralph. It's my fault." Tom thought it best to give Ralph a scapegoat rather than to make excuses. "I got me and Georgie caught leavin' the house and threw everythin' off."

"Caught?" Ralph seemed to recover from the irritation he had been showing a moment earlier. "Whatdya mean caught?"

"Tom's paw caught us leavin' the house. Seems he knew what was up all along. Sent us on our merry little way and said to be careful is all." George grinned at Ralph. "But he did hold us up some tellin' us to make sure we's home for dinner."

The fellas all chuckled softly and circled up together. "Well, I reckon we'd better come up with a bit more of a plan." Tom took charge. He wasn't sure, at the time, why he assumed the role of leader, but the fellas didn't object. Tom knealt and the others followed suit. "Did you figure out where them soldiers are camped out?"

Ralph nodded before speaking. "Yeah, I did." He spit out what looked to Tom like some of his father's chewing tobacco. "You know that big ole field cross from Miller's pond south o' town?" The fells all nodded. "Well, that big major has got them set up in tents in the field. Closer to the quarry than suits me, but I reckon that don't change things much."

"It changes one thing." Billy spoke up, and the others all looked in his direction. "We know that they aren't very concerned with whether the murderer is a danger to 'em."

"Yeah, Billy's right, ain't he?" James seemed to be mulling over the magnitude of what his brother had just said. "You think they didn't believe Sheriff Thompson 'bout the killin's?" James was incredulous.

"Naw, Jimmy, I think they believed that quick enough." Tom was rememberin the faint hint of a grin at the corner of the major's mouth the morning before. "I figure they know more about the killer than they're lettin' on."

"I agree with Tommy." Ralph joined in. "That troll was too fast to leave without gettin' no more information. If he was really in the dark 'bout stuff, he'd have stayed to hear what we found out stead of bargin' off like that."

George nodded his head slightly. "I'm with you fellas. There's somethin' bad wrong about that major."

"Okay, then. We know we don't trust 'em, but where do we go from here?" Billy seemed keen on getting back to the plan.

Tom scratched his cheek as he pondered the question. "Well." he started. "Didn't you say that old sergeant seemed a little uncomfortable with the major, Ralphie?"

Ralph nodded. "Yeah, he seemed real uncomfortable when that oaf interrupted Pastor Burton."

"I noticed that too." Billy's tone was characteristically steady. "He kept leaning on one foot then the other. Looked like he wanted to stand up to the major, to be honest."

"Yeah, that's exactly what I was thinkin'." The tension in Ralph's jaw had eased up some. He seemed to be a bit distracted by talking over the plan, and Tom was glad of it.

"Well, I figure we should see if we can't get to talkin' with that old sergeant. If he ain't happy about one thing the major did, he probably ain't happy about more too." Tom grinned slightly to himself mentally patting himself on the back for the brilliance of his plan.

"But how are we going to get close enough to him to talk about anything?" Billy had a knack for shooting holes in Tom's plans, but he was right. They would be hard pressed to get past the soldiers in order to talk with the sergeant.

"Dern it, Billy. You're always ruinin' my ideas." Tom wasn't really angry at Billy, but he was a bit frustrated by the realization that he hadn't been as clever as he had thought. "Okay, how 'bout this? We get in that field of hay cross from where they've got them tents set up and watch 'em a while. With a little luck, the sergeant might just step away, and we can talk to him then." All the other boys nodded along, and Tom assumed that meant that they were all in agreement. "Alright, then. It's already past six. We best be gettin' a move on before someone sees us." Tom adjusted his pack, hefted his rifle, and set off at a brisk pace through the tall grass behind the schoolhouse. He thought it best to stay off the road as much as possible; he wanted to avoid getting caught by anyone and having to explain what they were doing. The fewer people in on the plan, the better.

* * * * *

Tom had always loved the morning dew; the way it glistened in the early morning sun and made everything look fresh and clean warmed his heart, and the hearty smell of wet grass made it all the better. But that morning, Tom hated the dew, and he despised the wet grass. He wondered to himself what he had been thinking when he suggested hiding in the hayfield. Every one of the fellas was soaked to the bone by the morning dew as they lay on their bellies in the field with the hay stalks towering over their heads. Their clothes stuck to them and the muggy heat was becoming oppressive, but lay there they did, silently watching the small camp of soldiers. They had spotted the sergeant briefly as he walked from one tent to another and ducked in quickly. The second was the biggest tent in camp; so, Tom figured it must be where they took their meals. When the grizzled man reemerged rubbing his belly, Tom was fairly certain that he had guessed right. The sergeant took a few steps then ducked into a third tent; it was not as big as the mess tent, but it was noticeably larger than the other white structures surrounding it. Tom guessed that it must be the major's tent.

"Good grief." George groaned in his hoarse whisper. "We're gonna be here all summer, at this rate."

"Y'all figure that tent he's in right now belongs to the old troll?" James asked as though he already knew the answer.

"Yeah, I reckon it does." Tom tried to keep his voice down, but, on his belly, all his body weight was pushing on his lungs and threatened to expel his air too quickly. He took another breath and tried to control his exhale better as he continued. "I figure ole rusty there is the one that makes all the men get where they belong and such. They're probably talkin' 'bout what they're going to do today." The other boys nodded their agreement. Tom noticed how little and how slowly their heads moved as they bobbed up and down, and he was suddenly very glad that his friends had all grown up hunting; it wouldn't do to get caught due to someone scratching their nose too quickly or too noisily.

Tom lay there in silence focusing on controlling his breaths, hoping that might help the time pass by faster; it didn't. He carefully picked a long piece of grass and methodically tore it into pieces along its grain. When that one was done, he picked another, and another, and continued that way for at least an hour. The boys were all silently occupying themselves with one thing or another, but they always kept a close watch on the tent into which they had last seen the sergeant enter.

Finally, when Tom's pile of shredded grass had become precariously tall, he noticed the old soldier emerge once again and approach two soldiers who were sitting in the grass playing cards. The sergeant had a big voice, and Tom could easily hear him as he spoke to the soldiers. "You two!" The two dropped their cards, jumped to their feet and snapped to attention in one smooth motion. "Grab a trencher and go dig us some latrines. 'Round the corner of that patch 'o hay oughta do." With that, the two soldiers picked up two small spades and started walking.

"Tom!" Ralph was still whispering, but there was a panic in his voice. Tom looked toward him and noticed his face was growing white. "Them soldiers are coming right at us!"

Ralph was right, and Tom almost panicked. "Okay, quiet now. We gotta move." The boys all began crawling backward until they were about fifteen feet inside the field. They could still see the soldiers' boots, but they were certain that the soldiers couldn't see them.

"Why we always gotta dig the pots, Johnny?" One of the soldiers said to the other. He had an accent; it wasn't foreign, but Tom was having trouble placing it, just the same. "Why can't nobody else never dig no pots?" His voice was raspy, but he sounded to be very young. Tom reckoned that he couldn't be more than one or two years older than himself. "I mean there I am, drinkin' a cuppa coffee, and up comes dat sergeant again tellin' us to dig more pots. Don't nobody else know how ta dig a pot?!"

"We dig the latrines, 'cause Sarge Evans says so." The other voice was deeper, but Tom was sure its owner wasn't any older than the first's.

"I worked that much out meself, Mack. Question's why he's always tellin' *us* to do it. He could tell anybody to dig da pots, but he always comes lookin' for *us*." The accent was from up north somewhere. Was it New York?

"Don't matter. Don't care." The other voice said. Tom was sure the second soldier was from the South.

"Jus once I'd like a little consideration, ya know? Jus a little equal consideration." The first soldier complained as he began digging a hole at the edge of the hayfield.

"What did you think you were joinin', the *Salvation* Army? The sarge don't owe you no consideration. You're lucky he bothered to learn your name." The second soldier worked quickly hefting scoop after scoop of dirt into a pile quickly outpacing the first soldier.

The northern soldier exhaled hard as if about to counter his friend once more, but was interrupted by the distinctive rumble of a truck approaching. Tom heard the engine at the same instant and began craning his neck side to side trying to see who might be approaching. As the vehicle passed by, all Tom could see was the tires, which stayed in view as they approached the gathering of tents. Someone climbed out of the driver's side of the truck, but Tom couldn't identify them from his knee down perspective.

"Dat's dat stupid sheriff from town, ain't it Johnny?"

"It's him alright."

Sheriff Thompson!!! Tom's heart beat faster. He looked to George who was white as a sheet. Did the sheriff know what they were up to? Had Tom's father told him? Was he there to bring them back home? Tom's mind raced.

He heard some mumbling at the camp, and assumed the sheriff was asking about Tom and the fellas, but a moment later his assumption proved to be wrong.

"Get out of my camp!" The major wasted no time on false pleasantries this time.

"You and I have things to discuss." Sheriff Thompson's voice carried more than usual. Tom realized that he must be on the verge of shouting, but his tone was still even.

"Nope, we don't. If I wanted to *discuss* anything with you, I woulda done it yesterday at that pathetic meeting of yours." Major Clinton's voice practically dripped with venom.

"I never said you *want* to discuss anything. You don't get to *want* or not *want* anything." Sheriff Thomson had a no nonsense tone that made Tom nervous. "We're going to talk about what you know, and, if you're very lucky, I won't lock you up for interfering with a police investigation." Tom could tell that the words weren't simply a hollow threat; the sheriff fully intended to make good on it, if the major didn't comply.

"Ole Thompson is givin' him the what for." Jimmy whispered as quietly as his obvious excitement would allow, but the moment of glee that showed on his face was short-lived. As Tom tried feebly to return James' grin despite the uncertainty he was feeling, the air was shattered by the sound of a sickening crunch and a thud. When Tom looked back, John Thompson lay in a heap on the ground next to the truck tires, his face covered in blood. The major's distinctive tall leather boots stood astride him, and the sheriff wasn't moving. Tom held his breath deeply and could tell the fellas were doing the same. After a few moments, the major stepped away from the crumpled heap of a sheriff, and the sergeant knelt next to Sheriff Thompson and placed his hand on the side of his neck.

"He's alive." The boys all heard Sergeant Evans announce. "You two!" Evans was pointing toward where Tom and the others were concealed, and the two soldiers who had been digging the latrine holes snapped to attention. "Get over here, and pick this man up."

"Yes, get over here and *tie* this man up!" The major bellowed. Another pair of Army boots approached where the major was standing, and Tom heard some more mumbling. "Speak up Lieutenant! I can't hear you!" The major's voice sounded like he was barely containing his rage.

"Yessir!" The man who had approached the major responded. "I asked if it is wise to take an officer of the law prisoner, Sir."

Tom saw the major's feet pivot violently and heard an even more sickening crunch than the one that felled the sheriff. Evans rushed to the bloody mess that had dropped to the ground and fell to his knees next to the young man.

"Don't bother with that one, Evans. He's already dead." Major Clinton's voice was still loud, but it was no longer filled with rage. The only way Tom could think to describe it was bitter cold. It was the most terrible voice he'd ever heard. Every pair of boots in the camp had gathered around the scene, and Tom decided he had to get a better look. He began silently crawling toward the edge of the field once more. All the soldiers stood by and practically cowered before their commander in abject terror. Clinton slowly turned on the spot, surveying them all. He stopped and glared at the two latrine diggers, who had stopped near the sheriff. "Didn't I order you two to tie up that meddlesome fool?" His voice sent chills down Tom's spine. The two soldiers startled slightly and stooped to tie up the sheriff. One of them was slightly bigger than the other; Tom figured he must be the one with the deeper voice, the Southerner. The larger soldier seemed to be examining the sheriff for injuries as the major barked orders to the rest of the soldiers.

Tom glanced back at the fellas; all of their faces showed nothing but shock. Tom assumed his expression must be similar. *"What kind of man could kill another with a single blow?!"* Tom turned back to the activity in the camp. A medic was placing a blanket over the body of the dead lieutenant, and the two diggers were carrying Sheriff Thompson, bound and gagged, into the sergeant's tent. Tom crawled back to his friends, trying to make sense of everything he had just seen.

"Tommy, was that man really dead?" George's voice was a little hollow with disbelief.

"He sure looked like it to me, when that medic covered him up." Tom's voice sounded even more hollow as it escaped his lungs.

"What are we gonna do now, fellas?" Tom had never seen Jimmy further from a laugh in his life, not even when they had run away from the quarry.

"Be more careful." Billy chimed in, the constant voice of reason. "My vote is that we don't so much as move until dark."

"We can't do that, Billy." George was beginning to regain some composure. "If me and Tom ain't back for dinner, his paw and Uncle Garv will come lookin' for us. And that troll just might kill one of 'em."

"I ain't leavin' without talkin' to that sergeant." Ralph's voice was stone. The set of his jaw showed a stubborn determination beyond anything Tom had ever seen. "And I sure ain't leavin' Sheriff John in there to get beat to death by that man, neither."

Tom signed heavily. "Ralph is right." He started. "We can't leave the sheriff, and we need that sergeant's help." He sat upright, knowing that no one could see him that deep in the field. "But George is right too. We gotta get back before dinner to keep them from worrying about us and gettin' laid flat next to that dead lieutenant." Tom wearily wiped his brow with the back of his hand.

"Then what do you think we should do?" George was concerned. Tom could hear it in his voice.

"We can't risk anyone else coming down here and gettin' killed. That's for sure and for certain." Tom's mind was racing as he tried to decide what to do. "Maybe we oughta send somebody back to tell my paw what's going on. That'll give us at least two hours to figure out how..."

"Shhh!" Billy interrupted Tom with a harsh whisper. "Listen!"

Tom laid flat on his stomach once more and took in the sight of the boots hustling around the camp and the sounds of soldiers hurrying from one place to another. "Evans!" Clinton had re-emerged from his tent and was yelling for the sergeant once more.

"Sir!" Sergeant Evans had snapped to attention in front of the major.

"Evans, I'm not waiting until later. I'm heading to the quarry to see about sorting things out. We'll be back around dark." The major spat what looked to Tom like a chewed cigar on the ground. "Keep the meddlesome lawman tied up. I'll be wanting words with him if he ever wakes up." With that Major Clinton turned on his heel and marched to a truck similar to the sheriff's, climbed aboard with a handful of his troops, and set off down the road. One of the soldiers that had joined the major was the medic, which struck Tom as odd with an injured man and a corpse in camp. About a dozen soldiers remained with the sergeant, including the two diggers.

"Christ be praised." Billy exhaled quietly.

"Seems He's lookin' out for us." Tom agreed. "That's just what we needed." He sat up once again and looked to the other boys. "Billy and Jimmy, y'all head home. Tell your paw what we saw and make sure he's ready to take care of Sheriff Thompson when we get back." Tom was talking quickly, but he kept his voice low and measured. "Give my paw a call and tell him and Garv what happened too. Tell them we'll be home soon."

"Tommy, I don't plan on going nowhere." James wasn't keen on being left out of the action. "Billy can manage by himself."

"Jim." Ralph joined in. "You know better than that. Ain't nobody supposed to be walkin' around alone. Just standin' across the street from my house for a few minutes this mornin' was near the stupidest thing I've ever done."

"Ralphie's right. Y'all both oughta go." George agreed. "Billy needs you with him, and we need you to tell somebody what's going on here."

"I agree." Billy's even logic joined the fray. "It'd be idiotic to go traipsing around by myself. I need you with me, brother." Jimmy finally nodded his agreement.

"Ok, that's settled." Tom was once again interrupted by movement and sound from the camp.

"You there! Stand to!" Sergeant Evans bellowed to a few men milling about near Sheriff Thompson's truck who immediately snapped to attention. "The five of you grab Simmons, Whorley, and Mitchell. I want a patrol of the perimeter. Set out around the pond first. Check the treeline. MOVE!" The men practically jumped at the order. They bustled into the camp, grabbed weapons near campfires and headed out with the other three men Evans had mentioned. Evans then walked toward his own tent.

"We need a better look. Something is going on over there." Tom whispered raspily, his voice scratchy from the long morning of whispering. "Jim, Billy don't go just yet. We might have more for you to tell our paws."

The fellas all crawled forward to get a better look. Evans was quietly talking to the diggers who had been standing guard outside his tent. He waved over the only other soldier in the camp and whispered something to him. The third soldier nodded and walked into the mess tent. Evans resumed talking with the two latrine digging soldiers who seemed taken aback by what he told them. The Southern soldier nodded his astonished agreement, but the Northerner hesitated.

"What in the world is going on over there?" George thought aloud. "What's he got up his sleeve?"

Evans grabbed the Northern soldier by the front of his shirt and spoke animatedly and quietly close to the soldier's face. The soldier's eyes grew wide, and he began to nod. Evans released his shirt and the soldier ducked into the sergeant's tent.

"You figure we were wrong about him?" Ralph asked with obvious concern in his voice. "You think they'd hurt the sheriff while that oaf is gone?"

"Nah, I don't think so." Billy was obviously trying to puzzle out what was going on also. "It seems like he's trying to get something done that the Major wouldn't approve of him doing.

The third soldier emerged from the mess tent carrying a couple crates stacked atop one another followed by the cook carrying two more. They loaded them into the back of John Thompson's truck and returned to the mess tent once more.

Tom looked to George puzzled. George returned the twisted glance and simply shrugged his shoulders. "Dunno Tommy boy. Dunno."

The sergeant and the Southern soldier had begun loading other crates into the truck. They seemed to be heavy. Tom guessed they contained arms or ammunition. They worked in tandem and loaded every crate in sight. All the while, the other soldier and the cook seemed to be emptying the mess tent of every scrap of food. Tom couldn't quite figure out what was happening, but he was sure it was working in their favor. He glanced sidelong at the group the sergeant had sent on patrol. They had reached the far side of the very large pond and seemed to be investigating the rundown old mill that sat by the outlet to the creek. It'd take them minutes to cross the distance to the camp.

Tom looked to the others. "Fellas." He'd spoken aloud, not full voice but more than a whisper. They all looked to him, shocked. "It looks like God is on our side for sure." Billy seemed to be the first to catch Tom's drift.

"The sergeant is escaping and taking Sheriff John with him!" He whispered excitedly.

"That's just what I was thinkin', Bill." Tom grinned. "I figure it's 'bout time we let the sarge know we're here." He stood, as did the others, and began walking quickly toward the camp. They all kept their weapons slung across their backs; they didn't want their potential allies to shoot them in a panic.

When they were about twenty yards away the cook spotted them and let out a cry, though more quietly than Tom guessed he might normally have done. "Sarge!" He dropped the crates he had been carrying and pulled a revolver from a holster slung around his ample stomach. "We got visitors!" He half-shouted once more and glanced to where the sergeant was standing.

Evans strolled over to the boys. "Mornin'." He said, quite matter-of-factly. "What can I do for you boys?" The sergeant eyed the guns the fellas were carrying warily but did not draw his own.

"Sergeant. My name is Tom Haynes. These here are Billy and Jimmy Wilson, Ralphie Donnelson, and George Priestly. We're from Doughty." The sergeant nodded politely but didn't remove his casually laid hand from the grip of his service pistol. "We figured we'd take a gamble that you're on our side, whether you realize it yet or not. We been watchin' from that hayfield there all mornin'. We know that major done half-killed our sheriff, and we know you ain't too happy about it." Tom grinned at the sergeant whose calm visage had grown to a look of disbelief.

"Reb! Brooklyn!" The Southerner stepped around the corner of the truck where he had been hiding with his rifle leveled. The Northerner stuck his head out of the tent. Tom stole a glance across the pond; the patrol had moved on from the mill but still had not yet noticed he and the fellas' presence at the camp. "Did you know these fellas was hidin' in that hay right under your noses?!" He scorned the two latrine diggers. Tom could tell he was having a bit of trouble keeping his voice quiet.

"They was hidin' where?" The Southern soldier, Reb Tom supposed to be what the sergeant had called him, seemed numb with disbelief.

"I didn' see nobody neither, Sarge." Brooklyn must be where the Northern soldier called home.

"How did we ever win a war with troops like these...?" Sergeant Evans seemed to be talking to himself. "Well, what do you boys want then?" His hand had dropped from his pistol.

"We were hoping to help you get the sheriff back to town. And we were hoping you'd be able to help shed some light on what happened to our friends. Something killed them, and we mean to find out what." Tom's light tone was gone; the voice that replaced it was no nonsense and obviously meant business.

"Alright fellas. Alright. I reckon the time really has come for that." Evans seemed weary all of a sudden, but he recovered himself quickly enough. He spun to face his men. "Lower your weapons and get back to work. We've gotta be outa here fore that patrol gets back!" His voice was strong and harsh, but he kept his volume low. Everyone went back to work. "You three" He pointed to James, Billy, and George. "get up in the bed of that truck, spread out some blankets, stow them crates, and don't let anybody see ya do it." The boys got to work as if they'd been taking orders from the sergeant their whole lives. "You two, with me." Evans turned on his heel and set out for his tent.

Tom and Ralph locked step with him and strolled right into the tent to see the Northern soldier cleaning blood from the sheriff's face. It looked to Tom like John Thompson's nose and cheekbone were broken. "Is he gonna be alright?" Tom asked the sergeant.

"Should be. He took a heavy hit, but he oughta be fine if we get him to a doctor." Evans sounded angry.

"The Wilson boys' paw is our town doctor. We oughta take him to their house right off." Ralphie had softened considerably since that morning, but Tom could tell that it was just temporary.

"Then that's just what we'll do." Evans sounded resolute. He ducked his head out of the tent, checking on the progress of the truck. Tom glanced over his shoulder to see Reb nod slowly. "A'right fellas, this is it. We gotta move fast now, and that sheriff ain't no small man. Y'all gotta help us get him into the bed of that truck quick, or that patrol'll pepper us all full of holes." Evans was serious, and Tom was nervous. But he and Ralphie nodded along nonetheless.

Each of them grabbed one of the sheriff's arms or legs and hefted him up. Once out of the flap of the tent, they set off as briskly as they could toward the bed of the truck. About halfway there, Reb cranked the metal beast up, and moments later Tom could hear yelling and curses being hurled from behind; the patrol had caught wind of what was happening and was headed toward them. He glanced over his shoulder and saw that they were much closer than he'd expected. They must've quickened pace on the road side of the pond. Tom quickened his pace too, as did the other three as they carried the near lifeless sheriff. There was a loud metal clang followed by the report of a rifle. They were still a couple hundred yards off, but the patrol had opened fire. A hail of shots followed, and the harsh sounds of metal striking metal and gun blasts soon filled the air. Tom wondered if Roosevelt had felt much like this charging San Juan hill.

"Almost there Boys! Keep moving; keep pace!" Sergeant Evans cajoled them along, but Tom's legs had begun to burn fiercely.

The third soldier who had been helping the cook load food into the truck appeared near the tailgate. He knelt, raised his rifle, and began returning fire. He worked the bolt of his rifle faster than Tom had ever seen before. He fired his five shots, grabbed a stripper clip, reloaded, and commenced firing again. The report of the rifle so close at hand, and in front of Tom nonetheless, was practically deafening, but he could still make out the shots of the patrol ringing behind him. He had read stories that sometimes, in the heat of battle, you can be struck by a bullet and not realize it until later. He wondered if his back was spotted with his own blood and he urged himself on. They rounded the behemoth, and he felt the safe relief of cover. They hefted the sheriff into the truck with help from the cook and the Wilson boys.

"Let's get outa here!" Evans shouted. "Sanderson!" He shouted to the soldier who was returning fire just in time to see him catch a bullet in the head.

Tom screamed in disgust and surprise at the loss of the new found comrade, knowing that the man was dead even before he hit the ground. Evans whirled around ran to the cab and ordered the Southerner to drive. The cook and Brooklyn slammed the metal tailgate closed as the truck spun around onto the road, gears grinding all the while.

The patrol was less than one hundred yards off and was still firing every round they could find. Rounds rang off the truck as everyone dove into the bed for cover, but the Northern soldier was a moment too late; he caught a bullet beneath his shoulder. Tom didn't know much about wounds of that sort, but the amount of blood pouring from the hole unsettled him. The cook had begun pressing the heels of both hands firmly on the wound, but there was still blood leaking from it. Tom noticed that the soldier had passed out a moment before he realized that they had escaped the range of the patrol's rifles.

"Won't they follow us?!" Billy shouted to the cook.

"They can try, but they'll have a hard time getting' anywhere. We stole most of the gasoline in camp and emptied the rest into a big pot of soup I'd been makin' for lunch." The cook grinned as he kept pressure on Blooklyn's wound. "Shame to waste good soup, but some things can't be helped."

CHAPTER II

It was half past noon when the truck rumbled up to Dr. Wilson's office door at the back of the Wilson family home. The blanket under Brooklyn was soaked in blood, and both he and the sheriff were still unconscious. As the truck was coming to a stop Jimmy hurled himself from the vehicle and rushed to the house calling for his father. Tom helped George lower the tailgate, and Billy and Ralph stood ready to help move Sheriff Thompson.

"Someone's shot?!" Dr. Wilson called excitedly as he ran to the truck carrying his bag.

"Here, Doc! One under the shoulder. Think it went clean through him." The cook had kept his full weight on the heels of his hands in an attempt to stop the bleeding; his arms were beginning to shake.

"Does all of that blood belong to this man?" The doctor was eyeing the soaked blankets as he climbed into the bed of the truck.

"All his, Mr. Wilson." Tom heard himself say. He was remembering the blood from the butcher's cellar and felt an ire raising up in his guts.

"Keep that pressure on." Doc Wilson was slipping his hands under the soldier to feel for an exit wound. "You're right; passed right through. I know you're tired, but you probably saved this man's life. Hold on just a while longer." He got to work cutting Brooklyn's sleeve and field jacket away from the wound. The blood soaked material slid from beneath the cook's hands to reveal the soldier's pale skin. Tom couldn't tell if that was normal, but it occurred to him that the blood loss might have drained his color.

"What's the word?" Sergeant Evans had sidled up next to Tom and was looking on wearing obvious concern on his face. "Will he live?"

"Doc says the cook might've saved him, but I don't figure he's outa the woods just yet." George spoke up before Tom had formulated an answer. He couldn't look away from the blood and pale skin. Billy had taken up a spot next to his father and was helping tuck cotton batting underneath the wound.

"Ok, on the count of three lift your hands out of the way, and I'll put some sterile batting into the wound." The doctor was poised with the bandage, and the cook was looking right at him, wide-eyed. "One." The cook breathed out heavily. "Two." He took in a sharp breath and held it tight. "Three!" The cook moved as quickly as his exhausted arms would allow, and Doctor Wilson shoved an unbelievable portion of the batting directly into the wound. He then grabbed another tightly folded piece of batting and pressed it tightly over the wound with one hand while rolling Brooklyn onto his uninjured left side with his other hand. Billy helped and began pressing his bloodied gauze into the exit wound and reaching for another folded piece of batting to press firmly onto the soldier's shoulder blade. "Ok, son, let's wrap him and get him to the table." The two worked quickly to wrap a strip of white linen tightly around Brooklyn's chest tying a surgeon's knot over the entrance wound. "Tom, you and Georgie get him inside on the table while I take a quick look at the sheriff."

"I'll help ya." Reb had stepped up behind Tom without him taking notice.

"I'll help too." Jimmy had been lingering in the doorway telling his mother what they had seen. The four of them gingerly carried the injured soldier into Doctor Wilson's office, a smallish room all painted white with supplies all along the wall to Tom's left and a few cots against the righthand wall. In the middle of the room there was a tall examination table. They set Brooklyn on the table and waited for the doctor.

"Get him onto that first cot, fellas." Jack Wilson said to the others helping him carry the sheriff. "That's it now, gently. He's had a rough enough time without us jostlin' him about." Billy, Dr. Wilson, Sergeant Evans, and Ralphie lowered him carefully onto the bunk. Mrs. Wilson had followed them into the room. The doctor turned to everyone standing around and took a deep breath. "Ok, now. You've done your part; now give me some space. It's gonna be a long day, and these men have a ways to go before I'll call 'em safe."

"Come along gentlemen, outside if you please." Mrs. Wilson was donning a white apron and rolling up her sleeves. Billy followed suit. "James, please help everyone find a place to rest and recover while we try to help these men."

"Yes, ma'am." Jimmy patted Tom on the shoulder and headed toward the stairs to the kitchen. Reb and Evans were on his heels. Tom slowly followed George and Ralph through the doorway. Last he saw Doc Wilson was measuring medicines and suiting up in an apron of his own.

* * * * *

James had led them all through the kitchen door to wash their bloodied hands. They each took turns at the basin. The soldiers and cook all took seats around the decorative kitchen table. Tom, George, and Ralph each crowded around the Wilsons' phone to inform their families of their location and the fact that they were each safe before joining around the table. Mrs. Priestly was beside herself talking to George on the phone. He must have spent nearly thirty minutes consoling her and telling her that he was fine before finally hanging up the phone and sitting next to Tom at the table. An uneasy silence hung over them all, as Tom wondered who would be the first to start in on the many topics that they obviously needed to discuss. The Sergeant let out a slow sigh telling Tom that he would start things off.

"So, how about you boys tell me just what you were thinkin' waltzin' into camp like that?" Sergeant Evans obviously wanted to feel out the situation before telling anyone his side of things.

"Those dead doughboys weren't just bodies to us; we knew 'em." Ralph's tone was sharp and no nonsense.

"That's it?" The Sergeant seemed to be having a hard time believing that could be enough to push the fellas into such danger. "Sorry now, I don't wanna sound insensitive or nothin', but, having lost friends of my own, I have a hard time believing there ain't nothing else going on here."

"Sergeant, can I ask you a personal question?" Tom wasn't about to play games; he was getting right to the heart of the matter.

"I suppose so." The Sergeant seemed wary. "But I may not be inclined to answer it."

"I reckon that's fair." Tom sighed. "If somebody who was supposed to be protecting you mighta had somethin' to do with killin' people you knew, would you just sit around instead of doin' somethin'?"

The Sergeant was visibly taken aback. "Well, son, I'm a soldier."

"All due respect, Sergeant, I'm not your son. And, when it seems that soldiers are the ones abandonin' people to die, who other than regular folks are left?" Tom bristled a bit, but he was trying to keep the Sergeant on their side.

Evans sat up straighter in his chair. "Sorry, I guess you've got a point there. Tom, wasn't it?"

"It was. Still is, in fact." Tom's tone was a bit lighter but still no nonsense.

The grizzled sergeant let out a deep sigh, leaned back in his chair, and cupped his face with both hands. Tom and George exchanged glances.

"Look Sergeant, I don't know what's goin' on here, but I'm about done beatin' around the bush." Ralph was visibly irritated, though that was not much of a change from the norm of the last few days. "It's pretty dern clear that you ain't with that torpedo of a major, but don't nobody know who you're *with*."

Evans lowered his hands to his lap and sighed heavily again. "Alright, I figure you've got a point there. No sense in prevaricatin'." The sergeant balled his hands into fists on the table. "Truth be told, Major Clinton is a traitor, and I reckon that means I've been one myself lately."

Tom was taken aback. He knew the major wasn't what he appeared to be, but the term traitor was reserved for the worst of the worst. Immediately names such as Aaron Burr and Benedict Arnold sprang to the forefront of Tom's mind. The idea of the term being used began to worry Tom greatly. "Traitor? Just what do you mean when you call him a traitor?"

"Yeah, Sergeant, what do you mean? Is he one of them that tried to help the Hun?" George seemed quite concerned.

"No." Evans replied. "He ain't that kind of stupid. We saw a lot of men drug up before a firing squad as deserters or turn-coats." Evans paused and sighed. "Clinton is worse."

"Worse?" James was incredulous. "How could anybody be worse than that?!" It was obvious that James was struggling through a mixture of fear and disbelief.

"What's worse is that the man believes he's a patriot. He's committin' atrocities and thinks it's a good thing to do. The major is totally off his nut, to be honest." Evans sighed again and looked at James. "It's James ain't it?"

"Yeah, what of it?" James didn't appear to like being addressed directly.

"This is your place, right?" Evans had a note of concern in his voice.

"Yeah, my family's. What's it matter to you?" James was beginning to fray, and his gung ho attitude was headed in a bad direction.

"Don't mean any offense. I am just wonderin' if we need to do anythin' to make this place safe." Evans looked inquisitively at James. "Major Clinton might be coming after us when he finds the state we left the camp in."

James' demeanor changed from one of irritation to one of fear. "How would he know where to go?"

"Said yourself this is where folks go when they're hurt, right?" James nodded his answer. "Clinton knows we got at least one injured man with us don't he?" Tom, George, Reb, Ralphie, and the cook all added their nods in chorus. "Well, don't take a genius to know where we'd be headed after talkin' to that patrol."

"Jimmy, we need to get on the move." Tom took the lead once more. "How long you figure your dad will be?"

"About ten seconds I figure." Billy stood in the door wiping his hands on a white cloth. "He's coming right now."

"My soldier?" Evans asked, his voice laden heavy with concern.

"He'll live, we reckon." Billy grinned a tired grin. "He lost a lot of blood, but I think Paw saved him." Dr. Wilson slipped in the door behind Billy and began washing his hands in the basin.

"The bullet went clear through the muscle. Didn't hit anythin' vital." The physician turned wiping his hands on a kitchen towel and nodded at the cook. "You, sir, saved that man's life. Someone should give you a medal."

"Thanks Doc." The cook exhaled with obvious relief.

"Thanks for certain. Thought he was a goner." Reb seemed to have a weight physically lifted off him. They might argue, but Tom could tell that Brooklyn was a dear friend to the large soldier.

"We can't thank you enough, Doctor, but just this moment we got more pressing matters to attend to." Evans had resumed his tone of leadership, and, under the circumstances, Tom welcomed the determination it aroused within him. He felt the sergeant was a man he could trust and rely upon; he knew he could follow this man's orders with confidence. "How long until the men can be moved, doc?"

"Moved? Moved where? Why?" Dr. Wilson was obviously confused.

"Anywhere but here Paw." James interjected. "That Major is probably gonna follow us here, and we best not be here when he finds this place." Dr. Wilson's face registered a shock.

"Do you think he'd really hurt civilians in a doctor's office?" his face was aghast at the very prospect of such a thing.

"Hurt? No. He'd kill ever' one of us without a second thought." Tom could tell by Evans' face that Reb had spoken out of turn, but the grizzled old sergeant didn't disagree with the assessment.

"Mr. Wilson, he's right." Tom realized his take on things might urge the doctor to understand the seriousness of their circumstances.

"Paw, he murdered one of his own men; we watched 'im do it." Billy's even tone seemed to bring home to his father the reality of their desperate situation.

"I'll ask ya again, Doctor. How long 'til we can move them men?" Evans' tone was quite earnest.

"Two hours, maybe three." Jack Wilson was white as a sheet. He was a strong, tough man, but the idea of combat was obviously not one he relished.

"So, five o'clock at the latest?" The doctor nodded his assent. "Good. That means we can be on our way 'bout three hours afore the major gets back to camp. That oughta be plenty of head start, as long as none of them boys from camp high-tailed it down to tell him what we done pulled." Evans sighed heavily again. "Better pray hard that we get outa here 'fore Clinton shows up. We ain't got nearly enough guns to fight the fury he'd be bringin' with him.

"James. Bill. You fellas get the ambulance readied." Dr. Wilson took the lead. "Hitch the Belgians; they're more steady. Can't afford to be bouncing those men around when we move 'em." Tom, you get on the telephone to your dad. Let him know we're comin' that way and to be ready." Tom nodded and started back toward the phone mounted on the kitchen wall. "Is your spare room in the basement still empty?"

"The slave station?" Tom was puzzled as to why Dr. Wilson would be asking about that old piece of the Underground Railroad.

"Right. Is it empty?" The doctor answered adamantly.

"Yessir, it's empty. Too hard to get into and outa to be used much." Tom was still confused.

"Good. Ask your folks to get it cleaned as best they can 'fore we get there. We're gonna need to use it as a clinic." Tom thought he was beginning to get the drift. "George mah boy, head down to my office and get Mrs. Wilson to help you stow a few cots away to pack in the truck." George nodded and headed back down the stairs.

Tom now fully understood. He picked up the phone and asked the operator to connect him to his parents. The secret room in the basement would be a handy place to hide the injured men and other soldiers, if Clinton came looking for them. He glanced around the room while waiting for the connection; Dr. Wilson was spouting instructions, and Sergeant Evans was turning them into orders as he barked them at one person or another.

"Hello, Tom?" Richard Haynes' voice came over the telephone. "Is everything alright?"

"Hey Paw." Tom started in excitedly. "Everything ain't alright. We reckon that troll major is gonna be lookin' for us real soon."

"I hadn't considered that." Richard Haynes sounded concerned. "Should I grab some fellas and head over there? Could have fifteen guns between us"

"Nah, I think the Doc has a better plan, Paw." Tom wanted to get the plan out as fast as possible; there would be a lot to do, and he didn't want to waste time on the telephone. "You know that slave room in the basement?"

"Yeah, what about it?"

"Figure we could set up a clinic for Doc Wilson, the injured ones, and these other doughboys?" Tom didn't really remember how big the room was; he hadn't been in there in years, but he hoped it would work.

"It'd be a real tight fit, but I reckon we could get 'em in there." Tom's father seemed to be picking up the plan on his own. "We can find beds for the rest of the Wilsons."

"Thanks Paw. We'll get there as soon as we can." Tom felt some small measure of relief at the prospect of safety and his own bed. "We oughta be able to get there 'round five-thirty."

"Tom." Mr. Haynes' voice had taken a serious tone.

"Yeah Paw?"

"Whatever you do, be careful. Don't take chances, okay son?" Tom could hear emotion in his father's voice.

"Yeah Paw, I'll be careful. Trust me, I don't wanna get tangled up with that major." Tom didn't relish that idea whatsoever. He had seen what that man was capable of doing to a person, and Tom was not about to bring that on himself if it could be helped.

"Good man, Tom. Good man." Tom heard his father sigh over the telephone. "Your mother has been worried. To tell the truth, I've been a bit worried myself." Tom could hear his siblings playing in the background. "I know you can watch after yourself, but that doesn't stop me wondering if something might get after you."

"Paw, don't you worry. We was safe, and I think we're startin' to get answers. We'll see ya soon."

"Love you son. Watch after the others."

"Love you too, Paw. We'll be safe as houses. Promise." Tom hung up the telephone and got to helping Ralphie carefully wrap Dr. Wilson's guns and load them in a packing crate.

Chapter 12

Tom kept his vigil at the kitchen window, staring out over the fields of long grass behind the house. He resisted the urge to check the clock again; he knew it was about half past two o'clock. He scanned the treeline methodically and scoured every inch of the landscape for signs that someone might be approaching. George had taken a watching post a few feet away at the outside kitchen door. Tom could almost feel his friend's eyes working in concert with his own as they endeavored not to be taken by surprise. Tom knew that Jimmy and Reb were in the back bedroom keeping their own watch, and Ralph and Sergeant Evans kept watch in the parlor. The rest had taken up temporary residence in the basement, looking over the two injured men. The waiting grated Tom's nerves more than he would normally have expected. He was accustomed to waiting; he'd spent countless hours sitting under cedar trees or behind fallen logs in the woods waiting for prey. *"Patience is the hallmark of a good hunter."* his grandfather MacClairn had frequently reminded Tom when he was younger. The kindly patriarch had passed away when Tom was still a child, but Tom knew he would remember that piece of advice until the day he died. He had long been acclimated to that certain type of waiting, but this was very different. When hunting one hopes for the appearance of their quarry, but Tom was far from excited at the thought of anything appearing at the edge of those woods.

Movement! Tom's gaze was quickly drawn from the field to the treeline as he instinctively began to grip his rifle at the ready. Out of the corner of his eye he saw George do the same to his right. He peered deeply into the trees squinting his eyes across the distance. The treeline was more than 300 yards away. There was a riot of movement just beyond the treeline, but Tom was having a hard time figuring out what was lurking in the shadows.

"Can you tell what that is, Georgie?" He asked without turning his face away from the window.

"Not sure, Tommy boy. Might just be some deer or somethin'." George responded in turn, still staring out the window in the back door.

Just when Tom thought he would have to move to get a better look, they came bounding out of the trees. *Wolves!* There were too many to count at this distance, as they ran back and forth twisting and turning and weaving between one another.

"Good gracious..." George trailed off mid thought and paused for a few long seconds. "...I ain't never seen so many wolves all at once, Tom."

"Me neither, Georgie." Tom tried his best to count the bodies as they quickly moved back and forth and in and out amongst one another. "Gotta be more than two dozen, dontcha reckon?"

"That many easy." George answered. His voice betrayed the slight shock that Tom knew they both were likely wearing across their faces.

"How many you seen at one time before, Georgie?" Tom was still having trouble counting the mass of furry creatures as they began to gain a little pace while crossing the field that separated the trees from the house and outbuildings.

"Well..." Tom could almost hear the cogs whirring in George's mind as he tried to recall different wolf packs he had encountered. "Think the most I ever saw at once was maybe twenty."

"Yeah." Tom nodded to affirm his agreement. "Biggest pack I ever saw was two summers back." Tom paused as he tried once again to count the enormous group of wolves weaving their way through the field, knocking down the grass as they came. "That one was big, sure enough. But we only counted twenty-one that time."

"Yeah, that's a bunch, but this lot is bigger." George still had a tone of disbelief in his voice.

"I'm sure there's more'n thirty out there." Tom kept trying to count the wolves; then something else struck Tom as odd about the pack. Something that he hadn't noticed right away. Not all the wolves looked the same, even at this distance. "George?"

"Yeah, Tom?"

"That pack look funny to you at all?" Tom was trying hard to ascertain what was odd about them aside from their sheer numbers; he had a feeling that his mind was close to sorting it out, but he couldn't quite put his finger on what it was.

George hummed a low hum and put his face closer to the window in the door. "Now you mention it, they do look kinda funny." He hummed again, almost rhythmically. He was clearly puzzling about the wolves as much as his friend.

Tom had a sudden realization. No one wolf looked odd to him, but the group looked odd together. "Them wolves all look the same color to you Georgie?" Tom began to piece together what was odd about them.

"Ya know, I think you're onto somethin' there Tom." George had tone of both confusion and fascination in his voice. "Tommy… them ain't all the same kinda wolf...are they?"

Tom squinted harder across the distance. He was sure that some of the wolves were a reddish color. They were still twisting and turning their way across the field toward him, and his view become increasingly more clear. "George, some of them wolves are smaller too, not just younger. I can tell it more 'n more as they get closer." Tom adjusted his gun again, squeezed the grip with his right hand, and thoughtfully scratched his temple with his left before returning it to the forestock. "Might oughta go grab the Sergeant, Georgie. I'll keep watchin' in the meantime."

Tom heard George back away from the door slowly as he moved toward the hallway door that led to the front parlor. Tom was more than a little bewildered by what he was seeing, but he knew it meant something. He listened to George's footsteps moving away down the hallway and heard the muffled tones of Ralph's voice from the parlor.

"Sarg." He heard George's voice quietly wafting down the hall. "Yessir. There's somethin' we think you oughta see back here."

Tom kept his eyes on the wolves as he heard George's footsteps growing closer once more, accompanied by the heavier steps of the old soldier. The view of the animals crossing the grassy expanse grew ever clearer the closer they got to the house, and Tom was becoming more and more certain of what he was seeing.

"What we lookin' at here, Tom?" Evans' deep grisly voice preceded him into the room.

"Wolves, sir. A bunch of them." Tom nodded his head toward the window without turning to look at the sergeant. "A whole bunch in fact. And that ain't the only thing weird about 'em."

Tom glimpsed George and the sergeant from the corner of his eye, as they stepped up to the door and gazed out. He noticed the old soldier move side to side taking in the whole expanse of the field and treeline before focusing on the wolves in earnest. The movement reminded Tom of his father when they would hunt together. Either Evans was also a hunter, or hunting and warfare had more in common than Tom had previously realized.

"That's a tolerable lot o' wolves, ain't it?" Evans' tone made it evident that he knew very little about wolves.

"Yessir, it is." Tom confirmed. "But that ain't the oddest part, Sarg." He furrowed his brow one last time, making sure he was right. "Those ain't all the same kind of wolf."

"Whadya mean, Tom? A wolf's a wolf, ain't it?" Evans' tone had taken on more than a hint of sheer confusion.

"There's two kinds of wolf that lives around here, Sergeant Evans." George interjected. "You probably seen a timberwolf a time or two. They're real good size and usually grey."

"Yeah, I've seen a couple since I been posted in Virginia." Evans was still waiting for the other shoe to drop.

"Well, Sarge," Tom began again. "There's another kind of wolf 'round these parts. It's smaller and real skittish." Tom took a brief second to steal a sidelong glance at the sergeant before returning his eyes to the field. "The red wolf don't never associate with timberwolves. And I do mean *never*, Sarge."

"But there they is." George interrupted anew. "Plain as day, sir. They're runnin' together like a regular pack, and there must be thirty of 'em!"

"How big is a normal pack, fellas?" Evans' tone took on a new tint, one of determination and no-nonsense.

"Six usually. Maybe a dozen or more in big packs." Tom paused thoughtfully. "I don't think I ever even *heard* of this many wolves bein' all in one place at the same time before. Especially not all peaceable with reds and greys all mixed up together. It's downright bizarre."

"Creepy's what I call it." George stated matter-of-factly, and Tom decided that he wasn't wrong about that.

"Creepy is definitely the word for it." Tom agreed. Then, he had another realization. The wolves were no longer getting closer to the house. They had stooped moving across the field and were just weaving and circling about fifty yards from the fence. They seemed to be trying to keep their distance from the woods, but they also didn't seem keen on getting any closer to the buildings. The horses were hitched up to the ambulance in the driveway just outside. Tom had a clear view of them. They had clearly gotten a whiff of the scent of the wolves and were nervous, but they didn't seem as though they were ready to bolt. That also struck Tom as a bit odd, but Belgians did tend to be braver and less prone to panic than many other breeds.

"They're actin' right peculiar, Sarg." Tom reiterated. "Look how they're movin' in and out and circlin'."

"They don't seem to be gettin' any closer now, do they, Tom?" Evans took the words right out of Tom's mouth.

"No, they've stopped. Looks like they're tryin' to keep their distance from both us and the woods." The sergeant had noticed the same things that Tom had just been musing. He must have done some hunting in his day.

"Watch 'em close." Tom said absentmindedly. " Pick one out and watch 'im."

Tom centered his gaze on a large black timberwolf that seemed to be more dominant over the others. He might have been the pack leader. He circled in and out making long sweeping turns, barely looking at the other wolves. He would periodically lift his nose high sniffing the air in the direction of the house, then toward the woods. He barely took note of the field itself. Tom was certain that he was looking for something in particular.

"That sniffin' they're doin', Tom." George let the statement hang for a few seconds. "Don't it remind you of how they act when they think they're bein' hunted?"

"I was just thinkin' that, Georgie. Looks like how that one acted right before Mark shot him last week." Tom pondered about the lone wolf that had been trying to raid the chicken house. "He knew somethin' was up. He knew we was close, and he didn't like it none."

"Yeah, and these don't seem none too excited neither." George contributed. "But they don't seem near as worried about us as the woods. Anyhow, they's a lot closer to us than whatever they're runnin' from."

George had nailed it on the head. They were running from something, and whatever it was wasn't good. Tom felt a shiver run down his spine. Something bad enough to scare red wolves and timberwolves into the same pack that would lurk within rifle range of a house must be very dangerous. Could it be the soldiers were lurking in the woods planning to attack? Tom hoped that's all it was. Even hardened soldiers would be hesitant to slog through a battalion of wolves to get to the house, and Tom was certain that they would hear their rifles if they started shooting the animals to clear a path. The wolves might be a blessing in disguise, but they still made him feel uneasy.

"Y'all seem like the experts on this." Evans started in once more. "Figure we oughta start shootin' before they get more aggressive?"

George started to hem and haw a bit, but Tom knew the answer. "No, I don't reckon we should." He waited for someone to take the opposite position, but no one did; so, he continued. "I figure they ain't after us and ain't likely to bother us. The Wilsons ain't got no small livestock around, not even no cows. Them wolves ain't huntin'. They's scared. And, seems like to me, they might even make them soldiers think twice about sneakin' up on us through the woods." Tom could see the others nodding their head in his peripheral vision.

"Sounds good to me, Tom." The sergeant voiced his agreement. "Just keep on keepin' watch. Lemme know if anythin' changes."

Tom and George nodded their assent and continued their vigil, investigating every inch of the treeline and field while watching the wolves do their dance. Tom locked eyes on the big black timberwolf again, and he thought, for the briefest of moments, that the wolf returned his gaze.

* * * * *

Four o'clock came and went, but the patients still weren't ready to be moved. Brooklyn, in particular, was in touchy condition, it seemed. Long before the wolves had shown up, Tom and the others had gotten both Sheriff Thompson's truck and the ambulance pulled near the basement door and loaded down with more provisions and armament than Tom had ever seen. Tom glanced down at the driveway for probably the thousandth time; everything appeared to be fine. He scanned the treeline and field methodically once again before looking back to the wolves. He had long established there were nearly forty of them, but their constant movement made it very difficult to get an exact count. Tom sighed, hefted his gun with his right hand, rubbed his eyes with his left, then returned to his statuesque vigil.

"*Clang! Clang! Clang! Clang! Clang!*" The grandfather clock in the hallway sounded its notice that it was five o'clock.

"An hour behind schedule." George stated, his tone heavy with worry and nerves.

"Yep, I reckon you better phone the house again and let 'em know we still ain't ready to leave." Tom imperceptibly adjusted his shoulders to relieve the tension of standing watch for so many long hours.

"Reckon you're right, Tommy." George backed away from the window toward the far wall, keeping his eyes on the field as much as possible.

"*Click*" Tom heard George lift the receiver and ask the operator to connect him to Tom's house.

"Missus Haynes? Tom told me to call, it's George Priestley... Yes ma'am...Well, the injured men ain't ready to move yet...I told 'em...Yes ma'am I sure did...We're bein' real safe, promise...uh huh...We'll get movin' jus as soon as we can...Alrighty then." He returned the receiver to the hook and himself to his post, and Tom was certain they'd be standing just on those spots until morning, when Billy suddenly came running out of the basement stairwell still wearing his white apron.

"Brooklyn's in a bad way, fellas." He announced a bit more loudly than Tom thought was intended. Sergeant Evans must have heard Billy's statement, because Tom heard him coming back down the hallway. Tom tried to keep his eyes on the field but couldn't help stealing glances around the kitchen.

"What's the racket?" Evans asked a bit concerned seeing Billy in his apron.

"It's Brooklyn, Sergeant." Billy paused a brief moment while he tried to decide how to deliver the news.

"What about Brooklyn?" Reb had come into the hallway too.

"He's lost too much blood, and we gotta give him a transfusion or he ain't gonna make it."

"A transfusion?" Reb seemed concerned. "Don't people die from them sometimes?"

"This ain't field medicine private." Sergeant Evans had both sternness and fatherly kindness woven through his voice. "This doc knows what he's doin'. Don't you worry none."

Billy nodded at the Sergeant. "Tommy, you got Type O blood Paw says. That's what we need."

Tom fully turned away from the window for the first time in hours. "What do you mean? You gonna give him my blood?"

"Unless you got a better suggestion." Was all Billy said in response.

Tom didn't hesitate for even a second. "What we waitin' for?" He ran into the basement hot on Billy's heels.

"Tom, hurry up, my boy, we need to be quick about this." Mrs. Wilson said as he came through the door. "We had him conscious for a while, but he's passed out again now."

Doctor Wilson pulled over another surgical table and placed it next to the one where the injured soldier was laying. "Right here Tom." He said as he grabbed a wooden case from a shelf and began pulling rubber hoses, a glass jar, and several needles from it.

"Do I lay down?" Tom asked as he climbed onto the table and felt a sudden nervousness rush through him. He'd never given blood before, and he'd never been very fond of the idea of needles; even the small pricks from general checkups were less than pleasant, in Tom's recollection.

"Yes Tom, lay down and pull up your sleeve as far as you can without it getting tight." Dr. Wilson was obviously hurrying, but his movements were still very deft and precise. Tom pulled his sleeve up to his bicep and laid down trying to breathe slowly and keep his adrenaline in check. He glanced across the small room to see Billy caring for Sheriff Thompson. His face was heavily bandaged, particularly on the right side. Tom realized that the major must have punched him with his left hand and began mulling over what that meant. Either the Major was left handed or even more freakishly strong that Tom had previously thought. That would probably explain why the left handed strike only injured the sheriff where the soldier that took a hit just after died on the spot.

"Okay now Tom..." The doctor's voice brought Tom back to the moment. "...you're gonna feel a pinch here." Dr. Wilson prepared Tom for the needle, wiping his forearm with cotton batting and alcohol. "You might wanna look away for this part, my boy."

Tom breathed out and held it as he looked at the injured soldier and reminded himself again why he was on the table hoping that would give him some courage. Then he felt it, the needle stabbed sharply into his arm. But the initial pain was quickly overshadowed by the bizarre feeling of his blood pumping out of the hole in his arm. He looked again to see the red liquid running down through the tube attached to the needle in his arm. It flowed freely into a glass jar on a smaller table between the two surgical tables. The sight of it suddenly drove all other things from Tom's mind. He watched it pour and puddle in the glass container and meditated on the irony that is life. Tom had been accustomed to blood in many different contexts through his life. He had hunted, dressed the animals he had killed, butchered livestock, and dealt with minor injuries on nearly a daily basis since childhood. He had recently experienced the darker side of blood in the butcher's cellar, but he pushed those thoughts from his mind as he watched his own blood flowing into the jar. He continued musing about blood and realized that more than anything else, he had sung about blood in the old hymns each week in church. "There is a Fountain Filled with Blood", "Nothing But The Blood", and "There's Power in the Blood" all now took on new meaning. He contemplated anew the butcher's cellar; he saw the carnage again, with his waking eyes. He watched his own blood fill the glass jar a little at a time. And he suddenly realized the significance of blood. The soldier laying next to him would die without his gift of blood, and Tom would suffer eternal punishment without Christ's gift of His perfect blood on the cross. The doughboys didn't simply die. They were murdered; they had their lifeblood stolen away from them and strewn through a warehouse with a rough disdain that could only come from something that is intrinsically evil. Tom was once again aware that he was staring at the jar of blood. He felt slightly lightheaded, but he supposed that was normal. The jar was nearly full. He was surprised that so much blood had just come out of him.

"Alright there Tom. That'll be about enough." Dr. Wilson said as he pressed some more sterile cotton batting against Tom's arm and removed the needle. "Hold that tight and bend your elbow, Tom." Tom did as he was told and watched the doctor work quickly to prepare the blood to go into Brooklyn. He poured a small vile of liquid into the blood and stirred it with a glass rod.

"What was that Doc?" Tom asked inquisitively.

"It's heparin. It keeps the blood from clotting." Dr. Wilson answered as he continued to work quickly. He lifted the jar up to a metal rack and hung it above the soldier's head. He inserted a tube into the blood.

"Here Tom, you need to eat this." Mrs. Wilson handed him a small piece of chocolate and a biscuit with honey on it. Tom ate it slowly as he watched the doctor work. He had equipped the new tube with a needle and some kind of clamp. He then placed a small hand pump on the end of the needle and worked it quickly until a few drops seeped out the end and the whole tube was filled with Tom's blood. Tom continued nibbling on the snacks and wondering why his head felt so light. The doctor inserted the needle and removed the clamp to allow the blood to flow freely into his patient. Tom sat up slightly to get a better view, felt his head grow heavier as the remnants of the biscuit fell from his fingers, and he saw the darkness closing in like a tunnel.

Chapter 13

Some unnamed faceless terror was chasing him; Tom could feel it closing in behind him. Branches struck him roughly in the face, and thorns and brambles clutched viciously at his clothing tearing deeply enough to draw blood from his skin beneath. The darkness was all encompassing, pressing in on him from every side. Tom could barely tell where his feet were falling as he tore through the woods as fast as his legs and lungs would allow. The creature was hot on his heels; he could feel the distance between them closing steadily. He could almost smell its coppery breath still laden with the blood of his friends. He'd heard Ralph fall to its fangs and claws as they fled from the house and the terrible fate that had befallen the others, but even Ralphie's death wasn't enough to slack its bloodlust. It's eyes had glowed red in the darkness, and it's razor sharp teeth had flashed wildly in the ever so faint moonlight that had since been overtaken by the cloudcover that replaced it with a darkness so deep that he didn't even see the briar as it tore a deep gash of flesh from his forehead. He kept pushing himself harder through the darkness, but the pain in his head grew ever more intense, slowing his pace, as the blood flowed freely into his right eye. Then he heard it...the breathing. The beast was right behind him. It's breath was as slow and steady as his was fast, strained, and painful with every gasp. He tried to keep running, but his body was spent. His foot caught an unseen tree root and sent him flying face down in the leaves and thorns. He rolled to his side; as he turned he saw those horrible red eyes once again. The clouds finally relented enough for the tiny sliver of moon to reveal the outline of the beast. It was smaller than he had expected, but no less sinister. The moon glinted on its claws, as though it was being reflected by solid steel. It reached out its hand to rend him as it had his friends. But this time it moved differently; it had forsaken the swift terrible speed it had used to tear through the house in barely more than an instant. The menacingly slow and deliberate movement of the steely claws shook Tom to his very core. He tried to scream, but he couldn't conjure up enough breath to even speak. Finally, with lightening quickness, the hand slashed out.

Tom awoke abruptly and out of breath, in a cold sweat. His jerking motion had inadvertently knocked a blanket from the bottom of the surgical table on which he was laying. His head felt some better, but it still ached slightly. He sat up slowly concerned that he might faint again, but he didn't.

"Tom! You're awake. Good. How do you feel?" Dr. Wilson strolled over, trying to look nonchalant, took Tom's wrist and checked his pulse.

"My head hurts a bit, but I reckon I'm okay." In truth Tom was quickly feeling more like himself.

"Good, good. You seem to have recovered from your mishap." Jack Wilson seemed intent on Tom's condition alone, and it got Tom's curiosity working. He looked to his right and noticed the other table was empty.

"Where's Brooklyn?!" Tom was in an immediate panic. The adrenaline lessened the pain in his head, but he was no less concerned for the soldier.

"Calm down there fella." Tom heard a raspy voice with a distinctive accent from behind him. He wheeled to find that the adrenaline only helped so much, as he had to briefly steady himself on the table. Brooklyn was sitting up on a cot laughing at him. "Thanks for the blood, boss. Mighta been a goner without cha." The soldier had a good natured grin on his face, and Tom's worries were immediately lessened for a moment, until he noticed the windows...they were nearly dark.

"Doc?" Tom queried slowly, trying not to jump to conclusions again.

"Yes, Tom?"

"Is it just me, or is it dark out?"

"Just about. It's nearly eight o'clock." Doctor Wilson laid a hand on Tom's back to calm him even before Tom felt the panic rising up again.

"We're four hours late, Doc." Tom was keeping himself in check, but he was beginning to feel a more definite sense of urgency.

"We are, but we're ready to load up and leave as soon as you are. We didn't want to move until we were sure Brooklyn here wasn't gonna lose consciousness on us again." Dr. Wilson rounded the table and looked Tom in the eyes. "He seems to be on the mend. Letting you rest some was a bonus, but now we really do need to get out of here." His eyes were just as soft as ever, but his voice had a tone of urgency hidden in it. That was all Tom needed to get moving.

"Where's everybody?" He asked while hopping off of the table, hefting his Winchester from the bedside, deftly working its lever action, checking that it was still loaded, and carefully dropping the hammer as he moved toward the door. He also quickly scanned the room. Sheriff Thompson was still unconscious, but his breathing seemed deeper than it had been before.

"They're upstairs keeping their watches, Tom." Mrs. Wilson pointed to the stairwell door, as though Tom didn't know where it was. As he headed through the door and up the stairs, Tom mused that he must have gone out hard when he fainted. He tried to shake the terror of the red eyes from his memory as he ascended into the kitchen once more to find George still at his post.

"Look alive there, Georgie!" Tom startled his friend. George jumped slightly and Tom remembered what it was like to smile.

"Thank God, Tommy!" George's face registered relief as he realized who had given him a fright. "We gotta get outa here and quick!" He glanced once again out the darkening window toward the field. Tom could barely see the wolves still engaged in their continuous dance in and out and through and through. "We're almost outa daylight, and I sure don't like the idea of bein' stuck where that goblin can find us."

"Stole the words right outa my mouth, George." Tom clapped his friend on the shoulder and started back across the kitchen. "I'll grab the Sarg and everybody, so we can get outa here." Tom was already moving down the hall as the last words came out of his mouth.

Sergeant Evans was squinting out the window into the dying light as he leaned against the window sill. His brow furrowed deeply, and Tom couldn't tell if it was more from the strain of squinting into the near darkness or the worry of what might be lurking in those lengthening shadows. Ralph was half perched on the edge of Mrs. Wilson's reading desk with his back to Tom.

"Time to pull on out, Sergeant Evans." Tom's voice seemed to awaken Ralph from a daze.

"Sheesh Tommy, wear a bell, will ya?! Dern near stopped mah heart!" Ralph's expression was a combination of fright and relief. Tom realized that his friend had probably been worrying about both him and their overall safety.

"Sorry, Ralphie, forgot my bell at the house this mornin'." Tom chided good naturedly, and the shadow of Ralph's stereotypical smile creased his lips for a faint moment, but that was enough to buoy Tom's spirits a great deal.

"Brooklyn ready to move?" Evans appeared a bit relieved, but there was still considerable worry behind his eyes.

"He is. Seems to be doin' lots better."

"And you? How ya doin' there Tom?" The sergeant was a natural leader, assessing everything methodically and analyzing it as he made decisions.

"I'll be perfect in no time, if we get outa here before we run into any more setbacks." Tom's sense of urgency hadn't lessened since he'd run up the stairs. If anything, his sense of impending doom had increased. He had the ever present image of disquieting red glowing eyes floating in his mind, and he knew he wouldn't feel safe until they were well away from anywhere that Major Clinton was likely to find them.

"Alright then. What are we waiting for?" Evans hefted his rifle, threw his field bag over his shoulder, sidled past Tom into the hallway, and headed toward the kitchen.

"You go on ahead, Tommy." Ralph said as he gathered his own few things. "I'll grab Jim and Reb and head downstairs straightaway."

"Thanks Ralphie." Tom said patting his friend's shoulder as he passed into the hallway and headed for the front bedroom. Tom headed back down the hallway to the kitchen at as brisk a pace as he could manage without running.

"Evans went on down the stairs, Tom." George stated over his shoulder still keeping watch into the thickening gloom of twilight.

Tom didn't even respond as he hurried down the stairs; he knew that George didn't expect any response. Tom took the last three stairs in one leap, turning in midair to change directions at the landing. He entered the clinic almost as fast as he had exited just a few short minutes before. They had both Brooklyn and Sheriff Thompson on stretchers ready to move them to the ambulance as soon as everyone was assembled.

"Oh, Tom! Good!" Dr. Wilson greeted him as he entered the room. "Here's the plan." He returned to packing the last few things he had been using to treat his patients into a brown leather satchel. "We'll move both men at once." he pointed to Evans, "The sergeant will lead the way out the door and make sure it's as safe as we can make it." He then pointed to the cook. "Mr. Bosco here and Billy will carry Brooklyn to the ambulance right behind Sergeant Evans." His look was fatherly, but he also looked determined. Tom could tell he was concerned about things going exactly as they should. "Jimmy and me will carry Sheriff John right behind them."

Tom nodded. "Yessir. What about the rest of us?" As Tom finished the sentence, Ralph, Reb, and Jimmy arrived from upstairs.

Evans responded, "Reb'll pick up the rear down here and drive the truck when we head out." Evans pointed to Tom. "I'm relying on you to take care of things upstairs, Tom." He and Tom nodded to one another, trying to assure one another that Tom could handle that much. "You fellas'll keep a lookout from that porch outside the kitchen 'til we get to the vehicles, alright?"

It was Ralph's turn to speak up, "You can count on us, but I don't think them wolves is gonna be a problem."

"I agree with Ralph, Sergeant." Tom was sure that the wolves were much more concerned about whatever was in the woods than they were about the goings on at the house.

"Still, might be somethin' else out there that means us harm." Evans seemed much more concerned than he had, even that afternoon. Tom got the impression that the darkness was really worrying him. "Either which way, as soon as we got these men loaded up, you high tail it down from that porch, lickety split. No dilly dally, now. That's the most important thing." Evans looked from Tom to Ralph and back to Tom.

"Like Ralphie says, Sergeant. You can count on us." Tom felt confident in his ability to guard everyone from above, as he turned to head back upstairs with Ralph, but the sense of impending danger still lingered in his thoughts. He tried once more to push it to the back of his mind as he took the steps two at a time once more.

"What's the plan, Tommy boy?" George greeted him without turning. Tom was unsure whether he could tell who it was from his gait or if he had seen Tom's reflection in the ever darkening window.

"You, me, and Ralphie are gonna stand out on the porch and keep watch while they load up Brooklyn and Sheriff Thompson." Tom had crossed the room with Ralph close behind him. They each sidled up one on each side of their friend. George finally turned and looked first at Tom then Ralph. Each of the three adjusted their grip on their weapons and took a deep breath. This was it.

"Well fellas, there ain't no time like the present, right?" Ralph's voice held a bit of humor, but it barely concealed the nerves right below the surface telling Tom that he was no more keen on walking out into the near dark than any of the rest of them. They all knew something was off, and with the light fading the risk of attack was increasing substantially.

Tom looked to the treeline once more; he saw nothing moving, but the gloom was too deep for him to be sure that the shadows didn't conceal any enemies. His eyes drifted upward seeing the small slice of the sun hovering above the trees, and he knew it was now or never. He reached out his left hand to the doorknob, keeping his right securely on the grip of his rifle. The door swung outward squeaking only slightly on its hinges. Tom felt the sticky summer air strike his skin for the first time in hours. It was hotter than he expected after being holed up inside all afternoon. The faint caress of a breeze tickled the hairs on the back of his neck as he stepped fully out onto the elevated back porch, and he could feel George and Ralph flanking him to his back, as they exited and moved to either side scanning the wider view they achieved when they broke the plane of protection that the kitchen walls had afforded during their long vigil. Tom didn't know whether he enjoyed the freedom or feared it, but he knew that he had never felt more exposed, even when leaving his own home in the wee hours that same morning. The atmosphere around him was noticeably electric, and he was keenly aware of every small movement or alteration around him. He took note of everything assailing his senses all at once. He felt George and Ralph positioned beside and behind him, smelled the honeysuckle wafting from the fenceline, heard the horses snorting nervelessly, and saw the wolves as they continued their dance in the field.

"We're ready up here, Doc Wilson!" Tom shouted, hoping to get the vehicles loaded and get on their way as fast as possible. He heard the basement door open and close below him, and shortly Sergeant Evans had emerged from beneath the raised porch and was carefully investigating the edges of the house, looking around the corners, and checking underneath the vehicles.

"Okay there, all looks good out here. Hurry up with them patients." The sergeant called out to those in the house,

The Wilson men and the cook quickly emerged carrying their comrades to the ambulance as Mrs. Wilson continued to monitor the condition of the two injured men. Reb emerged last keeping a steady watch around the periphery of the yard, especially watching the field and fenceline, beyond which the wolves continued doing their dance, constantly moving and weaving in and out among each other. The big black alpha caught Tom's eye once more, gracefully trotting through the others taking no note whatsoever of the wounded men being loaded into the large wagon. Tom was certain that the smell of blood should at least make an impact on the wolves, but their focus remained on the distant treeline. Tom glanced down at the wagon to see that Brooklyn was already concealed within, the cook was now assisting Mrs. Wilson into the back to sit with the patients, and Billy had taken his spot on the driver's seat reins in hand. Tom's eyes then darted back to the treeline. *What had commanded the wolves attention so completely?* Tom scoured the shadows but saw nothing more than he had earlier. Once again, his eyes drifted to the sun which was now no more than a tiny sliver. Time was running out; Tom didn't know how he knew it, but he had never been more certain of anything this side of Heaven.

"All loaded!" Evans called to the three on the porch. Tom looked down to see Dr. Wilson closing himself inside the back of the ambulance as Jimmy joined Billy on the driver's perch and the wagon lurched into motion.

"Thank the good Lord for that!" Ralph exclaimed in relief, as at last they knew that they were mere moments from making good the escape they had been needing since just after breakfast.

"Coming on down now, Sergeant!" Tom called back as Reb climbed into the cab of Sheriff Thompson's truck and the grizzled older soldier stood in the bed of the truck watching the entire perimeter. It looked to Tom as though his head was on a swivel. "Come on boys." Tom said to his friends as he turned in the direction of the steps and headed toward the driveway below.

"Don't have to tell us twice, Tommy." George replied hot on his heels, with Ralph right behind him. Something suddenly caught Tom's attention, and he stopped his momentum a few steps from the ground and turned his eyes toward the wolves; they had stopped moving. Not only had their constant dance stopped in an instant, they had all turned fully away from the house to face the treeline. Tom could hear that George had stopped breathing and realized that he was also holding his breath. Despite the significant heat of the summer evening, a chill ran down his neck and his heart resumed its residence in his throat. Something was very wrong, and Tom was suddenly and very palpably aware of it.

"C'mon boys! Whatcha waitin' for?" Reb called out the window of the truck. Tom stole a glance in his direction but was more acutely aware of the fact that Sergeant Evans' attentions had centered on the field as well, and it appeared he had also bated his breath. From a full twenty yards away, despite the low light, Tom saw all color drain from the grizzled soldier's face. Evans slowly turned his eyes to the staircase, and Tom saw the look of sheer terror in his eyes.

"RUN!!!" Evans' voice shattered the moment and was immediately joined by a synchronous and raucous chorus of howls as the wolves all erupted at once.

The sudden discordant clamor shook Tom from his temporary paralysis and he leaped to the ground, hearing the other fellas hot on his heels. He tore across the distance separating him from truck and leaped into the bed of the truck, as George and Ralph followed suit and Reb shoved the behemoth into gear. They shakily spun slightly, turning toward the road, but the truck stopped jerkily and stalled; Tom felt terror fill him as he remembered the temperamental clutch on the sheriff's old army vehicle. He stood from the seat he had taken on the bench and looked toward the field that remained barely illuminated by the setting sun. A figure on all fours came sprinting at the wolf pack from the treeline. Time seemed to stop, as Tom realized that it wasn't the soldiers that had frightened the wolves into such bizarre behavior. He was barely aware of the growling that had erupted to take the place of the wolf pack's howls. The figure tore into the wolves at full tilt, swiping its long limbs this way and that, slinging blood as it went. The shower and spray of life-giving fluid looked black in the low light, and the extent of it's spray almost blocked all remaining light of the sun as it had just fallen behind the trees. He became aware that the wolves were charging at their attacker in force, but there was no evidence that it had slowed its pace even in the least, as it wreaked carnage across the field. Tom was focused so fully on the full tilt battle that had erupted only yards away that he didn't notice that Reb had managed to recrank the truck. The creature reached the fenceline, raised a massive grey wolf above its head, stood to its full height, and effortlessly tore it limb from limb. It lowered its arms, and Tom knew it was just as dangerous on two legs as when going on all fours. But what truly struck him in that moment were its glowing red eyes. He was certain that it was looking directly at him and savoring the moment before leaping the fence and rending him as it had the wolf. Tom was brought back to his senses as he felt the bed of the truck shake beneath his feet, grinding back into gear, and as he heard the report of Evans' rifle by his head. He saw the impact in the creature's shoulder, but it was barely shaken. Tom raised his own firearm as the truck gained speed. He took careful aim, unaccustomed as he was to shooting from a moving vehicle and was in the process of squeezing his trigger when a hulking black figure came soaring through the air behind the creature. The black alpha distended its massive jaws, teeth gleaming in the low light slamming its full weight into the monster, striking it full in the back as the wolf's long white teeth sank deeply into the base of the monster's neck, black blood spurting high into the air. As the truck spun onto the road, Tom saw other members of the pack sink teeth into every inch of the creature that they could reach, trying desperately to drag it to the ground. As they sped away toward safety, the last thing Tom remembered was the monster's high pitched howls of rage and pain as the black wolf savagely tore into it's neck, spraying blood with every shake of his heavily muscled jaws.

~160~

Chapter 14

As the truck slowed its pace to match the ambulance, Tom still couldn't manage to shake the sight of the horribly disfigured creature from his mind. Those glowing blood red eyes, savage slavering teeth, dripping claws, and grotesquely muscled shoulders haunted his waking thoughts. Tom had seen many things in his young life; he was sure he was familiar with every beast that God had placed in this land he called home, and he was certain that this creature was not among them.

Tom suddenly became aware of the fact that his mind was wandering, and he shook his head slightly. It wouldn't do to have his senses fogged while they were still in the open. He had no idea how many of those creatures there were or if the soldiers may also be lurking in the dark somewhere planning an ambush. He needed to be sharp. He glanced around the truck at shorn hayfields, wire fences, and dark distant trees. Discerning no movement, he turned his attention to the truck itself. He took note of his friends' faces. Understandably, George was lost in thought, but Sergeant Evans, still standing in the bed of the truck with his head on a swivel, had the most inscrutable expression on his face that Tom had ever seen; he had the set jaw and hollow eyes of a consummate soldier. Tom knew that he'd have to ask direct questions of the old warrior to get the answers he needed, but that would have to wait. Tom turned his attentions, once again, to Ralph. His face had fallen once more. His eyes were practically sunken, dark thoughts scrawling along behind them. His mouth hung slightly open, and the color had totally vacated his cheeks. It took very little imagination to know what he was thinking; Tom fought against his own mind trying to keep the thoughts at bay. No good could come of envisioning that brute ripping the doughboys apart as it had the wolf. Tom refused to allow his mind to wander there; he fought off the thought. He practically muscled it out of his mind. He didn't want to suppress the thoughts; he wanted to purge them completely.

"Ralphie." Tom called loudly, but with a gentleness in his voice. His friend's vacant eyes turned wearily upward to meet his own. "I can't see the treeline behind me very well from this bench. How 'bout you watch my back an' I'll watch yours?" Tom knew that putting his safety in Ralph's hands would tend to pull his friend out of his own mind; he wouldn't want to risk another friend's life.

Ralph nodded, his eyes clearing slightly. "Okay Tom. Might oughta do that, I reckon." His voice was far from cheery, but Tom knew the task would do what he intended for the time being.

"Georgie?" Tom turned his attention to his other friend. Who immediately started at the sound of his name.

"Yeah, Tommy? Somethin' up?" He stated with a hint of alarm as he began looking over one shoulder then the other scrutinizing their surroundings for some hidden terror.

"Naw George, ain't nothin' wrong. Just had a question is all." Tom's reassurance seemed to calm his friend's nerves slightly, as George looked toward him. "Figure we can do somethin' to make use of the barn and chicken coop if we get attacked? Was thinkin' that the place'd be more defensible if we had more lines o' sight, right?"

"Dunno Tommy. We'd have to work out some shooting holes in the barn, wouldn't we? An' that ole coop can't even keep out the winter breezes." Tom could see a renewed activity behind George's eyes; he knew the task would occupy his thoughts for a while and distract him from the creature for a while. "I'll have to think it over."

"Ok then, just lemme know if you come up with somethin'. Figure it's better to have 'em and not need 'em than the other, right?" Tom felt some relief knowing that his friends' were now occupied with something useful; it wouldn't do to have them distracted if they came under attack.

Tom glanced toward the Sergeant. The old soldier's eyes met his own, and Tom caught the tiniest hint of a smile on the man's face before he resumed his vigil of their surroundings.

* * * * *

Tom slowed his breathing, fighting the urge to sprint across the distance separating the treeline from the house. They had just hidden the truck fifty yards further into the forest in a thicket, and he knew that the deserters, Sheriff Thompson, and the Wilsons were all safely stowed away in the hidden room in the basement. He knew it had protected numerous runaway slaves from bounty hunters and unscrupulous lawmen who had scoured the countryside and harassed farmers, but Tom found himself, once again, fighting doubts about whether his friends and family would remain safe, as he saw soldiers swarming all over his home. He didn't see Major Clinton, and he knew that probably meant that he was inside the house, a thought that renewed his sense of panic. He felt his father lower himself to the ground to his left, and Tom followed his example, as he, once again, resisted the urge to run to the defense of his family.

"Paw?" Tom whispered so quietly that, for a moment, he was unsure if his father even heard him.

Richard Haynes very slowly turned his head a quarter turn toward his son, keeping his eyes fixed on the house, and whispered so softly that Tom felt as though he had practically screamed at his father the moment before. "Tom, we have to stay right here; it ain't the time to be a hero. It's in God's hands now. If we've done what we ought, then everybody'll be just fine. Understand me?"

Tom nodded, "Yes, Paw." But deep down his insides were screaming at him to move, to jump up and run to his mother, to sprint to his home shooting every soldier he saw, to rescue his siblings, to find Mark and protect him. The weight of the promise he had made to his brother descended on his mind like a falling anvil. He felt a stinging in the corners of his eyes as he thought of his brother and felt anger welling up inside him while he watched the soldiers invading his home. He gripped the stock of his rifle tighter and deftly wiped a tear from his cheek with the slightest movement of his head.

CRACK! Tom heard the snapping of a twig behind him and immediately was filled with a new fear. Had the creature survived it's battle with the wolves? Would his family be safer with the soldiers present to protect them from its fury? Would they find his mangled body the way he had found the doughboys? He felt the movement more than he saw it, and the singular twig snapping had been the only sound. Whatever was behind him had been moving slowly, methodically, cautiously, but he couldn't be certain that it was approaching him; it felt almost as though whatever it was had stopped moving the instant the sound had shattered the tender silence of the forest. Tom saw his father move his head ever so slightly to expand his peripheral vision to their left and arching his ear toward the noise; Tom followed his example angling to the right. If it was indeed the creature, it had changed its tactics, because, if it was still moving, it was doing so more slowly than Tom had previously imagined to be possible. Or was it more than that? Was it so stealthy that it could stalk at speed and still make no sound whatsoever? The thought sent a shiver of fear down Tom's spine as he felt the hairs on his neck and the back of his hands stand on end.

"See anything Tom?"

"No, Paw. Can't hear nothin' else neither." Tom was straining his every sense to find the source of the noise, but his father turned his attention back to the farmhouse and the soldiers. "Paw, what if it's the creature?"

Richard Haynes paused long before answering. Finally he released the softest of sighs. "If it's back there, then only a miracle can save us now. Best be looking to the enemy we know 'stead of worrying 'bout the one that lurks outside our observation."

Tom mulled over his father's words, feeling more peaceful by the moment. There was a sense of peace in the knowledge that, live or die, his choice was clear; he must look toward his family and known dangers rather than robbing himself of his wits looking for phantasms in the dark. He could hear his grandfather MacClairn's voice, *"Ole General Jackson used to say that faith in the Lord tells us to feel as safe in battle as we do in our beds. Act wisely, but don't never let worry rob you of your senses."* Tom turned his gaze back to the house and peaked his ears, listening for anything of interest, and he was surprised to find that the forest was alive with sounds he had drowned out scouring the night for some nameless, faceless fear. Squirrels, racoons, and owls scurried, wandered, and flapped deftly and quietly through the night, and Tom felt more easy and safe than he had in days.

BOOM! Major Clinton exited the back door in a rage, slamming the screen door open with such force that its top hinge splintered free of the wood, and the door hung lazily askew. He began barking orders to his men who jumped aboard the massive army truck as fast as if they had been fired from a cannon. The vehicle roared to life as Clinton climbed into the cab shouting obscenities at Tom's mother and Garv who stood in the doorway. He was still shouting as he pulled the door closed and the truck raced out of the driveway.

It was several agonizingly long moments before Tom's father moved. "I think we're in the clear, son." His voice softly shattered the silence, and Tom realized he had been holding his breath.

The two men, father and son, slowly and deliberately stood, and Tom felt the cool night air against his chest for the first time since he had flattened himself against the forest floor. They stood quietly for several more moments investigating their surroundings. Tom stole several piercing glances into the woods behind them, but he found no trace of the source of the sound that had terrified him just a short while before. The magnitude of the peace he now felt impressed itself upon him once again, as he almost laughed at his earlier panic and felt a new appreciation for his father's wisdom.

After what seemed both an eternity and the shortest of moments, Tom was sure that standing there any longer would be nothing but a waste of their time and a foolhardy delay in the open, where there still lurked a dangerous fiend and a pack of ravenous wolves. "Think we oughta head to the house, Paw?"

"Was about to suggest the very same thing, Son." Tom's father stated in almost full voice as he took his first cautious step toward the house. They moved carefully, alert to every movement or sound around them. They startled a fox in the field, and several mice that it had undoubtedly been hunting. A pheasant stirred from its nest as they passed, and an owl swooped after it. Tom couldn't tell if it had become a meal or a survivor.

The steps between the house seemed to be interminable. With every step his curiosity about what had occurred within the house and his desire to sprint the final distance increased. He kept his eyes moving and his head ever turning, as he probed the darkness for signs of danger, but the peace he felt spread throughout him more and more with every second. Then he saw it, smoke, near the barn. He barely hesitated, but he kept the presence of mind to keep moving forward. He turned his head back toward the forest as though checking behind them and whispered, "Paw, you see the smoke by the barn?"

Richard Haynes made a movement like he was wiping his cheek on his forearm to cover his own mouth as he spoke. "Good eyes son. Pretty sure its a sentry left behind." They both kept pace as though they hadn't seen the man, knowing that, if he hadn't already, he'd see them any second. The only course of action they had was to keep pace toward the house and force him to take action.

"*What do I do if he opens up on us with his rifle?*" Tom thought to himself, surprised that the thought didn't even make a dent in his feeling of safety and peace. "*Can I hit him from here?*" Tom wondered, adjusting his grip on his Winchester, knowing that, in all likelihood, his father would take the shot; Tom was confident that either of them could strike true at this distance under normal circumstances, but he was also quite aware that he was unaccustomed to shooting at targets that shoot back.

Movement!

Tom saw something lurch forward by the barn where he had noticed the smoke, but he didn't hear a shot. "*Had the creature gotten the soldier?!*" Tom's imagination began to run as he heard a scuffle in the area and saw a man's hands flailing as his rifle flew free of his grasp, and the soldier landed face down in the dust of the barnyard. Then Tom laughed in earnest for the first time in the seeming eternity since he and the fellas had first met the doughboys. Mark stood over the soldier holding one of his father's old lever action rifles, while Garv and George pounced on the soldier tying his hands behind his back. Tom and his father started off at a jog to close the hundred yards that separated them from the scuffle; they ducked through the cattle gate deftly and entered the barnyard, still laughing to themselves. The sentry had already been secured and was seated, leaned against the outer wall of the barn, obviously rattled and seething. Mark, George, and Mr. Garvin were all engaged in a hearty laugh at the soldier's expense.

"Hiya fellas." Richard Haynes chuckled to the group as he came to a halt with Tom at his heels, still laughing heartily.

"Rick, you're right on time. We thought this here sentry was gonna be trouble, but he was so focused on you two that he didn't even hear us comin'." Garv chortled as he spoke.

"Lookin' good there boys." Tom laughed to George and his brother, beaming with pride.

"Well, let's not stay out here all night. Haul him up, and get 'im into the kitchen." Richard Haynes laughed.

Ralph held the door for them as they dragged the private into the kitchen. The group was still a bit out of breath from laughter as they shoved the man down onto the bench at the table which Tom loved so dearly. "Sit, ya delinquent." Garv grouched at the man through his continued chortles. "If ya behave yerself, we might even get ya a bite to eat. If ya don't, then yer hurt pride'll be the least of yer worries. Understand?"

"Alls I understand is that you folks are in for quite a hurting when the Major finds out what you done to me. Best you could do right now is let me loose." The soldier's eyes were full of disdain, arrogance, and fury, but Tom felt no fear of the man. In fact, Tom simply pitied him.

Richard Haynes took a seat across the table from the young sentry, his face impassive and calculating, as the initial laughter had now worn off. "Listen here son. You're the one that don't understand his position. You're surrounded, outnumbered, outmatched, outgunned, and outclassed in a room full of people who you've wronged and who could easily do you harm if they so wished." He paused letting his words sink in, as he allowed the slightest of smirks to crease his lips. Tom knew he would never harm any man if he could help it, much less an unarmed and immobilized prisoner, but he had to admit that there was a sense of impending doom implied behind his steely blue eyes and calculated smirk. "Then again, with a commander like Clinton, we could torture you to death, and you'd still be better off than going back and telling him that a crippled pharmacist, handful of kids, and a farmer caught you off guard and took you captive." Rick smiled fully at his prisoner, showing the confidence he felt in his victory over the soldier.

Tom looked to the soldier once again, feeling a shock that he hadn't earlier noticed that the private couldn't be older than eighteen. Tom knew that the young soldier's blood must be running cold at the realization that this small town lawyer was not only right but was his only hope to avoid a mocking and terrible death at the hands of his own commander. Sheer terror flooded the sentry's face as his mouth gaped slightly; he didn't know what to make of the man who he faced across the table, but he was obviously certain that going back to camp meant certain death. "What do you want?" The sound of defeat permeated his voice.

"George, why don't you go fetch the sergeant." William Garvin stated with a hint of menace in his voice. Mr. Garvin was a kindly man, mostly, but he was certainly not one to cross lightly.

The ticking of the grandfather clock filled Tom with a warm feeling of home and safety that he hadn't felt since his game of dominoes with his brother the day before. Other than the solemn *Tick! Tock!* of the clock, the room was utterly silent, as the men from Doughty stared down the soldier whose eyes nervously flitted from one person to another; even Mark's young gaze seemed to unnerve and terrify him, and Tom couldn't blame him. Finally, he heard footfalls on the basement stairs followed by George, Evans, the cook, and Reb entering the kitchen. From the new look of dread on the soldier's face, one might've thought that the men emerging from the basement were none other than Satan, Beelzebub, Apollyon, and the Grim Reaper coming to take him away into eternal death.

"Well, Finney" Sergeant Evans began slowly. "Looks like you done stepped into quite a quagmire this time, don't it?" Evans took a seat next to Tom's father, clasped his hands on the table, and leaned toward the frightened private. "And we gotta answer ourselves a question, now. Just how do you want this thing to end?" Evans paused long staring into the soldier's eyes. "See, here's your situation. You're caught, and you wanna stay caught; that much we know for good and for certain. Clinton ain't a forgiving man, and you know it as well as I do. So, you can either help us, and get treated friendly like, or you can fight us and get treated like a prisoner." Evans smiled, showing his coffee stained front teeth. The grin was a mixture of amusement, ingratiating friendliness, and intimidation.

Finney held his gaze as long as he could before breaking, but it was a losing battle. "Alright! You got me!" He cried out loudly, visibly shaken. "What do you WANT from me?!"

Evans stared at him for another long moment before turning to Tom's father. "Mr. Haynes, he's all yours."

Richard Haynes scrutinized the young man for a few moments before speaking. "Tom."

"Yeah, Paw?"

"Cut 'im loose. He ain't goin' anywhere." Mr. Haynes held the soldier's gaze who still wasn't sure what to expect in the next few moments, and he visibly startled when Tom drew his knife to cut his bonds. But his terror seemed to lessen somewhat as the ropes holding his wrists were released.

"Reb, go fetch the Doc." Evans gave the order over his shoulder, and the hulking soldier disappeared down the stairs.

"Finney is it?" Garv stated as he took a seat on Richard Haynes' right side. The soldier nodded, while he rubbed his wrists nervously. "Well, Finney, you and us are gonna have us a nice little chat about Clinton. And you're gonna tell us everything he's been doing since the Sergeant here saved Sheriff Thompson. That clear?"

The soldier hesitated a moment, then cleared his throat before answering hoarsely. "Yessir."

"And I'm gonna tell 'em everything there is to know about Sector Five and Clinton's obsession with Herr Haber." Evans kept his eyes locked on the young soldier who seemed both relieved and disturbed by that revelation.

"Sir?" Finney addressed Tom's father who nodded his response. "If you wanna know all that, you might wanna make some coffee, cause we're gonna be talkin' for a good while."

"Mark," Tom's father began, "go fetch your mother. Coffee is a good idea, and we could use some dinner too." Mark hurried off down the hall, and George followed after him. "Tom. Ralph. You might want to have a seat. It sounds like this is going to be a long story." Tom took a seat in his father's normal spot at the head of the table, facing the back door and holding his rifle across his lap.

"Sergeant Evans." Reb announced his arrival with Doctor Wilson.

"Reb, Bosco," Evans addressed the big soldier and the cook with an official tone in his voice, "each one of you take a seat next to Private Finney here, so's he feels more comfortable, all surrounded by friends." The two men complied, and Tom could see Finney shift uneasily in his seat as he clasped and reclasped his hands on the table in front of him. Finney's eyes darted nervously to the door as George and Mark, still carrying their guns, reentered the kitchen followed by the two mothers who went immediately to the stove and began busying themselves with the dinner and coffee.

"Alright, enough dilly dally." Evans let out a sigh. "I reckon we oughta start at the very beginning. I probably shoulda told this story to General Pershing two years ago, but better late than never." He cleared his throat and started into the story, his voice sounding a bit scratchy. "In May of 1917, I, along with, then *Captain*, Clinton and about ten thousand other Americans, climbed off boats in France as the first troops in the Expeditionary Force. I wasn't a young man, but I was a lot more innocent than I am today." He cleared his throat, his voice still sounding quite rough. Tom noticed Mrs. Priestly filling a glass with water that he was sure was intended for the Sergeant. "It weren't long at all afore we saw action. They stuck us right in with the Brits and Frenchies and Belgians and Aussies and whoever else they could get to fight along side a bunch of doughboys." George's mother set the glass in front of Evans who thanked her and took a sip before continuing, sounding only slightly refreshed. "In our first skirmish, them Krauts used mustard gas on us. That stuff ain't what you might think. It ain't an easy death, and the masks don't protect too well. We all got burns and scars from it. It comes in heavy and yella. It itches and burns and eats away at any skin you ain't got covered up. The masks save your lungs, but that's all." He took another sip of water and collected his thoughts. "If ya lose yer mask though, them burns on yer skin happen to yer insides too. One of our fellas had a faulty mask. He didn't make it. His name was Danny." He paused. "He was a good fella."

Evans coughed slightly and stopped to drink fully from his glass for the first time, pausing, and Tom finally realized the reason for the catch in his throat; it wasn't simply scratchy. Evans was telling a story that, for him, was just as hard to tell as it was for Tom to talk about the doughboys and the butcher's cellar, and he suddenly felt a twinge of compassion for the grizzled soldier. "But it ain't as simple as that. A man don't just fall over and die from that garbage. No. It's long, and it's painful. And it's daggum messy. He coughed his lungs out into his mask and drowned in his own blood and snot and bile. Some of us tried to help him seal his mask, got his blood all over us in the process. We tried." He clenched his fist on the table. "When it was over, I sat back against the wall of our trench and just cried into my mask. Never told anybody that afore. Never admitted it. But I did. I cried like a baby. Didn't even hear the whistle sound that the Gerries were attacking at first. That's how they did, ya know. They'd set the gas loose and wait. Then, when everything was hidden by the haze and the chaos of blood and guts and horror was happenin', they'd attack, quiet like. No shelling. No machine guns at first. They'd just sneak across No Man's Land and up to our trenches and bayonet us in the backs, if they got the chance." He sipped again. "Finally, Clinton kicked my boots hard and pulled me out of my daze. He was hollerin' about the attack, his eyes full of excitement and fury. Danny dying didn't bother him at all, no, but the attack got 'im riled up. The attack was short. We shot 'em down as they came at us. A few men made it into the trenches, still full up to the brim with that mustard from Hell. We killed 'em. All but one. He stumbled at the edge and knocked 'imself unconscious as he fell into the trench." Evans sighed heavily again. "The fella was young. His uniform was new. Looked a lot like Danny, truth be told. He was layin' there, unconscious, when his Kraut buddies retreated, leaving 'im for dead. That's when it happened. Clinton stooped down over top of the guy, threw his weapons aside, and shook 'im til he woke up."

Evans had been staring at his hands the whole time he spoke, but he now lifted his eyes and glanced around the table. Tom followed his gaze from left to right as he looked at Garv, Mr. Haynes, and the backs of the ladies who had obviously been busying themselves with the food and attempting not to hear the story. Then he looked to Bosco whose face was sorrowful, Finney who looked like he'd been slapped hard, Reb whose stiff jaw betrayed his gritted teeth that were holding back his emotions, and Ralph whose face was full of anger once again. Then the Sergeant looked to Tom, who finally saw tear streaks down the old soldier's face. Tom couldn't imagine what expression his own face displayed, but he could no longer follow Evans' eyes as they looked to whoever was standing behind him. Tom felt a single tear roll down his right cheek, as he suddenly knew what the Sergeant was about to tell them.

Evans grunted to clear his throat, then began again, "I can still remember it like it was yesterday. The mustard hanging heavy around us, the itching on my hands, ears, neck. The look of surprise and fear in the German's eyes through the thick lenses of his mask. Then, without warning, Clinton ripped the man's mask off." Evans choked hard and slammed his clenched fist onto the table. He bowed his head, jaw clenched tightly, for several long moments before starting again. "It took only seconds for that young Kraut to start choking. His eyes oozed snot, and his nose ran; then they both were leaking blood as he coughed harder by the second, Clinton just kneeling over him barely two feet from the boy's face as it slowly exploded. When the coughs and hacks started chucking out his lungs, Clinton started in, taunting 'im.

'Come on Fritz! Gimme that blood boy! Give it to me!' on and on and on." Evans was crying freely now. "When it was over, the boy was unidentifiable. His skin was burned, and his insides were on the outside. He was soaked in his own blood and snot and guts." The Sergeant let out a long heavily shaking breath, took another sip of water, and began anew. "It was the worst thing I had ever seen; wish I could say it didn't get no worse, but I'd be lyin'. Clinton stood up, kicked in the side of the boy's head to mix his brains in with the mess, and started laughin'. Laughin'!" Evans' sorrow was steadily turning into rage. "That was just the beginnin' of Clinton's debaucheries. He never let up, the whole time we was over there. Always torturin' folks, drownin' 'em, beatin' 'em, and such. But he was obsessed with the gas and the flame throwers and other such garbage. He never let up on that. He'd hoot and holler anytime the Krauts let the gas loose, never saw 'im more excited." He had recovered some of his composure and sipped his water again. "He tore through everythin' he could get his hands on when we took a German trench or base and even learned some German to find out more about the gas. And he found out a lot. He found out that this one fella was the guy behind it all, name of Fritz Haber."

"Haber?!" Mr. Haynes exclaimed. "The Nobel Prize winner?!"

Evans nodded, "None other. He was the one that made chlorine and mustard and everything else you can think of. He was doin' experiments too, learnin' how different chemical stuff affected people. He'd stick needles in folks and shoot 'em full of whatever and watch what happened. Ya know, kinda figurin' how long it took to die with different ones and such." Evans shook his head. "Clinton got us assigned to a special unit in September of 1918. There was ten of us from our old platoon and a bunch from other places. Most of 'em was crazy. They'd all been accused of stuff like Clinton, all but me. Dunno why Clinton wanted me there, but he ain't left me alone since that first battle. Anyway, we took off behind enemy lines. We went lookin' for German science garbage of one kind or another. And Clinton took it on hisself to go lookin' for Haber's labs. Weren't long afore we found 'em neither." Evans let silence hang for a moment as the gravity of what he was about to tell us sank in. "We found Haber's labs, sure enough, outside Berlin in the countryside, but in 'em we found more than we bargained for. Notes upon notes upon notes about every chemical you can imagine. Boxes and boxes. And we stole 'em all. After Clinton gassed the scientists that was unlucky enough to be there workin' late the night Hank Clinton came callin'. It was like watchin' the Devil 'imself, Clinton laughin' again as them scientists coughed up their lungs and died in puddles of their own guts." He sipped again and cleared his throat. "But Clinton didn't give all them notes to the Army, like he was supposedta. He kept the worst of it for 'imself. kept the notes about chemicals that'll turn a man wild to hisself. Kept notes on how to turn a man into a beast. A *monster*."

Mrs. Priestly gasped audibly at the very moment that Tom realized what Evans was saying. Richard Haynes interrupted, "Are you telling us that the creature out there that killed them boys is a man?!" The incredulity in his voice was thick.

"Name's Corporal Bobby Moretti." Finney answered before Evans had a chance. "Or at least it used to be. Now he don't listen much and talks even less. Don't know if he even remembers who he was before, but he ain't that man nomore nohow; so, I reckon it don't matter too much."

"A man? A soldier?!" Garv was livid. "Clinton turned a soldier into an animal?!"

"He volunteered, as I heard it." Finney shrugged.

"He did. He's an animal now, for sure, but he wasn't much different as a man, neither, as I recall." Evans scratched the scar on his cheek. "He was almost as bad as Clinton, in the war. He was a true believer in what Clinton wanted to do. Followed blindly. And, when Hank asked for a volunteer to become the perfect chemical weapon, there weren't no stoppin' 'im."

"We saw 'im paw." Tom choked out, through the shock of the revelation. "We saw 'im at the Wilsons'. It coulda been a man. Stranger than any man I ever known, but he went on two feet some and had arms insteada front legs. Weren't no wolf or cat, that's for sure. Was killin' wolves right and left."

"But he got took down by them wolves at the end." George interjected. Tom looked in his direction and realized that Mark had left the room; he hoped that his younger brother hadn't heard the story from Sergeant Evans. "Them wolves mighta killed 'im!" Tom's best friend was invigorated by the idea, but Tom was sure that was too easy.

"Unlikely. He's stronger than you realize. That trick he pulled, rippin' that wolf in half with his hands, ain't the half of what he can do. And he heals fast too. I reckon he's good and hurt. Oughta be outa commission for a day or so, but I doubt he's done for just yet. Even with a couple slugs in 'im, he'll probably be back at it before week's end."

"So, you're saying that we've probably got about two days to find him and finish the job?" Rick inquired.

"That ain't a half bad idea." Evans sounded impressed.

Mollie Haynes cleared her throat, standing at the edge of the huge table commanding the attention of the embattled men. "It's time to eat. Y'all can finish this discussion after dinner. Just put your dirty dishes in the sink when you're done; we're headed to bed." With that, Mrs. Haynes halted the violence and impending battle with a wave of her spatula, and the men began serving themselves from the stovetop. The night was far from over, but the hot meal was a welcome respite.

Chapter 15

Tom lay awake in his bed listening to Mark lightly snore and staring at the ceiling, as the first light of dawn gradually fought back the darkness. He was having a hard time coming to grips with what he had just heard. Was it really possible that the creature that murdered the doughboys, that had torn a metal door to shreds, that had ripped a grown wolf in half with its bare hands was some perversion of a man? Could injecting chemicals into a person really change him that much? Sergeant Evans had said that this man, Moretti, had been a lot like that troll Clinton even before they started injecting chemicals into him; maybe the change was purely physical. Tom suddenly remembered a verse that his grandfather MacClairn used to quote. "The heart is deceitful above all things, and desperately wicked: who can know it?" Jeremiah 17:9. Yes, it was definitely possible that the creature that now stalked their quiet town, having had his body destroyed, perverted, and mangled by the machinations of evil was no more wicked now than he was before. Tom nodded to himself; yes, it's more likely that the creature simply became more capable of acting on his violent impulses through twisting his body in Clinton's grotesque experiments.

Tom rolled onto his side and looked at his brother. He was glad that Mark had left the room before hearing the details of Clinton's wickedness; the things Tom had learned had robbed him of the few hours of sleep the night might have afforded once they finished their long talk, but, Mark at least, was able to sleep unencumbered by the mental images of battlefield destruction and the systematic conversion of a human being into an iniquitous aberration. Tom envied his brother's innocence, and that struck him as odd. Only a few days earlier, he would have gladly gone to Europe to fight another Great War, but now he found himself wishing that he had never become aware of the depth of corruption that the world contains. He softly laughed to himself. Who would have ever thought that the very adventures that he had always dreamed of having would be the cure to his juvenile delusions of battlefield glory and excitement? How had he ever been so naive as to believe that war could be a desirable adventure?

Tom rolled onto his stomach and turned his face toward the wall. His thoughts began to jumble in his head. Flashes of the last few days came in no particular order as he pondered what was coming next. He glanced at the still barely visible ceiling and guessed the time to be just minutes before 6:00; just four hours until his father planned to meet together with other men from town to plan what action to take to stop Corporal Moretti, once and for all. Tom once again succumbed to his disparate thoughts and finally drifted off into a fitful dreamy sleep.

* * * * *

"Tommy! Wake up!" Tom was being shaken roughly as someone spoke firmly to the back of his head. "Come on Tommy! Daddy said to get you up!" Tom's eyes blinked open and he found himself looking at the same blank spot of wall he had been staring at when he fell asleep. "Toooommmmmmyyyyyyyy!!!" The voice belonged to Tom's nine year old sister, Ruth.

"Ok, ok, ok. I'm awake, Ruthie. Stop the shaking already!" Tom rubbed his achy eyes, as his younger sister stopped yelling at the back of his head. He realized he still had some pain there from when he had fainted the day before, but it was manageable. "What time is it, Ruth?"

"It's nine o'clock already!" The impatience in Ruth's young voice was heavy; Tom could tell she had used up all the patience her little body contained trying to rouse him.

"Excellent!" Tom exclaimed in mock satisfaction. "I got a whole three hours of sleep!" he laughed slightly. Tom rubbed his eyes again; then, without warning, rolled over quickly, grabbed his sister and tickled her roughly, as Ruthie let out shrill giggles and punched and kicked every inch of her big brother that her little limbs could reach. Tom began laughing so hard that he had to stop tickling Ruth, as he fell into a series of laughing coughs.

"You're a big meanie!" Ruth excalimed, still laughing.

"Daggum right!" Tom chortled. "But it's my job, after all. I am a big brother, ya know." Tom swung his legs out of bed and Ruthie straightened herself up.

"Momma saved you some breakfast, but you better hurry. Daddy says he wants ya to look at somethin' in the woods with 'im." Ruth bounced her way out of his room, and closed his door behind her, pigtails bobbing as she went.

Moments later, Tom emerged from his room, having thrown on clean clothes and his boots and grabbed his rifle with such feverish pace that one might have thought that his very life depended on it; he mused that he should have been a Revolutionary Minute Man. He had fallen asleep wishing for the blissful ignorance of his younger years, but he had woken with the sense of determination and duty of a man twice his age. Tom was not going to shirk his responsibilities, no matter how much he would prefer to stay in bed and pretend that death had never visited Doughty. He tore down the stairs, picked up five year old Mary who was playing in the front foyer, carried her into the kitchen with him while she told him that he was in trouble for sleeping too late, dodged their mother who was busied with the dirty dishes, kissed Mary on her little blonde head as he set her down to run back to her games, leaned his Winchester against the kitchen table, grabbed a biscuit, filled it full of eggs and bacon, slathered it in maple syrup, and took one huge bite.

"Tom," his mother began with her eyes still focused on the dishes she was washing, "your father is out in the barn with George, Mr. Garvin, and the Sergeant. Mark is on the roof of the front porch with Ralph, watching for trouble; oh, that big soldier y'all call Reb is up there with them." She placed her last dish in the draining rack and pulled the plug to let her dish water drain before turning to look at Tom while drying her dishpan hands. "Your dad wants you to come see him as soon as you're ready."

Tom swallowed his second huge bite of biscuit "Yes ma'am." He wiped his mouth on his sleeve. "You alright Momma?" He looked his mother right in the eyes; she looked tired. He noticed some wrinkles on the skirt of her apron. Those wrinkles always meant she'd spent a good bit of time kneeling and praying.

"I'm alright, son. Just a bit tired. This whole thing has got me a bit worried. Just keep praying that God'll watch over us and help me to put things in His hands." She looked to the counter as she draped the dishtowel over her freshly washed dishes to help it dry as well.

Tom took a step toward his mother, put his arm around her, squeezed her slightly and kissed her on the forehead. "God has got us, Momma. Don't fret. I think we finally know what we need to know to end this thing." Tom was shocked to realize that the optimism in his voice was genuine. He didn't know what had changed since he struggled to sleep the night before, but he silently gave God the credit. "Love ya, Momma." Tom kissed his mother's forehead a second time.

"Love you, Tom." Mollie Haynes put her arm around her son and squeezed him back. "Now, get goin'. Your Paw seems pretty anxious to get moving."

Tom shoved a third and final enormous bite of biscuit into his mouth, chewed it roughly as he snatched up his rifle, and barged out the screen door that had been hastily repaired after Major Clinton's manhandling of it the night before. His father and the others were milling around the barnyard, talking, and nodding this way and that, always keeping their guns at the ready. It had become clear to everyone in their long night of discussion, that the creature was unlikely to attack again for at least a couple days, but, with Clinton and his troops still out there, they were taking no chances.

"I say we keep two men in the loft at all times. One rifle and one scattergun." Evans grouched slightly as he made the suggestion. Since everyone else seemed to be in agreement, Tom assumed his tone was due to strain and lack of sleep.

"When did they say to expect a call, Sergeant?" Rick Haynes asked as Tom ducked through the cattle gate.

"His secretary said to expect a call from the colonel around eleven o'clock."

"Hey Paw." Tom half-whispered as he sidled up next to his father.

"Eleven, huh?" Rick Haynes chewed his cheek slightly, thinking. "I reckon that'll have to do."

"Momma says you wanna see me." Tom didn't want to change the subject, but he was curious why his father had sent his sister after him.

"Yeah, Tom." Mr. Haynes paused. "I was thinking over things this morning and think we should take a walk through the woods again." Richard Haynes motioned with his rifle barrel in the direction of where they had exited the trees the night before.

"See what was making that noise, ya reckon?" Tom found himself thinking the exact same thing. It was possible that the creature may be licking his wounds nearby, exposed, and vulnerable, and Tom thought it would be a good idea to get out there and see what they could find. If it couldn't attack them the night before, he was fairly confident that they could handle him in broad daylight.

Richard Haynes nodded. "Mmm hmm. Figure it probably wasn't Moretti, but it's worth a look anyhow." He wiped a trickle of sweat from his cheek onto the shoulder of his linen farm shirt and wiped one palm at a time on his canvas pants. "Sergeant Evans, mind keeping us some company?"

"Be my pleasure, Mr. Haynes." Evans hefted his own rifle slightly, adjusting his grip. "If there's a chance to be done with this right now, then I say let's get to it."

"George and me'll take up watch in hayloft, Rick." Garv started limping toward the barn. Tom realized for the first time that the old pharmacist was carrying a rifle with a shotgun strapped across his back. It looked to Tom that he was loaded for mountain lion; say what they might, nobody could reasonably deny that Mr. Gavin was tough.

"Alright Tom." Richard Haynes' voice called Tom's attention back once more. "Let's get to it." Mr. Haynes started toward the trees without waiting for a response from either Tom or Sergeant Evans.

Tom fell in slightly behind his father and to his left. Sergeant Evans mirrored Tom to Rick's right. They scanned the grass, trees, fences, buildings, and anything that could offer cover to an attacker. Each man seemed to know his role in the company. Their fields of vision overlapped slightly, and Tom and Evans alternated looking behind them as well. With the injuries he sustained, even the creature would have a hard time approaching this cadre without falling under a hail of gunfire. Rick would pause periodically and scan the ground. At one such interval, Sergeant Evans stepped up next to Mr. Haynes and followed his line of sight.

"What're we lookin' for here, Mr. Haynes?" Evans seemed legitimately confused.

"Trying to follow our path from last night back into the woods. Wanna be as close to where we heard something moving as we can be. Sometimes I lose our footsteps for a moment or two."

"You can track footsteps in dry grass?" Evans sounded astounded by the very idea. Now that Tom found himself thinking about it, he could see how that might not be a skill that everyone would have. He had often used it to track injured prey or find his way back out of the woods if he lost his bearings, but it was certainly a skill learned through experience.

"Just gotta know what to look for." Richard Haynes stated matter-of-factly as he started forward once again.

As they reached the treeline, their trail became more pronounced. The disturbed leaves where they had lain the night before, trying to avoid attracting the notice of Clinton and his men, were easily identifiable. The three men walked right to the center of the disturbed leaves and each took a knee, listening and scanning the forest. Tom replayed the events of the night before in his mind and looked in the direction where he first heard the twig snap. His view of a small depression in the area was skewed by his perspective on his knee. "We heard the twig from over there, Paw." Tom gestured to the area. He was certain that he would be unable to see anything of note from this vantage point; so, he slowly rose to his feet, scanning the forest all the while. At his full height, he could see something black in the depressed earth where he had heard the twig. There were also a lot of disturbed leaves surrounding the depression. "Paw, there's something over there. Not sure what, but I'm pretty sure it ain't Moretti."

"Where?" Tom's father asked as he rose to his feet as well.

"Right there." Tom pointed to the spot, keeping his trigger hand on the grip of his rifle. He could see Evans standing up in his peripheral vision.

"Yeah, I see somethin' over there too, Mr. Haynes."

"Call me Rick, Sergeant Evans. You calling me Mister makes me feel awful old." Richard Haynes leaned one way then the other inspecting the area as thoroughly as he could from this distance. "Yeah, somethin' is there, alright. Can see a little movement too. Might be breathing. Reckon we better head over there. Keep your guns ready and stay about fifteen feet apart, alright?" Tom and Evans grunted their agreement and each took a few steps away from Mr. Haynes.

Tom was slightly uphill from the other two men and had a better view of the depression. It was only about twenty yards from where they had lain on their bellies the night before. As he moved very slowly toward it, he could distinguish fur, black fur. And it was definitely breathing. "Paw, it ain't Moretti. It's got fur." Rick Haynes and Sergeant Evans both acknowledged they had heard Tom's revelation. He angled a little more to his left and saw whatever it was move in earnest. He caught glimpse of a huge amber eye, looking at him; then he heard something, a whine. *The WOLF!* "Paw! Wait!"

Mr. Haynes and Sergeant Evans both stopped in their tracks. "What is it son?" Rick asked, as he angled slightly and raised his rifle to the ready.

"It's the wolf!" Tom exclaimed aloud.

"What wolf?!" Rick was noticeably alarmed. Wolves were rarely good news for a farmer. "One of the ones that fought with Moretti?"

"Yeah, Paw. It's their leader, I reckon. The one that got a piece of him. The black one. I think he's hurt." Tom took several more cautious steps toward the wolf. It raised its head toward him, sniffed, lowered his head to the ground again, and resumed his whining. "He's definitely hurt, Paw. I'm gonna check on 'im."

"You think that's smart Tom?" Richard Haynes had no love for wolves; they had been his natural enemy since he moved to Doughty, frequently attacking his livestock.

"Yeah, I think it'll be ok, Paw. He don't seem worried about me." Tom took two more steps toward the wolf, and its only response was to increase its whining. Tom was only about five feet away now. He stooped slightly. "It's alright now." he said soothingly to the wolf. "I ain't gonna hurt you none. I'm just here to help." He carefully laid his rifle on the ground as he continued to slowly approach the wolf. The massive animal was laying on its belly. It had some gashes that were coated with dried blood on its side; they didn't look too deep to Tom. The creature must've only landed a glancing blow on it. As he stooped over the wolf, it rolled onto its side to reveal that one of its front legs was slightly displaced, setting at an odd angle and not moving properly when the wolf rolled over.

"He's got some gashes and a dislocated shoulder, looks like, Paw." Tom spoke quietly over his shoulder as to not frighten to wolf. "I think he's gonna be okay, but he needs some help."

"What exactly do you propose we do with it?" Evans was incredulous. The very thought of helping a wolf seemed foreign to him. Tom knew it would've seemed, at the very least, unusual to him if the roles were reversed, but something told him he should help this animal, after all, it might've gotten those injuries saving his life.

"I'm gonna see if I can do anything with this leg. Stay back. I don't think he'll hurt me. Think he knows I'm here to help." Tom slowly reached out his hand toward the wolfs face, looking the huge animal in the eyes. "Steady now, boy. I ain't gonna hurt ya. Promise. I'm a friend. Gonna try to help now, okay fella?" The wolf sniffed Tom's hand then licked the tips of his fingers. Tom gently stroked its muzzle with his fingers, then ran his hand up its cheek and scratched its ear. The wolf whined slightly, closed his eyes, and leaned into Tom's touch. "Okay, now, boy. I gotta do somethin' with this leg. It's gonna hurt. Just don't eat my face off, if you can help it, okay?" Tom reached out his other hand and gingerly touched the wolf's gouged ribs. The animal winced, but didn't lash out. Tom was right; those wounds were superficial. He was certain that they were very painful, but he was sure they just needed to be cleaned and left to heal on their own. Now was the moment of truth. Tom slid his hand along the animal's side toward its injured front leg. It panted heavily and turned its head away, as he got closer, but it made no indications that it would attack when he touched it.

"Tom, be careful. That's a wild animal there, not a dog. It might not understand that you're tryin' to help it." Rick Haynes had silently sidled up behind Tom and was now only a few feet to his left, pointing his rifle at the wolf's head.

"I know, Paw. It'll be alright. Not sure why, but I think he trusts me." Tom placed his right hand on the wolf's shoulder, and it winced again but didn't attack. He then reached down with his left hand and grabbed the wolf's paw; it turned its head away slightly and closed its eyes a bit tighter. In one simultaneous motion, Tom straightened the leg with his left hand while putting pressure on the shoulder with his right; the leg popped right back into the socket, and the wolf jerked slightly and let out a low howl. Tom released the leg, and the animal reached its head over slowly and licked itself on the shoulder for a few moments. It then hesitantly began to sit up. It put some weight on its leg, whined a little, adjusted, then sat upright. The wolf was huge. Sitting on its haunches, it was taller than Tom was on his knees. It began panting and glancing at the three men before licking Tom squarely on the face.

"If that don't beat all!" Evans exclaimed, dumbfounded. "In all my years, I ain't never seen nothin' like that. A full-grown, wild wolf takin' a shine to a man like that?"

"Well done, Tom." Richard Haynes congratulated his son, proudly. Tom looked at his father and saw that look of pride once again; it warmed his heart. "Now, if you're done doctoring wild animals in the woods, we oughta get back. We've got bigger problems to deal with."

Tom nodded, scratched the wolf's ear once again, and stood to leave, retrieving his rifle from the leaves. The three men started back to the house in the same formation they used to enter the woods, but, when Tom scanned behind them, he realized that the wolf was limping along behind them. It seemed dead set on following Tom. "Paw?" Tom paused as his father responded.

"Yeah, Tom?"

"The wolf is following us." Tom said with a hint of amusement in his voice, as the three of them stopped and turned to see the wolf laboriously limping toward them. It didn't slow its pace at all until it was directly in front of Tom. It sat on its haunches, licked Tom's hand, and looked right up at him, panting. "I don't think we're going to be able to leave it behind." Tom said, stooping to scratch the animal's head once again.

"We can't exactly take it with us." Rick said, amused but obviously uncertain what to do.

"Reckon our only other option is to shoot 'im, Paw. And that don't seem fittin'." Tom looked the animal in the eyes again. It was clear that the wolf had taken to him and was not going to be easily turned aside.

"What if it gets after the livestock?"

"Or attacks somebody?" Evans threw his hat in the ring.

"How about this?" Tom answered. "We take 'im to the house. We'll lock 'im in one of the empty barn stalls and treat the gashes on his side." Tom looked to his father, nodding at Mr. Haynes as he spoke. "Then, once he can walk right again and is healed up some, we'll take 'im in a truck well outside of town and set 'im loose. That sound fair?"

Tom's father's face betrayed the fact that he knew this was an argument he wasn't going to win. And his furtive glances around them reminded Tom that they had bigger worries right now. "Okay Tom, we can try it, but I don't know if it'll work. The horses ain't likely to accept a wolf in the barn."

"Okay, how about the cistern under the house?" Tom knew they needed to move, but he couldn't bear the thought of this wolf being left on its own, injured. It had saved his life, and he wanted to return the favor. "He can't get outa there, and there ain't nobody there to bother." Tom didn't wait for an answer. He handed his rifle to his father, hefted the wolf into his arms, and started toward the house. The wolf seemed uncomfortable at first, but it settled in after just a few steps and rested its head over Tom's shoulder. It was huge. Tom was sure it weighed every ounce of 140 pounds, but carrying it like that made it feel more like a giant rag-doll.

"Guess you got a new pet." Evans laughed, as he and Mr. Haynes fell in behind Tom and headed back to the house.

CHAPTER 16

"That's it, Cinder. We'll be done soon." Tom sat on the stone floor next to the wolf with a basin and clean cotton rags dabbing the dried blood from its wounded ribs. The gashes weren't deep, but they had gotten very matted as he pulled himself through the forest with only three functioning legs.

"Did you just call that beast Cinder?" Mollie Haynes asked from the doorway to the basement cistern that was off the opposite side of the main room as the slave hideaway.

"Reckoned he needed a name. Can't just call 'im *that wolf* or some such nonsense, now can I?" Tom chided playfully.

"I suppose you have a point there son." Mollie wasn't initially keen on keeping a wolf in the house but, when Cinder hobbled over to where little Hannah was playing on the floor and laid his massive head in her lap as gently as a giant, black, shaggy sheepdog might've, her protest quickly ceased. It became obvious to everyone that this was no ordinary wolf.

"I don't know how he covered that much distance with his leg like that, Momma." Tom deftly manipulated the skin on each side of the gashes on his new pet's side taking note of whether they were fully cleaned and how deep they were. The investigation confirmed that they were less severe than the amount of matting and clotted blood might otherwise indicate. Tom reached over and began carefully moving the animal's injured foreleg around to test its range of motion. Slight whining told him that the leg was still in some pain, but it didn't appear that any major or permanent damage had been done. "He must be mighty tough to have tangled with that monster and come away with no more damage than he did."

"I've been thinking that same thing, Thomas. How can an animal, a predator, be so adept at inflicting damage on another creature in one moment just to turn practically puppy dog in the next instant? He could've swallowed Hannah whole if he wanted, but he just acted like he'd known her since he was a pup." Tom looked to his mother; she was shaking her head in disbelief.

"The way I see it, Momma, ole Cinder here knows good from bad the same as most creatures. He knows that Moretti is evil, and he knows we don't mean him no harm."

"Could be. Best hurry up now, son. There's still a lot to be done." Tom turned to look at his mother, as she patted him on the shoulder and headed toward the basement stairs.

"Reckon she's right, huh Cinder?" The wolf blinked his big amber eyes at Tom impassively. He seemed perfectly content in his surroundings. That struck Tom as more than a little bit odd, but after discovering a violent monster roaming the outskirts of town and frightening wolf packs into other unusual behaviors, Cinder's acceptance of the house was practically normal. Tom finished cleaning the gashes in the wolf's side and stood to leave. Cinder whined lightly signaling to Tom that his absence was unwelcome. "I'll be right back, boy." Tom bent and scratched the wolf behind the ear, turned, hefted his rifle, left the cistern, and secured the door behind him. Listening at the door for a moment, he heard no more whining and hurried up the stairs.

Tom passed his sisters, who were sitting at the table reading their summer books together, as he crossed the kitchen and exited the house. Sergeant Evans, Mr. Garvin, and Tom's father were, once again looking about the farm warily from their position in the barnyard. Tom retraced his steps from a couple hours earlier as he ducked through the cattle gate once more.

"So, what did the colonel say?" Richard Haynes asked the grizzled sergeant.

"Didn't say anything." Sergeant Evans had spoken to someone on the phone, but this didn't sound promising. "In fact, I didn't even talk to Colonel Price."

"He didn't bother to call you back?!" Garv was clearly agitated at the thought that the Army couldn't even be bothered to follow up on their call for help.

"Thing is, the colonel ain't at Camp Lee." Evans clearly was unsure how to describe what he had discovered over the telephone. "I spoke directly with General Pershing. Called direct from Washington."

"Pershing?" Tom was incredulous. "Blackjack Pershing? . . . Commander of the Expedition?"

"That's right, but I don't recommend you call him Blackjack when he gets here tomorrow."

"Pershing is coming here?" Rick Haynes took his turn at being incredulous.

"So they DID take you seriously!" George was hanging out of the hayloft eavesdropping.

"Seems that way. In fact, Colonel Price is headed here from Petersburg right now." Sergeant Evans cracked a grin. "He's got a full company of infantry with him, all loaded up on trucks, more'n a hundred men."

"Whoo-ee!" Tom had never seen Garv so excited. "Don't that beat all?! Let the Army clean up their own mess!"

"That does seem an answer to prayer." Richard Haynes was visibly relieved.

"Well, it ain't that simple. Colonel is making his way to the soldiers' camp south of town, where you boys helped us with the sheriff." Sergeant Evans nodded, first to Tom, then to George, still hanging from the hayloft above. "We gotta go meet 'em there and let 'em know what they're up against." Evans' smile faded a bit.

"I'm coming along." Tom stated matter-of-factly. "I need to see this thing through."

"I agree, son." Tom's father nodded at him bracingly. "In fact, I think all you fellas should be given the option of coming along."

"Thanks, Mr. Haynes, but no thanks." George called from the hayloft. "I've had enough adventure. Sides, somebody oughta stick around and keep watch over the place."

"I'll stay with my nephew and keep a lookout. Not much good in open ground anyway." Garv chuckled and thumped his bad leg.

"Ralph should be there." Tom knew his friend needed to see justice for Wil and the other doughboys. "But I figure the Wilsons'll all stick around here."

* * * * *

It was almost noon when they headed toward the encampment. Mr. Haynes, Sergeant Evans, Tom, and Ralph all loaded into Sheriff Thompson's truck once it had been retrieved from the forest. Reb and Mr. Bosco had been left behind to help watch the farm and guard Finney. Tom was sure that the sergeant also hoped to shield them from any discipline the colonel might impose for being involved in Clinton's treason. Tom, Ralph, and Sergeant Evans were in the bed of the truck, once more, watching for trouble. Tom's spirits felt buoyed considerably; the soldiers on their way to help were part of the reason, but the daylight illuminating every shadow along the way was more responsible.

"This the same way we came last night?" Sergeant Evans directed the question at Tom, but he kept his eyes on the tree lines on each side of the road, looking for any signs of trouble.

"It is."

"Looks a bit different in daylight." Evans glanced over his shoulder down the road ahead. "Something I always noticed during the war. Different days, different weather, makes things look different. It's easy to get lost when you don't know the terrain."

Tom had never been anywhere much away from Doughty; so, he had never had occasion to experience that, and at the moment, he found himself glad of the hometown advantage, however small it might be.

"How far to the doc's?" Evans kept his head on a swivel.

"Half mile." Tom responded, stealing a glance at Ralph amid his constant scanning of the west side of the road. "Should be able to see it through a stand of trees dead ahead."

"I see it." Tom hadn't even seen Evans' glance.

They had decided it would be wise to stop at the Wilsons' house and see what they could find out about Moretti's injuries and which way he headed after the fracas the night before. It would be unwise to arrive at the camp too far ahead of the colonel, and it would be best to have as much information as possible when they did arrive.

"Here we go!" Rick called out the driver's window, and Tom felt the truck slow and turn into the Wilsons' driveway.

"Keep your eyes pealed, now." Evans was at the tailgate, rifle at the ready, his gaze piercing every inch of the area.

"We've got blood trails." Richard Haynes called out from in front of the truck.

"House still looks secure." Tom called from the bed of the truck.

"Don't look like any of the blood leads to the barn." Ralph seemed more himself since the news of the soldiers coming to take the situation in hand. "I reckon he dragged hisself in another direction."

"Could be, but he might've gone in the back." Rick cautioned.

"Alright, Rick, you're the tracker. It's your show. Where to first?" Evans was good at leading soldiers, but he was even better at deferring to experience and expertise when the situation called for it.

"I say we make our way to where you last saw the fiend and track him straightaway. That seems safest and fastest from where I stand."

"Yessir, I thought that might be your call." Evans hopped down from the bed of the truck and started toward Mr. Haynes. "Let's move it fellas. I don't like being out in the open without more guns to level on 'im."

Tom and Ralph each piled over the side of the truck bed and joined Rick and Evans at the front of the truck. Each knew his place and moved deftly right up behind Tom's father, Tom on the left, Ralph on the right, and the sergeant bringing up the rear, walking backwards. Rick set a slow pace, scanning the ground for sign and prints; a few paces toward the fence, Tom noticed the tracks the truck had left the night before amid his scanning of the trees and house, but still no blood. Rick paused twice for several moments before they reached the fence, and he redirected their path to avoid disturbing tracks. Tom had tried to avoid looking at the mass of bodies by the fence and littered through the field as long as he could, but eventually he had to look. There were wolves piled here and there and scattered like refuse. Most of them were barely touched, having only one swipe of the creature's claws, but one swipe was enough for most.

"Cinder was mighty fortunate to come away with no more damage than he got." Tom mused out loud.

"Moretti better hope them soldiers get to him first, if he still knows how to hope." Ralph had hurt in his voice, but also purpose. Tom could tell without looking at him that he was choking back tears. "If I get to him before then, he ain't gonna have a chance to do this again."

"Can't say I blame ya for that." Evans was still walking backward watching the truck and guarding them against attack from behind. "Even still, hurt as he is, Moretti's dangerous; don't let your anger get you careless."

"I'll take care, but he's got it comin' either way."

"Justice is a good thing, Ralph, but don't let yourself fall into looking for revenge." Rick's words of wisdom hung in the air for a few moments. "Look here now, Tom."

Tom glanced to where his father's rifle was pointing. The distinctive tracks from the quarry were plain to see, in the bloody mud. Two army issued boots and long five fingered talons. It seemed so obvious to him now that all the tracks were made by one thing, one man, one villain, but Clinton was just as guilty as if he had killed Wil and the others himself. Tom made a solemn, silent promise to himself and to God; Clinton would be made to stand to account for what he had done. The tracks headed off toward the south end of the field where there was a creek.

"Paw?"

"Yeah, Tom."

"Figure he headed toward the creek to recover?" Tom kept his vigil to the north, but kept stealing glances toward the creek. "There's some caves and such down there."

"He might've. The tracks definitely head that way. And the strides are shorter than at the quarry. Looks mighty injured."

"He took two slugs from me, and one from Ralph here." Evans stated.

That was news to Tom; he hadn't realized that Ralph had gotten a shot off at the creature. Tom had let go his trigger without firing when Cinder sank his teeth into Moretti's neck.

"I hit him low, though." Ralph sounded almost embarrassed to admit that his aim had been a bit low.

"All the better." Evans confided. "Moretti is different now, but he's still a man. A gut-shot isn't an easy thing to overcome. Doubt he'd make it long if he didn't get to the lab."

"Lab?" Tom asked.

"Under that warehouse at the quarry." Evans stated flatly. "Through that stairwell where you found your friends. There's a secret door."

"I checked every inch of that room, up to my elbows in blood most of the time. Where's the door?" Tom was exasperated at the thought he had missed something that could have prevented things from getting this far.

"There's a secret switch next to one of them light bulbs. Remind me and I'll show you when this is all over." Evans' tone redirected their attention to tracking Moretti.

"Well." Rick paused, clearly analyzing their next move. "If he's headed back to the quarry, then this way looks about as fast a path as he could get." Tom's father paused again, wiping sweat from his cheek onto the shoulder of his linen field jacket. "Still, I reckon we'd best follow his trail at least as far as the creek to be certain." He paused again, but no one answered. Richard Haynes took that for agreement and started off along the fence line toward the barn, keeping his eyes on the blood trail all the while. After several slow paces, he led them through the split rail fence into the field beyond. They kept their positions and the slow steady pace they had adopted upon exiting the truck. Tom's father paused periodically, scouring one curiosity or another until he was certain that his path was true or until he was sure that they were as safe as he was able to keep them.

Tom, being on the left side of the cadre, had the blood trail in full view through the grassy field. He expected the blood to relent after some time, assuming that most of it was likely from the wolves, but the blood persisted, thick enough for even a small child to follow.

"Paw?" Tom's curiosity finally won out.

"Yeah, Tom?" Rick paused, still investigating his surroundings.

"Don't that seem like an awful lot of blood?"

"It surely does, son."

"You figure that's all from Moretti hisself?" Tom could hardly believe that a creature could lose so much blood.

"Seems like it. He might be injured worse than we thought."

"Even still, Rick, best stay careful." Evans sounded nervous. "No more dangerous person than one that thinks they ain't got nothin' to lose."

"I agree with you there, Sergeant." Rick Haynes began moving forward again, as slow as ever. Some several yards further on, they had fully passed the barn.

"Barn looks closed tight on this side too, Mr. Haynes." Ralph had the best view of the barn, but Tom was sure that Moretti's trail was headed straight across the field with no indications of turning back toward the barn.

After what felt to Tom like an eternity, they reached the bank of the creek. The blood trail was just as thick as ever, if not thicker. Moretti's trail had gotten more erratic as it went, changing from all fours to a standing stagger and back again several times. He certainly had not been moving very quickly, at least not compared to the terrifying speed that Tom had observed from him at the outset of the attack on the wolves.

"He's in a bad way, or was at least." Evans stated flatly, though Tom thought he heard a tinge of compassion in his voice.

"I'd say you're right about that, Sergeant." Rick Haynes stated over his shoulder. "He clearly tumbled into the creek here."

Tom could see uprooted grasses and gouges in the mud down the embankment; it was quite clear that Moretti was much less nimble than he had been. "Blood increases on the other side too, Paw." The trail was exceptionally heavy in the mud, and it had practically painted the tall brown grasses through the field headed south.

"It's from the water." Evans had a tone of sage experience in his voice. "Mixed with the blood, and that spread it around more. Like getting shot in the rain, makes the bleed seem heavier than it really is."

"I'd say Sergeant Evans is right, there. Still, that's no small amount of blood." Richard Haynes had a tone of amazement in his voice. "Between how much blood he's losing and the fact that Ralph caught him in the stomach, I can hardly believe he was still moving when he got this far."

"Looks like he turned even more toward the quarry, don't it?" Ralph's voice had more determination in it. Tom mused that knowing how much damage he'd inflicted on the monster may have helped him feel as though he had at least struck a blow for justice, for the doughboys.

"Looks like he did." Rick responded. "Looks like he was keepin' a steady pace too. Slow but definitely steady."

"Way I figure, one of two things is true." Evans said. "Either he headed toward the lab, didn't make it, and is layin' dead out there somewhere. Or he did make it and is still there lickin' his wounds. Either way, I reckon we followed as far as we need for the time bein'. Figure we'd best go meet the colonel."

"I think you're right, Sergeant." Rick Haynes arched his back slightly, stretching. "Let's head back. Just the way we came, now. Don't want to run into Clinton unawares."

CHAPTER 17

Tom was musing that his position in the side ditch might be even more dreary and hot than the hayfield had been the morning before. They had left the truck about one hundred yards behind them and crawled through the ditch to the crest of a small hill, staying low and out of sight. Sergeant Evans had his field glasses out taking account of what was happening in the camp, but, even without binoculars, Tom could tell that the colonel had yet to arrive. The soldiers in the camp seemed to be going about their business, unaware of the hailstorm of retribution the United States Army was about to rain down around them. Colonel Arthur Price had a thunderous reputation as one who had no tolerance for misconduct within the ranks, and complicity in the murder of four veterans more than qualified one for his wrath.

"Do you see Clinton?" Richard Haynes asked in a low whisper.

"No, I don't see him. But he'd probably be in his tent right about now." Evans was scouring the encampment through his field glasses, looking for any signs of trouble.

"See that?" Ralph quietly asked the question to no one in particular. "On the Petersburg road? Somebody's kickin' up an awful lot of dust."

Tom looked into the distance to the east and saw what Ralph had pointed out. It was still some few miles away, but Tom could tell that someone was coming.

"Hold on, now." Sergeant Evans came to life. "There he is. Clinton's in the camp."

Tom looked back to the group of dirty, white, canvas tents and could tell that there was a commotion. Clinton was recognizable even in spite of the three hundred yards that separated them. He was a big man, but his real notoriety was his boisterous manner. He was shouting at soldiers, waving his arms, pointing his finger, throwing stray items at those who annoyed him. It seemed to Tom that he was even more unhinged than when he had killed his lieutenant, if that was even possible.

"That's it, Hank. You just keep on shoutin'. Keep everybody distracted from the trucks comin' at ya." Evans quietly encouraged the major to continue his tirade. "Shoot!"

"What's wrong, Sergeant?" Rick Haynes' voice held some concern as he asked the question.

"Looks like a private has seen the dust. He's tryin' to get Clinton's attention." Evans started drumming his finger on the side of his binoculars. "I think we oughta head down there."

"The colonel looks like he's still close to four miles out." Rick had a sound in his voice like a friend trying to reason through options.

"If we don't get headed down there, the colonel will be walkin' into an ambush." Evans' voice had urgency behind it. "The colonel is good, and'll win a fight with Clinton's men if he has to fight one, but he's probably gonna lose men in the process. Personally, I want them fellas' help huntin' Moretti rather than fillin' graves."

"I'm with the sergeant." Ralph had set his jaw with determination. "Let's get down there and settle this thing."

"Alright, but let's not make any mistakes. I don't want any of us filling graves either." Rick's tone was steady, but there was caution behind his words, much the same as when he sent Tom and George out into the dark morning a day earlier.

The four made their way back to Sheriff Thompson's truck, as quickly as possible without opening themselves up to exposure, should an ambush be hidden on the side of the road. They covered the ground quite quickly in the formation that was beginning to be second nature to Tom. Moments later they were cresting the hill in the behemoth headed toward Clinton's encampment at a steady pace, trying to draw his attention.

"Don't shoot unless you have to, now fellas." Evans was between Tom and Ralph all leaning over the cab in the front of the truck bed. He was checking the load of each of his weapons. Rifle first, then each pistol in succession. "These fellas are soldiers followin' orders, and they've all seen fightin' before. We don't want them shooting at us if we can help it." Evans checked the breach of his Springfield a second time, racked the bolt home, and waited.

It didn't take long for Clinton's men to notice the flanking maneuver. The sheriff's truck wasn't huge, but Clinton was down five men; his unit was in no shape to face a company of the Army's best troops on one front and four riflemen on another. Chaos ensued in the camp, men running here and running there as the men from Doughty fell upon them, led by their own sergeant. Colonel Price and his infantry was closing quickly also, ten trucks full of infantry, bayonets glinting in the Virginia sun. Tom's heart was pounding in his throat once more, as he tried to steady himself; he didn't relish the idea of coming under a hail of bullets again, but he grit his teeth, regripped his 1895 Winchester, and steeled his will, mastering his desire to lay down in the bed of the truck and hide.

"If this is what the war was like, then I'm GLAD that the Army didn't take me." Tom mused, chuckling to himself and thanking God for the first time, that his beard didn't grow in at an early age. The thought lightened his spirits some, and his heart slowed ever so slightly. It wasn't much, but it would do.

Their truck and the trucks of the Colonel arrived at nearly the same moment, converging on the startled traitors all at once. The confusion was so great that Clinton's men began yelling at one another, some laying down their arms with hands raised high above their head and some threatening violence against ally and enemy alike. From everywhere around the military trucks rifle barrels appeared, leveled at the confused and disorganized group of soldiers huddled with the tents at their backs. As the dust settled and the shouting decreased, a commanding voice came ringing from among the Army trucks.

"Lay down your arms and surrender, and I'll promise you a fair court-martial. In fact, for most of you, General Pershing probably won't even let me hang you." The voice was no nonsense, and Tom was glad that the remarks weren't directed at him. "This is Colonel Arthur Price, United States Army, and I'll give you three seconds before I give the command to gun y'all down where you stand. That'd tie this matter up nice and tidy for me, but I reckon you lot wouldn't enjoy it so much. Now, what's it gonna be?"

Some of Clinton's soldiers still holding their rifles exchanged glances, but it was a vain gesture. Once the first of the holdouts dropped his Springfield in the dust, the rest followed like dominoes.

"Can't say I'm not disappointed that I don't get to shoot any of you traitors, but I figure you ain't quite as dumb as you look." An immaculate officer in a spotless green uniform strolled forward from between two trucks, his 1917 service revolver leveled at one particularly nervous looking corporal, hand-wrapped cigarette dangling from just below his heavily waxed handlebar mustache. Tom thought him to be the very picture of a military officer. "My name is Colonel Arthur Brimley Price. You may know me as the Bulldog of the Argonne. I'm an officer of little patience and less forgiveness." Colonel Price paused, removed his cigarette from his mouth with his left hand, wiped some loose tobacco from his bottom lip, puffed twice, then looked over the prisoners once more. "Now, I have a question for you degenerates, and the first man to answer me gets a prize." Colonel Price let the idea hang in the air for a few moments. "The first man to answer my question gets my endorsement as a cooperator when General Pershing arrives tomorrow." A low rumble of confusion and fear spread through Clinton's soldiers, hands still raised high above their heads. "Tell me now. Where is Major Henry Clinton?"

There were a few short moments of silence before half of Clinton's soldiers erupted at once shouting answers in a garbled tangle of voices. The corporal at which Price had been pointing his revolver roared in disgust and punched a private standing next to him.

BLAM!!!

A shot rang out, silencing the entire uproar. Clinton's loyal corporal lay dead, a mess of blood covering his chest where the .45 caliber slug had impacted, cutting short his treasonous life. Smoke billowed from Price's cigarette and revolver barrel alike. He drew hard on tobacco, exhaled slowly, threw the cigarette into the dirt, ground it out with the toe of his tall cavalry boots, and looked to the private that had been on the receiving end of the corporal's punch.

"Private?"

"Alexander." The young soldier answered, a bit of a crack in his voice.

"Private Alexander, I'm about to give you a golden opportunity." Price grinned ingratiatingly at the young soldier. "You tell me honestly where Clinton is, and I'll suggest leniency at your court-martial."

"Sir, I don't rightly know what happened. We was all lining up on his commands. Then we saw that other truck comin' in, and he turned tail. Went off on foot. Cross the fields. If I didn't know better, I'd say he turned full coward." Private Alexander pointed off toward the south in the general direction of Miller's pond.

"Did he now?" Price's tone was that of a school teacher eliciting more information from a student. "Now how long have you been with this unit?"

"Just transferred, sir. Was in the ninety-first infantry division in France, sir. Fought under you and the General in the Argonne. Didn't sign up for this." The private seemed less scared and more ready to be done with Clinton once and for all. "Thought this transfer was a career posting, but the major is off his nut. Killin' our own men, assaultin' civilians. Say nothin' about that fiend Moretti; don't hardly look human no more." The private made a sound of disgust before continuing. "No offense sir, but if that's what the Army is comin' to, then I'd just as soon live out my days in the stockade."

"Freddy!" Colonel Price called over his shoulder in Tom's direction.

"Yes Colonel!" Sergeant Evans answered to Tom's surprise.

"Come on over here, Sergeant." Price kept eye contact with Private Alexander.

Evans patted Tom's back and climbed out of the truck, rifle slung over his shoulder, briskly marched to where the colonel stood with the private, and snapped to attention with a salute.

"Tell me, Freddy, what's your impression of this soldier."

Still saluting Evans answered, "Sir, seems the good sort. Always kept his head down and stayed as far from Clinton as he could without attracting attention. Honestly, Colonel, there's several here that wouldn't be if they'd known what they was gettin' into, myself included."

"Captain Moore!" Colonel Price called toward his own trucks this time.

A sharp looking young officer marched to within a few paces of the colonel, snapped to attention, and saluted.

"Captain, process these soldiers, shackle all of them save the good sergeant, separate out the trouble makers, and start questioning them." Price returned the salute, and the captain got busy with his orders.

"Sergeant MacDowell!" Another soldier stepped forward taking his turn at saluting his commanding officer. "Take first platoon and clear the camp, starting with the command tent, then take charge of setting up a defensible perimeter."

"Yessir!" The sergeant whistled shrilly, pointed to the encampment, and was followed by a dozen tough looking soldiers into Clinton's tent, then out into the rest of the camp.

"Sergeant Evans, if you don't mind." Price holstered his revolver and set off toward the tent.

Evans motioned for Rick, Ralph, and Tom to join him. They exited the truck, slung their rifles over their shoulders, and joined the grizzled sergeant.

"Freddy?" Rick asked quietly as they set off toward Clinton's command tent. "Know the colonel well, Sergeant?"

"I was Colonel Price's ordinance sergeant when we were chasin' Pancho Villa through Texas. Seems a lifetime ago now." Evans absent-mindedly scratched the scar beneath his eye. "Arthur was a good friend in those days, but I can't say that'll mean much after all I've helped Clinton do."

Ralph reached the tent slightly ahead of the rest of the men and drew the flap back for the others to enter. Colonel Price had taken a seat behind Clinton's field desk and was sifting through the papers scattered over its surface. To Tom, he looked every inch of an Army commander, in his pressed uniform, complete with jodhpurs trousers, highly polished cavalry boots, and trooper campaign hat. He tossed some papers aside, leaned back in his chair, and started rolling another cigarette.

"What's all this about, Freddy?"

"Sir..."

"Enough of that *sir* garbage. Arthur's always been good enough before. I might have to court-martial you; might even have to see you hanged, but I ain't gonna listen to you grovel to me, not after you saved my life at Guerrero." Price removed his imposing hat, revealing his thinning hair, tossed it on the desk, and lit his cigarette.

"Arthur, we're a long way from Guerrero." Evans sighed heavily. "The war wasn't Mexico, and Clinton isn't you. The man is mad. He's obsessed with chemicals and Fritz Haber. Thinks he can use his methods to change soldiers into killing machines. He's already twisted one poor soul beyond recognition, and there's rumors he's been working on someone else. Don't think he ever really trusted me, but he wouldn't let me transfer out, no matter how many times I asked."

"Tell me about this twisted soul, as you put it."

"He killed my friends, colonel." Ralph interrupted.

"Did he? Who were these friends?" Price was clearly not pleased with being interrupted, but he was not without compassion for the loss of a friend.

"Soldiers, sir. Doughboys, fresh back from the war and just looking for jobs. Four of 'em. Lieutenant William Sweet, Sergeant Hosea Rosenthal, Private Micah Lange, and Private Harrison Caine." Ralph choked slightly. Tom looked at him and saw tears streaming down his face.

"Clinton's creature, Corporal Moretti, tore 'em up, Colonel." Tom interrupted. He wasn't about to let Ralph suffer in this alone; Tom had a part in this business, and he wanted justice for the doughboys as well. Price would understand; they would make him understand. "He's a fiend, if he's still alive. He murdered those fellas for pure sport." The tears began to flow from Tom's eyes as well. "We found 'em, a tangled mess, torn limb from limb, eyes and mouths gaped open in a silent scream." His tears fell heavily, but Tom didn't even attempt to wipe them away; he wanted the colonel to see what Moretti had done, what Clinton had done. "I spent hours, Colonel, carrying little bits of their bodies out his lair. Hours of sifting through their blood, knee deep, almost. Standing in the middle of men that I knew, men that I liked. Clinton is to blame. And Moretti."

"And you, Freddy? Are you to blame?"

"I am. Arthur, I'm to blame too. I didn't kill those fellas. I didn't twist Moretti's mind and body. I didn't agree with it from the very beginning, but neither did I stop it. So, yes, I'm to blame." Evans was crying as well, tears streaking his wrinkled cheeks.

Colonel Price let out a heavy sigh, leaned forward onto the desk, ground out his cigarette on the glass of a framed photo of Clinton, and folded his hands. "This is quite a mess, Freddy. Quite a mess indeed." He sighed again and started twisting the end of his mustache. "Not sure I can protect you from the general staff. You'll probably face a court-martial."

"It's been a long while comin', Arthur."

"Well, the general will probably relieve you of duty when he gets here tomorrow, but, until then, you're my advisor on operations here. What's our next move? Doesn't sound like they've found Clinton. Where do you think he's headed?"

"The same place as Moretti, if he survived that entanglement last night, back to the basement lab at the quarry."

Chapter 18

Tom shifted on his hard bench seat in the back of the Army truck; he was sandwiched between his father and a beefy soldier whose name he didn't know. Tom stole a glance at Ralph, who was sitting across from Richard Haynes; his ginger mustache didn't have its characteristic twitch, as though ready to laugh at any minute, but Tom thought his friend seemed to be on the mend.

They had left five trucks, including Sheriff Thompson's behemoth, fifty-six soldiers, three heavy Browning M1917 machine guns, Captain Moore, and Clinton's shackled unit behind as they pulled away from the camp in search of Clinton and Moretti. The remaining six trucks were loaded down with men and munitions as they rumbled toward the quarry. Tom had never seen such a show of force in his life. The Colonel had mobilized a full company of regular infantry and three platoons of military police who specialized in apprehending dangerous soldiers who were outside their orders; all together, the force was comprised of more than 150 soldiers. Sergeant MacDowell commanded the MP's, and Tom couldn't deny that they were intimidating. Most of the infantry and MP's carried .30-06 Springfield rifles, but several of the hardened soldiers carried trench sweeper shotguns and double automatic handguns, Colt 1911's. One particularly impressive MP corporal, who Tom thought was simply the largest man he had ever seen, carried a Lewis gun; Tom had seen the weapon in news reals, but he had never imagined he would be sitting across from a soldier that carried one. The Lewis gun was large, by any standard, weighing nearly thirty pounds; it carried a 97 round magazine and could fire at a rate of 600 rounds per minute. The giant corporal had one magazine on the machine gun and four more strapped to his gunner's vest. Tom found himself almost pitying Clinton and Moretti when he thought of the terror that was about to fall upon them.

The truck slowed slightly and rocked hard to the left, as the driver followed the lead truck off of the Petersburg road onto the dirt and gravel laden trail leading to the quarry. Tom rechecked his Winchester, working the lever halfway back, returning it to firing position, and lowering the hammer. He felt his heart start to creep back into his throat as he turned his attention toward the forest, watching for anything suspicious.

The trucks were traveling fast, considering how rough the deeply rutted road had become through years of quarry trucks traveling it loaded down with thousands of pounds of stone and ore. Tom found himself wondering if they might beat the major to his destination. He wasn't keen on facing Clinton and his monstrous creation side by side in some underground lair, but he was no more keen on giving Clinton room to maneuver. *"The colonel knows what he's doing."* Tom reprimanded himself. *"Focus on yourself. Pay attention!"* Tom blinked hard, shook his head slightly, and refocused his attention on the trees whirring past him. It wasn't long before he spotted the redirected creek running closer to them toward the quarry. They were close. Tom regripped his rifle again and said a silent prayer.

As the trucks rolled into the clearing surrounding the quarry, some swung left, some right, and Tom's truck lead three others into a fan shaped position by the lake itself, facing the warehouse in which Tom knew he would, once again, confront the butcher's cellar and the creature responsible for it. All the soldiers leapt from the trucks and assumed combat positions, each scanning a particular portion of the quarry, weapons at the ready.

"Tom, Ralph..." Richard Haynes called their attention and they both directed their eyes to him. "Stay close to Sergeant Evans and me. We don't want to give Clinton or Moretti a chance to hurt anyone else." Tom nodded and looked to Ralph.

"Yessir, Mr. Haynes. I'm just ready for this to be done." Ralph's eyes looked tired; Tom wasn't sure if his friend had slept at all since the night they spent in the treehouse. Rick nodded at the young man whose ginger mustache drooped slightly, betraying the grim, tight line his lips had become.

"Rick, y'all are with us." Sergeant Evans stood waiting at the tailgate with Colonel Price.

"Wouldn't have it any other way," Richard Haynes stated, patted Ralph's knee with his left hand, then reassuringly nudged Tom with his shoulder.

Tom hopped from the truck, rifle poised to unleash his four heavy .30 caliber rounds at either Clinton or Moretti if needed. He fell in next to his father as they walked to the front of the truck. On the ground he saw Moretti's tracks and a continued trail of blood leading to the door of the warehouse. The cadre assumed a formation with Evans and Colonel Price in the lead. On either side of their smaller group, MP's fell in, guns leveled on the front of the rusted metal building. They took their time, following along the trail of blood and grotesque claw tracks, advancing slowly...cautiously. When they were ten yards from the ripped and mangled door, now shut once again, the colonel motioned for the group to stop.

"MacDowell." Colonel Price stated just loud enough to be heard. Tom could tell by the tone that it was an order. The MP sergeant stepped forward from the left of the group with the massive corporal advancing from the right. They stopped just to either side of the door, as Tom and the fellas had just days before. Tom could see them dig in their feet and coil like vipers, preparing to strike. Sergeant MacDowell looked to the soldier whose Lewis gun was poised toward the opening. The corporal nodded, indicating that he was ready, and MacDowell launched a savage kick against the door, slamming it open in an instant. The corporal unleashed a hail of fire into the building, first to the left, then slowly sweeping right. It took only seconds to empty the entire magazine into the bowels of the rusted and blood painted room. Smoke and the smell of gun powder hung heavily in the air, as the corporal removed the disk magazine from atop his devastating weapon and replaced it with another fully loaded one.

"Colonel?" MacDowell asked loudly, and Tom realized that his ears were ringing from the report of the machine gun. He glanced sidelong to see the colonel slowly and authoritatively nod his head. The MP's all jumped into action, charging into the warehouse. Colonel Price and Sergeant Evans leading in their wake as the three men from Doughty followed closely behind, Tom to the left, Ralph to the right.

Tom glanced above the door at the rusted metal exterior of the building just before ducking inside the darkened room. It was even hotter than he remembered. It still carried the sickly sweet smell of stale blood, though the floors were no longer sticky. Soldiers were everywhere, investigating every corner of the warehouse; nothing seemed amiss until Tom noticed that the doors to the basement were closed.

"Where's the lab, Freddy?" Price asked in a commanding tone.

"Middle aisle, Colonel." Evans had resumed his respectful terms. Tom assumed it was for the benefit of the other soldiers.

"Lead the way." Colonel Price gestured with his revolver for the sergeant to show them the entrance. "MacDowell, Jennings, breaching maneuver again, if you please." He shouted in no particular direction.

Evans cautiously approached the trap doors in the middle of the large room, stooped by the acid stained split where the two doors met, shifted small hatches Tom hadn't noticed before, and inserted two hooks attached to woven military cord.

"Ralph?"

"Yes Sergeant?" Ralph seemed taken aback at having been addressed directly.

"Mind helping me open these doors?"

Ralph's response was to follow Evans' example by slinging his rifle over his shoulder, grabbing the end of one of the cords, and standing well clear of the doors. Two privates stepped forward to help Sergeant Evans and Ralph muscle the doors open.

"Sergeant MacDowell." Evans got the other sergeant's attention. "I'll count three, and we'll swing the doors open. There's stairs going down just underneath here and a small room with another door that leads to the left." MacDowell nodded, as did the huge corporal, and both knelt slightly, eyes focused on the doors. "One...two...three." Ralph and Sergeant Evans pulled hard on the cords with aid from the two soldiers, and the two heavy metal doors swung upward. MacDowell and Jennings rose from kneeling positions as the doors swung open, then slowly advanced toward the stairs, weapons leveled at the hole in the floor. Tom couldn't see what lay beyond, aside from the faint flicker of electric light from within, but the lack of hellfire from the Lewis gun told him that neither Moretti nor Clinton were waiting within.

"Don't see no door, Sarg." Jennings rumbled loudly with the lowest bass voice Tom had ever heard. "You sure there's one down there?"

"There is. Must be latched tight. It's hidden." Evans leveled his rifle at the hole and sidled up on MacDowell's left side. "Yep, it's latched. I'll have to open it." Evans led the other two men down into the butcher's cellar, and Price led Tom and Rick to the top of the steps where Ralph rejoined them.

"Just here?" MacDowell asked over his shoulder to Evans with his trench sweeper pointed at the bare tile wall. Tom noticed that the six inches of blood that had flooded the cellar when last he saw it was gone; a thick sticky film of blood painting the floors and walls was all that remained.

"That's it." Evans responded. "You'll hear it click. When it does, the door'll be free to swing open." MacDowell nodded, and Evans reached above his head to the light fixture. It was a cage covering one dim bulb; most of the light in the cellar came from bulbs along the tops of the walls, but this one fixture was different. Tom had been so intent on searching the walls when they found the doughboys that he had taken almost no note of the fixture. Sergeant Evans gripped it and twisted. The fixture turned, and Tom heard a popping noise from the wall to the left. As he had when entering the warehouse, MacDowell kicked the wall hard, and the hidden door swung open. Jennings stepped forward and fired a few rounds, but stopped well short of emptying another magazine.

"Nothing there, Sarg." The hulking corporal stated loudly, but Tom wasn't sure which sergeant he had been addressing. Both Evans and MacDowell angled to one side or the other of Jennings and looked intently through the door.

"This hallway is clear Colonel." Sergeant MacDowell stated, sounding almost disappointed.

Colonel Price led the way down the stairs as the two sergeants and Jennings filed through the hidden door. Tom descended the left side of the stairs next to his father, fighting away thoughts of the doughboys once again. The sight of Mike's hollow eyes kept flashing into his eyes. He remembered the feeling of their blood soaking into his socks, splashing up on his pants, coating his fingernails as he scratched every inch of the walls and floors of the butcher's cellar. The room had been sealed off, and the blood hadn't dried yet, as it had in the warehouse above. It was still sticky causing his boots to stick to the floor with every step. Worst of all, it flooded his lungs with the smell of death, the smell of his murdered friends. Rage and nausea were fighting a battle in his guts, and Tom tried desperately to fight off both of them. He gritted his teeth and refocused on the door to his left. It was almost the entire width of the wall, a full six feet. He could tell by the glow within that the space beyond the door was also lit with electric bulbs.

Colonel Price marched through the opening, and the men from Doughty followed suit. Tom found himself at one end of a long hallway, nearly twenty feet wide and at least sixty feet long. The floor and bases of the walls were coated with a thick film of blood that tapered off further down the hall; it looked to Tom as though it had flooded in from the butcher's cellar when the door was opened before their arrival.

"This is worse'n the war." Jennings stated aloud, clearly disturbed by the sight of so much blood.

"I only wish you were right about that, Corporal." MacDowell's voice sounded heavy, sad. Tom mused that he had more than just his rank in common with Evans; both men had clearly seen far too much death.

"What's in that room at the other end, Freddy?"

"The lab proper." Evans sighed. "You can see the start of it from here, but it spreads out to our right. That's where we'll find Moretti." Evans pointed to Moretti's distinctive tracks in the blood.

"And Clinton?" MacDowell asked.

"There's only one set of tracks." Rick Haynes answered confidently from next to Tom. The soldiers all glanced in his direction.

"I've never met a better tracker, Arthur. I'd take his word for gospel."

"It certainly doesn't look like more than one pair of boots from where I stand, Colonel." MacDowell added his assent.

"We'll deal with the major soon enough." Price growled, clearly annoyed that this was going to be more difficult than he had hoped. "Let's handle Moretti and regroup."

MacDowell took the lead, Evans slightly behind him to the left and Jennings mirroring the grizzled sergeant on the right. Price followed a few paces behind, and the Haynes men and Ralph brought up the rear in formation. The hallway was a disturbing mix of sticky and slippery, the blood even less dried than in the butcher's cellar behind them. Tom fought off another wave of grief, jaw ever tightening as he clenched his teeth until they hurt.

Tom focused on the hallway ahead and Moretti's tracks to steady himself. The portion of the room that they could see ahead of them was tiled as well and empty, aside from the bullet holes from Jennings' Lewis gun and the bloody tracks and smears that Moretti had left behind when he had entered. The tracks were closer together than Tom has seen them before, and they often were accompanied by long smears where Moretti had dragged himself along the hallway. At one place, it looked as though Moretti had fallen fully against the wall, as there was a huge smear of blood, some fresh, and sprawling prints from his disfigured hands to either side.

"He's as injured as we thought." Evans stated over his shoulder. "But even injured, don't forget how dangerous he is."

MacDowell motioned for the group to stop and pointed to the righthand corner at the end of the hallway. Jennings silently stalked toward the corner and ever so slowly began to rotate to his left, sweeping the entire room with the muzzle of his lethal Lewis machine gun. Tom held his breath waiting for Jennings to unleash another rain of bullets into the room, but the hulking corporal never pulled the trigger. He stepped fully into the room looking toward Tom's right, where Sergeant Evans had said Moretti would be.

"Sir." Jennings started slowly. "If I didn't know no better, I'd say I was looking at a dead animal." Evans and MacDowell rushed into the room and took their positions to Jennings' left, trench sweeper and rifle leveled at something beyond what Tom could see.

"He might be dead, Arthur. He doesn't seem to be moving." Tom could sense Ralph tense up to his right. He stole a glance to see an anguished look on his friend's face. Tears streaked his cheeks and dripped from the ends of his ginger mustache, and rage flickered in and out of his deep green eyes.

"Best be certain." Price stated matter-of-factly, as he started forward, Tom, Rick, and Ralph in his wake. They stepped up behind MacDowell, Evans, and Jennings, and the entire party started forward. Tom could see Moretti, covered in blood, not appearing to breathe. The disfigured man seemed to have been further mangled by the ravages of wolves, the impact of bullets, and even dragging himself cross country to return to the bleak, cold, tiled room shut away underground and cut off from anything good or wholesome. Tom felt a pang of compassion for what had once been a man.

The group stopped a couple yards from where Moretti lay grotesquely twisted on a metal laboratory table, limbs falling at unnatural angles. Tom heard a faint gurgle from the creature, and pulled his Winchester to a better position, should he need to fire. Moretti had plainly not succumbed to his wounds yet.

"Moretti." Colonel Price stated loudly, revolver aimed directly at the creature's forehead. "Corporal Robert Moretti. Can you hear me?" A disturbing seething sound emitted from the tangled mess of torn flesh, clotted blood, and twisted limbs. "I'm Colonel Arthur Price." Another seething sound. "You're outside your orders and will be taken to Camp Lee for treatment, confinement to the stockade, and court-martial. Do you understand me?"

A deep guttural gurgle came boiling out of the corporal's mouth. It sounded to Tom as though he had a mouth full of water. Moretti's muscles tensed with immense effort as he tried in vain to lift his head and shift himself onto his side. He collapsed even further than he had been; long, lean, and completely destroyed on the table.

"Moretti?" Evans called to the man in a tone both commanding and gentle. Tom was surprised by the sound of the sergeant's voice.

"Saarrrrge..." Moretti's distorted voice came gurgling from his lips. "It's too...too late." He coughed lightly, inhaled a labored breath, sighed slightly, and began again. "I'm done, Saarrrrge." His breathing seemed to get even more difficult.

"We've got a medic, Bobby. Let's get you sorted."

Another sickening breath escaped the young monstrous body. "Better this way." He slowly managed to reply. "Don't tell..." He hacked slightly and inhaled again. "Don't tell my momma..." His body slumped more as his breath became shallower yet. "Prayyy fooor meeeeee..." his breath just seemed to escape his lungs as he slumped flat against the table.

Tom stared hard, watching for signs of breathing. He watched for several long moments, listening for any sounds that might come from the creature that had so terrified him only a few short minutes before, but his vigil was in vain. Evans' shoulders slumped as he stepped closer to Moretti and took him by the wrist; the long horrible fingers and claws of his right hand hung limp from the sergeant's grip.

"He's dead." Evans stated at last. The tone in his voice was odd; Tom couldn't place it, but it resonated in his own heart.

"Probably just as well, Freddy." Price sighed. "He was right. Nobody would benefit from seeing this disaster. What Clinton did here is a crime against God and man." Price spit his unlit cigarette onto the floor in disgust.

Tom felt his heart sink from his throat, through his chest, and settle in his stomach. The monster that had killed his friends was dead, but he didn't feel any relief. The fear that had haunted Doughty for days could finally begin to come to an end, but Tom felt no comfort. All he felt was sadness. All he felt was pity. That's what he had heard in Evans' voice, pity. This young soldier had been twisted and abused by the machinations of an evil man; he'd been groomed for evil purposes by the worst wickedness that Tom could imagine, and he had succumbed to the leadership of a man absorbed with hate and corruption. But, in the end, Moretti had sought peace; he had found shame for his actions, and he had sought prayer. Tom pitied him deeply. Moretti was only a few years Tom's senior; he had volunteered to serve his country in the Great War, and he had been led astray by his commanding officer. Tom was reminded of his rejection from the Army and how angry he was, but for the grace of God, Tom might've fallen under Clinton's command and become this twisted, iniquitous wretch. He found himself praying for Moretti's mother. He found himself feeling sorry for Bobby Moretti, as silent tears streaked his face, and he found himself hoping that the poor mangled wretch on the table in front of him had found redemption before it was too late.

Chapter 19

"I can't believe he's just...well...dead." Tom mused aloud.

"You think I killed him?" Ralph's voice was a mix of so many emotions that Tom could hardly tell what his friend was feeling.

"I don't think you shooting him did the job by itself, but I'm sure it didn't make it easier for him to get healed up."

"When Sergeant Evans first told us about how bad I hurt him with that bullet, I was kinda proud of myself." Ralph coughed hard, clearing his throat. "I don't know what I am anymore, but I sure ain't proud."

Tom glanced at his friend, sitting next to him perched on the tailgate of an Army truck, as soldiers went this way and that, investigating and securing the area. Ralph had tears streaking his face, and he kept clenching and unclenching his fists alternating with wringing one hand with the other. Tom could tell that Ralph was struggling; he didn't know how hard it could be on a person to wonder if they had killed another human being, but he was fairly certain that more was going on with Ralph than he had previously thought.

"You didn't do nothin' wrong, Ralphie."

"No? You so sure about that?" Ralph had more than a little anger in his voice. He wiped tears from his cheeks before continuing. "I know it ain't always wrong to kill somebody. Moretti was a bad man. He killed Wil and the others. He woulda killed us, if he got half a chance. I had plenty of reason to shoot him. I coulda shot 'im in self-defense last night, but I didn't."

Tom was confused. "I don't understand Ralphie. He was comin' after us. How ain't that self-defense?"

"Tommy, what matters ain't what he was gonna do. What matters is what I did." Ralph looked Tom straight in the eyes. Tom could see anguish behind Ralph's green eyes as they continued leaking tears. "I didn't shoot 'im cause I was scared of him. I didn't shoot 'im cause he was comin' after us. I shot 'im cause I hated 'im and wanted him dead for what he did to them fellas." The tears streamed even faster now, and Tom finally understood.

"I ain't gonna lie to ya, Ralphie. That don't sound good." Tom paused letting his friend hurt for one second longer. "But that ain't the end of things. That ain't all there is." He paused again, as Ralph's face became confused, even frightened. "Look, it ain't good to shoot somebody in anger. It ain't good to go lookin' for revenge. But God can use that for good just the same. Was it bad for you to pull that trigger the way you did? Yeah! I ain't gonna lie to ya; it mighta been the wrong thing to do, shootin' 'im in anger. BUT! It wasn't wrong to pull the trigger at all; you just can't have the wrong heart about it."

"That's the whole point, Tom! How can that be anythin' other'n murder?!"

"Well, we don't rightly know what killed 'im, but I'd reckon it was them wolves mostly. Truth is, Cinder's probably the one that did 'im in, not you. But still, if you hadn't shot 'im, the Army woulda done it at a firing squad." Tom sighed heavily. "But that ain't the point neither. I been wonderin' if God is teaching us all somethin' here." He clapped Ralph on the shoulder and stared hard into his watery eyes. "How about this, Ralphie? If he had lunged at us down there today, would you have shot him again?"

"Yeah, course I woulda. Wasn't about to let 'im kill nobody else." Ralph's eyes started streaming afresh.

"But you wouldn't been shooting outa hate, would ya?" Tom waited for Ralph to shake his head before continuing. "Tell me Ralphie, you hate Moretti now?"

"Naw, I don't hate 'im."

"You hope he went straight to Hell?"

"You kidding?! That's awful Tom!"

"Answer the question, Ralph!"

"Course not! Don't wish that on nobody! Besides, you see him down there? You hear 'im?" Ralph was crying harder than ever. "Hear 'im crying for his momma? Askin' us to pray for 'im?" His ginger mustache was soaked in tears as he choked slightly. "Pray for 'im, Tommy. He asked us to pray for 'im." Ralph began to fully weep and buried his face in his hands.

"That's right. He did." Tom paused again and put his hand on his friend's heaving, shaking back as he wept. "And we oughta be prayin' for his family, dontcha think?"

"I have been." Ralph sobbed loudly. "Been prayin' for his poor momma."

"Now tell me this, Ralphie. You hate Clinton?" Tom paused as his question sank in. "You hate him for making Moretti what he was and sending 'im to his death?"

"I dunno, Tom." Ralph's weeping slowed as fear replaced his grief.

"You want 'im to pay for what he's done?"

"I want him caught, if that's whatcha mean."

"No, I wanna know if you wanna hunt 'im down and shoot him yourself. I wanna know if you wanna watch 'im die like we watched Moretti. You wanna see the life drain outa his eyes? Make his eyes look like Mike's and Wil's and the others'? That what you want?"

"Stop it Tom, that ain't funny."

"I'm not tryin' to be funny, Ralphie. I'm serious. Is that what you want?"

"NO!" Ralph yelled in Tom's face. "That's terrible Tom! How could I ever want that?! I'm not a monster!"

"That's right Ralph. You ain't a monster." Tom's response confused Ralph again. "Those are the kinds of things Clinton wants, not you. So, tell me again, Ralph. When you shot Moretti, what were you tryin' to do?"

"Stop him!" Ralph said exasperatedly. "I was trying to stop 'im from killin' anything or anybody else. I just wanted him to stop!"

"So, you didn't just want 'im to die? Didn't just wanna kill 'im? Weren't just thinkin' about revenge?"

"No, I don't reckon I did." Ralph began to understand what Tom was saying. "I wanted the killin' to stop...wanted the dyin' to stop."

"That's what I figured, Ralphie." Tom smiled at his friend; it was hard to manage a smile after everything they had endured, but Ralph needed it. "You ain't a murderer Ralphie, not really. You shot 'im, but you weren't trying to kill 'im. You mighta hated 'im, and that was wrong; that was a sin, but we all sin, Ralph, all of us. And you feel sorry for how you felt before. That's your conscience. Hatin' him for a time didn't turn you into a murderer, and we oughta be thankful for that." Tom patted his friend hard on the back and cracked a bigger grin. "Don't want none of my friends turnin' murderer after all."

Ralph weakly returned the grin. "Reckon that's true enough Tom. Thank you."

"Anytime, Ralphie. Anytime."

"So what's next?"

"Reckon we got lessons to learn from this whole thing. That'll probably take a while. And I reckon the Army'll be after Clinton." Silence fell between the two friends as Tom became lost in thought, drumming his fingers on the stock of his lever action rifle, and slowly scanning the treeline, a habit he might never shake, after all that Clinton and Moretti had put him through. Eventually his attention fell on a group of soldiers milling about another truck and pointing in one direction or another, clearly engaged in discussion about one plan of action or another. Tom was uncertain how long they had sat there lost in their own thoughts before his father strolled up with Sergeant Evans.

"Tom. Ralph. We're headed back." Richard Haynes' voice was weary.

"What's up, Paw?" Tom asked his father, concerned.

"Not a whole lot, Tom. The colonel is leaving some soldiers here to wrap things up and we're headed back to camp then home to fetch Sergeant Evans' other soldiers, or at least those that are safe to move."

"Think we convinced Arthur to recommend me for court-martial, but just slap them with no more'n a few days in the stockade." Evans sighed. "They're good fellas, and most have only been with us a few weeks."

"What about you?" Ralph's voice was heavy with concern.

"Don't you worry about me. The General does a good service in justice. I'll get a fair shake, sure thing." Evans smiled slightly. "I'll just be glad to be rid of Hank Clinton, even if that means spending the rest of my days behind bars or breaking rocks." He chuckled under his breath. "Truth be told, I could use a vacation." With that, the grizzled sergeant who Tom had come to admire climbed into the bed of the truck and took a seat followed by Richard Haynes.

"Any idea where Clinton got off to, Sergeant?" Tom's father asked.

"Not a clue. Never took 'im for a coward, but it seems that he'll never stop surprising me with faults I didn't know he had." Evans sighed heavily. "He's probably long gone. Got friends as bad as he is scattered all over the world. No tellin' where he's headed off to."

Tom and Ralph took their seats as the rest of the soldiers began filing into their positions along benches or setting up a camp in a defensible position where the base of the hill met the edge of the lake. They had four M1917 machine guns placed and manned before Tom felt the truck shudder under his feet and head back toward the campsite and home.

* * * * *

The drive had been without incident; they had left Colonel Price and his men at Clinton's camp, retrieved Sheriff Thompson's old truck, and headed on to the Haynes' farm. Tom had never been more relieved to see the old white farmhouse, barn, and even chicken coop than he was when his father turned the cantankerous behemoth into the driveway. *"Tonight, I get to sleep."* Tom thought to himself. *"I'll probably sleep for days, and it'll be glorious."* Tom twisted slightly in his seat to stretch his sore back, as the truck came to a halt by the fence line and he saw George's familiar face poking out of the hayloft window. Tom stood up in the bed of the truck, raised his arms high above his head, yawning, and heard his father shut off the truck's rumbling engine.

"Back already?" Tom heard Mr. Garvin call out as he stepped out of the barn door.

"Moretti's dead." Richard Haynes shouted back as he exited the cab of the truck. "Clinton's troops are locked up awaiting trial, and the major himself is in the wind."

"Well, that's good news! So, why the long faces?" George was climbing down from the hayloft.

"I've gotta gather my men and report back to the colonel. Gotta stand trial myself." Evans dropped the bombshell.

Tom noticed that George had stopped midway down the ladder that was mounted directly on the front of the barn with his jaw hanging open. George's expression described how Tom felt; it was as though they had just won a war simply to be told that their general was going to be arrested for helping them succeed. Tom slung his Winchester across his back, and started toward the tailgate with his shoulders slumped.

"They're puttin' you on trial?" Mr. Garvin was incredulous as he hobbled toward the house.

"They're putting who on trial?" Mollie Haynes asked the question before she was even halfway out of the screened door to the kitchen.

"Sergeant Evans, Honey. They're court-martialing him." Richard Haynes' tone was sad but resigned. "I've offered him my services as counsel at the proceedings, but we haven't gotten far down that road yet."

"Oh, Rick! That's terrible!" Mollie Haynes looked as though she was on the verge of tears. "I'm so sorry, Sergeant Evans. If we can do anything at all for you, testify, write letters, anything, please don't hesitate to ask." Tom's mother held the door for Sergeant Evans as she ushered him into the kitchen. Tom took the door from his mother and held it for the rest of the group as they entered.

"But there's good news too, Mrs. Haynes." George's tone was one of a person trying to encourage those who were only seeing the worst in a situation.

"What good news?" Mollie asked.

"Mollie, Moretti is dead." Rick pulled her to him with one arm around her shoulder. "And Major Clinton has disappeared, running from the Army most likely."

"Hopefully he's caught soon." Mollie's face betrayed the deep concern she was trying to hide. "Poor boy's mother. I can't imagine the pain of losing a son." She said quietly. "Were you with him when he died?" She asked her husband.

"We all was, Mrs. Haynes." Ralph spoke up, choking slightly. Tears had come and gone frequently on the ride back to the Haynes' home. Tom tried not to notice, hoping not to embarrass his friend. "We was all there at the end. He asked us to pray for him." Tom felt his eyes begin to swell with tears as well.

"Pray for him?" George was clearly taken aback. "He asked you to pray for him?" He looked from person to person, as they each nodded their heads in response. George looked sheepish. "Maybe I wasn't right to call it good news. Don't know what to make of all that, to be honest." He lowered his gaze.

"Him dyin' is a mixed bag." Garvin spoke up. "Can't hurt nobody else now, but sounds like he felt bad about the bad he did."

"I think he did." Evans began, sighed heavily, then continued. "I think he regretted it at the end, but I think he knew he was dyin'. I think he wanted to make peace before he died. I think that what led him to that remorse was his own death." He sighed again. "Saw it a lot in the war, but it don't make it any easier."

A heavy silence hung in the air for several long moments as each person was lost in their thoughts. Finally, Tom couldn't take the silence anymore. "Ma, where's Marky?"

"What?" Mollie Haynes blinked briefly trying to refocus on the question. "Oh. He's on top of the front porch with the Wilson boys. Private Matthews went downstairs to check on Private Eames." Mollie Haynes responded.

"Private Matthews? Private Eames?" Tom was genuinely confused.

"Oh, I couldn't stand calling them 'Reb' and 'Brooklyn'; so, I asked them their real names." Mollie grinned slightly.

"Speaking of, I should go down and let them know what has happened." Evans sighed and headed into the kitchen and toward the stairs.

"I'll come with you Sergeant." Ralph shouldered his rifle and headed down the stairs.

"Wanna help me check on Cinder, Georgie?" Tom asked, looking for a respite from so much hurt.

"I reckon I could do that." The amiable soda jerk agreed.

"Rick, Bill, would you mind helping me with the children in the parlor? Agnes is watching them by herself. I think we could all use a dose of their laughter." Mollie led the way as the men followed her down the hall.

Tom followed Sergeant Evans down the staircase into the basement with George and Ralph right behind him. He was eager to see how the wolf was doing. He realized he was eager to pet the animal and thank him for protecting them from Moretti. He was eager to tell him that it was all over, that they were safe. Tom sighed a sigh of relief, as he adjusted the Winchester on his back. *"As soon as I get done with Cinder, I'm putting this rifle back in the cabinet."* He thought to himself. *"Hopefully I'll only need it for hunting deer from now on."* Evans turned left toward the secret door to the Underground Railroad room, and Tom turned right toward the cistern.

"Ralph! Lookout!" Tom heard George scream from behind him and turned just in time to see Henry Clinton's left fist connect with Ralph's ginger clad face, sending him flying down the last five stairs. Tom's affable ginger friend hit the stone floor hard and didn't move. Evans wheeled from his spot by the door, training his rifle on his former commander, but Clinton's pistol was too fast. The brutish villain fired three rounds into Evans' chest, and the sergeant fell against the wall then to the floor, blood soaking through his jacket.

Tom unslung his Winchester as Clinton turned his Colt on him and George. Clinton pulled his trigger again and again, narrowly missing Tom's right ear before tearing a groove across the left side of his forehead. Tom went down too; the bullet's graze burned hot, and his head began to ache. He felt something else tear past his shoulder as he crouched cradling his face. Then he heard it, a scream more terrible than anything he had ever heard and growling, loud vicious growling. Tom forced his eyes open through the pain and saw a jumbled mess of green uniform, pale skin, scarlet blood, and black fur rolling down the stairs and onto the floor. Clinton's pistol went flying as the massive black wolf violently shook his heavily muscled head and neck back and forth, the major's throat crushed between his jaws, mouth open in a silent scream. It was mere moments before Cinder released the dead officer to slump on the floor and trotted over to where Tom knelt. Tom rubbed the wolf's shaggy neck and head, gratefully, as he dragged himself to where Ralph lay motionless on the floor.

"Doc! Doc Wilson! Get out here quick!" George Priestly screamed frantic, pushing his hands hard against Sergeant Evans' wounds. "Doc! He's dying! Hurry!" George's voice cracked as tears mixed with blood and he pressed ever harder, trying in vain to stop the bleeding.

Tom rolled Ralph onto his back. His ginger mustache was hidden beneath all the blood that had leaked from his savagely shattered nose and cheek, broken teeth lying on the floor beside him. Ralph didn't seem to be breathing.

"Evie! Hurry with my kit!" Doctor Wilson shouted to his wife. "Hurry! We're losing him!" He was helping George press hard on Sergeant Evans' wounds.

There was chaos swirling all around him, as Tom cradled his friend's head in his lap. Tears flowed freely as he felt Cinder lick his wounded face. He wept deeply until his tears blurred his vision, or was it something else? The light seemed to be fading around him. Tom shook his head, but the movement only seemed to darken his vision further, as tears streamed ever more freely from his eyes. He blinked hard, trying to clear the tears and his vision, but his head began to throb and dizziness began to overwhelm him. He was passing out; he could feel himself losing consciousness. *I'm sorry Ralphie.* He thought. *I'm sorry I couldn't save you.*

Chapter 20

The weather seemed appropriate, as they stood quietly together; they sky was overcast and grey, and the summer heat had relented slightly. Tom thought it had to be the coolest Virginia day in at least a month. He shifted from one foot to the other uncomfortably, waiting. It had been four days, but his head still throbbed. Dr. Wilson had been very worried about his concussion; the bullet had struck his skull very hard, but Clinton's wild aim had saved his life. The holes in the brick wall of their basement gave testimony that Tom had been fortunate, much more fortunate than so many others. He pressed hard on the bandage, confirming that it was still holding in its proper place.

"Leave it alone, Tom." Mollie Haynes whispered to her eldest son. "If you keep fiddling with it, it's going to come loose."

Tom had to confess to himself that his mother was probably correct; he tried to distract himself by looking around at the other families in attendance. To his right was the Priestly family, Agnes, Mr. Garvin, and George; the younger children had been left at the Haynes' house with Tom's youngest siblings, Janey Williams, and Mr. Garvin. George was staring at the ground, his lips a grim line as he pursed them tightly in a manner that was very uncharacteristic for Tom's best friend. *He's taking this pretty hard."* Tom thought to himself, forcing back tears and pulling his gaze from the soda jerk's pained face.

Next to the Priestlys stood the Wilsons. Dr. Wilson stood statuesque as his wife gripped his arm, crying openly. *"All these years as a nurse, and she's still sensitive about people."* Tom thought fondly of Mrs. Wilson; she was a gentle sort, and kind. The twins stood next to their mother, more difficult than ever to tell apart in their matching suits. Jimmy's face had never been further from a smile, not even on the morning they had awoken distressed in the treehouse. Billy looked just as pained as his mirror image, logic put aside on this occasion in favor of emotion.

Tom hated funerals. He hated the ceremony. He hated the darkness as everyone dressed in black. He hated the weeping. He hated the eulogies and songs. He hated the lowering of caskets. And he hated the loss. He hated the feeling that he got when he realized that he had to live the remainder of his life on earth before he was again able to see people he loved. He hated knowing that it would be years before he was able to speak to them again. He found himself missing people from his past. He thought of his grandparents and began to squint hard resisting the tears that began to form in the corners of his eyes. He thought of Old Lady Givens and her hard candies, and the first tear streaked down his face. He thought of Wil and Hosea and Mike and Harry; Tom's tears began to flow freely, and he thought for the thousandth time in those few days about Ralph.

At the foot of the graves stood the Donnelsons. Tom was crying hard as he gazed at his friend's family. When he looked at Mr. Donnelson, it was clear where Ralph had gotten his ginger mustache; Bruce Donnelson had the largest red beard that Tom could imagine. Ralph's mother was petite with blonde hair that showed flecks of grey; she was a beautiful woman and pleasant, always with a laugh on her lips...except for then, that moment, by the graveside. Mrs. Donnelson had tears streaming down her alabaster cheeks, as she cradled her arm around the man next to her. Tom wept hard, feeling more than he knew how to handle as he looked at them; Ralph was seated in a wheelchair next to his mother. The injuries that Henry Clinton had inflicted on him had been substantial; Ralph had lost several teeth, had a fractured jaw, broken nose, and crushed cheekbone. The doctor had not been very optimistic about his recovery when he phoned Ralph's parents, asking them to hurry home to see their son. Tom had spent hours by his bedside weeping, reading Scripture aloud to him, and begging God to spare his life; Ralph's parents had rushed home to be with their son, and had spent a silent vigil praying in the clinic in Dr. Wilson's basement. After two, long, hard days with little rest and even less sleep, their prayer and fasting in desperate begging for Ralph's recovery had ended in prayers of thankfulness and rejoicing; Ralph had opened his eyes, struggled to a sitting position in bed, and asked for a glass of water. He would live! Tom locked eyes with his affable friend, and both wept freely for several moments before Tom tore his eyes away to take in the rest of the scene.

At Tom's feet lay open the first of seven graves. *"So many dead men."* Tom thought, distraught. *"So many lives lost, for what?"* He wept on, not wiping his tears. *"I wish I had never heard the name of Henry Clinton."* He looked to his left, up a hill toward the city beyond. Framed against the grey sky was Arlington House, like a monument to those who lay all around it. Thousands of graves covered the green hills that lay along the southern bank of the Potomac River. Tom's tears began to slow as he took it all in. He was taken aback by the sheer enormity of the death that surrounded him, and he found himself pondering the same question as he looked from grave to grave to grave. *"What did you die for?"* He kept silently asking headstone after headstone after headstone. *"What was it that you were fighting to protect? What was it that you were fighting to overcome? What was it that you were fighting to destroy?"*

Tom looked again to the Donnelsons, then to those standing next to them. He saw faces he didn't recognize, faces of family members of those who had lost their lives in Doughty. He saw tall fathers, curly haired brothers, weeping mothers, distraught sisters, and grandparents who were near collapse under age and grief. Tom felt for them and mourned with them. The men he was here to honor had been taken from this world before their time, by evil men. Tom wept in grief and compassion; he had never felt so much loss in his life, and it was almost unbearable. He tore his eyes away from the familes and tried to regain his composure. He slowly wiped his tearstained cheeks as respectfully as he could, trying to remain dignified at the somber affair.

Tom gazed directly across the graves as the officers and Pastor Burton took their places. General John Pershing and Colonel Arthur Price were arrayed in their finest uniforms, as they stood in stately parade with an array of general staff officers about them and rank after rank of enlisted men in finest dress uniforms standing at attention behind them. The color guard held polished rifles and magnificent banners that all seemed to glow despite the sun being hidden behind the heavy clouds. Between Tom and the funeral officials lay seven simple caskets. The headstones were not ornate, nor were the coffins, but there was a grandeur to the event, nonetheless. The mood of respectful admiration shone through the grief they all felt for the fallen soldiers.

A single soldier slowly marched forward from the ranks, past the color guard and next to the officers, carrying a bugle. He stiffly raised the brass instrument to his lips and began to blow. The mournful strains of Taps began to cry forth from his bell. Tears began falling freely from the mourners once again. When he was finished playing, the soldier slowly lowered his instrument, turned on his heel, and retook his position in the ranks.

"Death affects us all." Pastor Burton began. "In our lifetimes, we will all confront the specter of death. No one is immune to the ravages of this world. Every man must eventually confront death, whether that of another or of himself. But it has not always been thus. God created man to live with Him in eternity, to share in His communion together, and to worship Him free of infirmity. But sin entered this world through Adam after Eve was deceived by Satan dressed as a serpent. And sin had a companion; death came along with it; death, the grave, and the risk of punishment in Hell.

But God didn't end our story there; no, He gave us a chance to regain our communion with Him. He gave His own son that we might experience redemption. Yes, Jesus Christ came to this earth to buy us back from our sins with the highest payment He could muster, His own blood, the very blood of our Creator, spilled for us. Over the last several days, I have been given the honor and privilege of meeting with the families of these fine men, honored in our midst. Sharing in their grief I was blessed by learning more about the men these families have lost. In my meeting with them, we discussed the issues of sin and redemption, and I was asked by each of the families to speak over their sons and brothers here today. And I want to share with you this piece of comfort. If you have accepted the gift of Christ's redemption, then you have a hope of seeing these men one day in glory. The families of these men are confident that they have met the LORD in His glory and made that decision, to follow Him." Pastor Burton paused and breathed heavily. "Let us pray." He bowed his head indicating for those congregated on the hillside to follow his example. "Oh gracious and mighty Heavenly Father, you are holy, holy, holy on your throne of grace. May we ever endeavor to follow you daily, taking up our cross in the example of Christ, opposing evil, rejoicing in good, and loving one another. Thank you for the bravery and sacrifice shown by each during the Great War and in the recent days when sorrow and wickedness have visited us. Bless us, we pray, as we honor these men, and show your peace and comfort to us in our affliction. In the holy, precious, and majestic name of Christ Jesus we pray. Amen." The entire hillside echoed his "Amen." And the stately clergyman retook his position.

Next Colonel Price stepped toward the families, accompanied by seven officers carrying fine wooden and glass boxes. Each officer took his place in front of his respective family, and General Pershing stepped forward. If Colonel Price was impressive, the general was downright intimidating. On the breast of his immaculate green uniform hung more medals than Tom had ever seen. He mused that they must have weighed forty pounds. General

Pershing was tall and stiff as a flagpole. His officer's cap was set low to shield his eyes from the nearly nonexistent sun; there was no denying that this man was a seasoned field officer. His light grey hair was neatly cropped above his ears and around the back of his head. His still dark but greying mustache was trimmed more perfectly than Tom would have thought possible. His tall brown boots were polished so deeply they looked as though one could use them as a mirror.

"Of the duties that have been entrusted to me by this, the United States Army," The general began in his booming voice, his tone somber. "This is both the greatest honor and the most fearful of all." He paused dramatically before continuing. "No other responsibility in this mighty military force can compare with the magnitude of this one, the honoring of a fallen brother in arms." Another pause. "On this day, I am ashamed of myself. On this day, I must confess that the lives of these men ended, not out of necessity, but out of betrayal. I was not present when these men were killed, nor was I aware of the circumstances that led to their murders. I was unaware, because I had been deceived by a man under my command. Nonetheless, a breakdown in my command led to these tragic deaths, and, for that, I must share some responsibility." He paused again as his voice faltered ever so slightly. When he continued, his tone was even more resolute and commanding. "When I became aware of the events of these recent days, I immediately appealed to my generals for records of each of these men. In the end, it became obvious that posthumous awards were not only appropriate, but necessary here today."

"We honor the sacrifices of Lieutenant Robert Harlow and Private Nicholas Sanderson in their service to the United States on the date of June 14, 1920." General Pershing nodded ever so slightly to Colonel Price who retrieved one of the wooden cases from an officer and turned to face a short middle-aged couple. "To Private Harrison Caine," The general began. "The Army awards the silver star for exemplary service in France on the date of

September 29, 1918." Colonel Price handed the case to Harry's mother and father and repeated his ceremonious approach of the next couple. "To Private Micah Lange, the Army awards the silver star for bravery in combat in repelling a counter offensive maneuver in France on the date of October 11, 1918." Mike's parents received his medal amidst a fresh flow of tears, and the colonel approached a couple who both had thick, black, curly hair. "For service to his unit in France on the date of October 11, 1918, despite immense personal danger while already wounded, the Army awards Sergeant Hosea Rosenthal the silver star." Hosea's parents received the case silently and gazed at it with clear anguish on their faces. "To Lieutenant William Sweet, the Army awards the silver star for exceptional leadership and courage in the face of stiff resistance during the Battle of the Argonne Forest from the dates of September 26, 1918 to November 11, 1918." Wil's father was even taller than Wil had been, thin and strong; his mother was fair-skinned and slender, the very picture of propriety and respect. They received his medal with expressions of gratitude to Colonel Price. "Finally, to Sergeant Wilfred Evans, the Army awards the Distinguished Service Medal for a career of exceptional service by a soldier whose dedication to duty is beyond reproach." Colonel Price gently delivered the case to Sergeant Evans' elderly parents and embraced the sergeant's mother as she wept.

Tom was still watching the elderly Mrs. Evans with tears streaming freely down his cheeks when he was shaken from his musings by the report of gunfire. The honor guard delivered a customary twenty-one gun salute to the fallen soldiers, and the ceremony ended quietly with the caskets being lowered into their graves. When he looked back later, the time spent sharing condolences and weeping together was little more than a blur before the long trip back to Doughty. He had always wanted to visit a big city, but, when he arrived in Washington for the funeral, he couldn't stomach the thought of sight-seeing with so many friends being committed to the earth. They left directly from the cemetery, and Tom could think of nothing but home

Epilogue

It had been almost a year since the funeral, and things had returned to almost normal; deep down. Though, Tom knew he would never be the same. The kinds of things they had all seen and endured change people, some for the better and some for the worse. Thankfully, it seemed to Tom that Doughty had grown stronger through it all. *"I guess that the fellas and me are closer than ever, at least."* He mused to himself, while he kicked his bare feet in the water. Tom gazed about himself at the clearing; it was truly beautiful. The Army had purchased the quarry, demolished the buildings and every remnant of Clinton's debauchery within days of the funeral; it had been donated to the town and converted into a public park, and, where the warehouse had once stood, there was a simple stone monument bearing only the names of the men who died in Doughty in June of 1920.

"Come on fellas!" Ralph shouted, shaking Tom from his musings. "We come here to swim or to nap?!" His ginger mustache quivered with excitement. If he was invigorating before the tragedies they experienced, then Ralph had become downright electric after. He never let an adventure pass them by and never hesitated for even the briefest moment to help a person in need.

Tom followed the other fellas up the hill by the lake, right along the edge of the cliff. When they reached the point where Tom had first seen the doughboys leaping into the water they all stopped and looked at one another.

"For Harry!" Billy shouted before leaping into the water; his fear of heights long since forgotten; such things seem to die, when we begin to really live our lives.

"And Hosea!" James followed his brother off the cliff.

"For Mike!" George leapt well clear of the precipice and plummeted to the water below.

Ralph turned to look at Tom. "For Wil." He stated with a mix of pride and sadness behind his smile.

"For Evans." Tom replied and the two friends ran together, soaring over the edge of the cliff and into the water below in their own salute to fallen brothers.

ACKNOWLEDGMENTS

The successful release of this novel is the direct result of an outpouring of support of me and my dream by my amazing community of supporters. A special thanks to those who displayed an extra measure of generosity in taking this project from the computer screen to the completed text.

Joanna Buckwalter

Russ Presson

Marsha Presson

Shawn Presson

Jared Johnson

Anna Hendrickson

Nikki Williams

Caitlin Bowen

Justin Rossbacher

Beth Pelaccio

Elizabeth and Barry Agnew

And to one special benefactor who requested not to be named, Thank you for your continued support and generosity.